MAKE-BELIEVE
AND ARTIFICE

Polestars

1. Strange Attractors – **Jaine Fenn**
2. Umbilical – **Teika Marija Smits**
3. The Glasshouse – **Emma Coleman**
4. Our Savage Heart – **Justina Robson**
5. Elephants in Bloom – **Cécile Cristofari**
6. Drive or Be Driven – **Aliya Whiteley**
7. Back Through the Flaming Door – **Liz Williams**
8. Human Resources – **Fiona Moore**
9. Into the Dark – **Patrice Sarath**
10. Different Times and Other Places – **Juliet E. McKenna**
11. Make-Believe and Artifice – **Rose Biggin**
12. Futures to Live By – **Ana Sun**

MAKE-BELIEVE
AND ARTIFICE

POLESTARS 11

Rose Biggin

NewCon Press
England

First edition, published in the UK September 2025
by NewCon Press
41 Wheatsheaf Road, Alconbury Weston, Cambs, PE28 4LF, UK

NCP349 (hardback)
NCP350 (softback)

10 9 8 7 6 5 4 3 2 1

Cover Art by Gary Northfield.
Cover design by Ian Whates
Editing and typesetting by Ian Whates

Contents:

Introduction by Jared Shurin   7
Chanticleer and the Peacock   11
The Gunman Who Came in from the Door   23
The Modjeska Waltz   27
A Map to Camelot   45
The Ghost of Cock Lane   55
The New Woman   69
Miss Scarlett   117
A Game Proposition   131
The Chandelier Bid *(with Keir Cooper)*   141
Golden Girl   161
The Tartest of Flavours   165
The Diamond Twenty Thousand Times
        Bigger than the Ritz   181
Mrs Pepper's Ghost   195
Helen/Hermione   205
The Arousing Adventures of Gelato Parlour   213
About the Author   228
Acknowledgements   229

Begin Where You Are.
Then Go Anywhere Else.

An Introduction by Jared Shurin

Where to begin with Rose Biggin?

I can, at least, tell the story of my journey. Back in 2013, I was pulling together an anthology called *Irregularity*. It was themed around the Age of Reason, with a particular focus on the un-reasonable. Imagine a time, historically speaking, where everyone is doing an excellent job of putting things into boxes. Now imagine the things (or Things) that cannot be boxed, or tidied, or *systemised* in any way.

Due to various factors, including my own limited capacity (and patience), *Irregularity* was not for open submissions. I was, as many can testify, mildly obsessed with this book, and going well above and beyond my normal (lax) standards of perfectionism. As befitting my (pretentious) vision for the volume, the contributors were a hand-picked crew.

Imagine my surprise when I received, unsolicited and unexpected, a story. This is not how publishing works. The anthology wasn't even announced, but somehow a tale had manifested itself in my inbox. This mysterious submission, which I read – because, who wouldn't? – was "A Game Proposition" (qv).

The entire experience felt otherworldly. A mysterious story from an unknown entity; throwing my meticulous plans completely awry. Ironically, appropriately, karmically, *whichever,* this story introduced the chaos that my book needed. My own Reasonable boxes went quickly out the window, and I contracted the story as quickly as I could, because, as you will soon see, Rose Biggin is an amazing, incredible author.

The mystery deepened when I received a note from Claire North a few weeks later. As well as her own story (which *was* solicited, and, for the record, also brilliant), she congratulated me on my fine taste in acquiring a Rose Biggin original. *Wait*, I asked, *how did you know that? What have I done here?! Is she famous?!*

Her reply:

She isn't a famous writer. She will be one day. She is, however, a regular guest on my sofa bed. About nine months ago, her arrival on my sofa bed coincided with my receiving a certain brief for a short story... [The brief] was so right up her street we could have flippin' named the street after her.

Claire North is, as always, correct. With *Make-Believe and Artifice* we get one step closer to that inevitable and well-deserved 'one day'. The Case of the Phantom Story was closed, and Rose's story was the answer to the question I didn't even know I was asking.

Within *Make-Believe and Artifice*, you'll find that Rose has gone to answer many more questions over the years. Questions that only she has been insightful enough to ask – and imaginative enough to answer. She's unafraid to tilt against (and lance) icons of literature. You'll encounter her interpretations of stalwarts ranging from Chanticleer to King Arthur; adding new perspectives to F. Scott Fitzgerald and Mary Shelley. She's unafraid of Shakespeare and even willing to tackle *Cluedo*. Rose's approach is neither pastiche nor imitation, but a deep understanding of their themes and their spirit.

These stories incautiously, *gloriously*, adventure far further than you might ever expect: while undeniably respecting the source material, Rose also sees what it lacks. She gives Helen of Troy agency. She grants a Chandlerian 'dick' some wry self-awareness.

She even graces Sherlock Holmes with the gift of human frailty – not cruelly, but with warmth. Her stories, as you'll soon see, are subversive without being sly; challenging without being 'edgy'. I hasten to add that these are not retellings, or even re-imaginings. Even with these familiar characters, Rose, in the words of Kathy Acker, 'lives in her own world, because she makes the world hers'.

Chaos, as you will quickly find, is one of the underlying themes in Rose's work. Not in the Moorcockian capital-C sense, but in an appreciation of the whimsical, quirky and generally un-boxable. The greatest vice, these stories argue, is simply being too serious about things. It is okay to obsess, to worry, to strive. Ambition is laudable, as is a sense of purpose. There's nothing inherently wrong with quests. In fact, they're admirable endeavours. Even vanity – whether that's Chanticleer's pride of place or a space billionaire's atomic mansion – is forgivable. But to take yourself *too* seriously; to lose one's self-awareness or respect for the absurd – that, well, *that* crosses the line into hubris. Rose's stories deal out nemesis gently but firmly. The inevitable comeuppance arrives in a variety of forms, from heartbreak to ice cream.

From her uncanny perspective into known worlds to her ability to fashion her own, Rose is undeniably one of the most fascinating – most unabashedly creative – voices in literature today. What *Make-Believe and Artifice* holds is merely the tip of the iceberg; an introduction to Rose Biggin's achievements *so far*. This is not a retrospective, but an opportunity. If you have 'slumbered… while these visions did appear', worry not, for there is far more yet to come.

– Jared Shurin
London, June 2025

Chanticleer and the Peacock

Chanticleer – dilettante, bon vivant, raconteur, a flâneur of course, and a poet; fearless gambler, virtuosic foxtrotter, amateur alchemist and leader of the call, fluent at raising the sun in over two dozen languages and composer of symphonies in two dozen more – Chanticleer, mighty and unquestionable king of the farmyard, his red hair curled and his featherlight shirt freshly pressed, strode languidly from the coop at the tail-end of a fine summer's night and lit a cigarette. He leaned against the splintered wood and breathed the sage-and-rosemary smoke deep into his noble chest, then blew it out in sharp lines from his beak. He watched the smoke rise into the sky, weaving between the stretches of magenta and apricot that at that very moment were making their way through the gaps in the clouds. He smiled at the sight.

Chanticleer, all in red, in his bespoke suit of crushed velvet and silk, and shoes of the deepest bottle-green, as shiny as if freshly dipped into syrup. Is that real leather? Best not to ask.

A gorgeous morning is preparing to spread itself over the farmyard. The sky, as mentioned, will shake off the clouds and embrace a new spectrum of pinks and reds, and the air will change its texture, open itself up to new experiences and take on a warmth, and the sunflowers growing by the biggest barn will know something is about to kick off and turn to follow the action; and then, finally, the beginning's finale, the truest moment of the start of the day, the highlight of the calendar and let joy be unconfined, the sun itself will rise. The hilltops will glow a superb orange, crackling like new fire, and the whole horizon will blaze with that red-hot rope for a long and languorous and luminous minute, and only Chanticleer – sun worshipper, morning person, early starter, espresso devotee – will be around to see it.

At least, that's the plan. Chanticleer has to do something, of course, to bring the whole process to the boil.

The sun answers to Chanticleer; everyone in the farmyard knows this, nobody more so than Chanticleer himself. It's a lot of responsibility and could certainly flummox a lesser cockerel, but our Chanticleer has never let it go to his head.

Every day, across the whole farm, he wakes first – no matter how raucous the night before, no matter what revelry in the coop, he never lets the farmyard down – Chanticleer is there, stepping out onto the sawdust and dirt floor while the sky is still dark. He goes straight to one of his high points – the nearest and (frankly) dirtiest move is to stand on the top of the coop, which he'll do, if the party the night before was *particularly* out of control and merits a rude awakening: or the corner of the potting shed roof will do, or the handle of the broken wheelbarrow that sits vertically half-immersed on top of the compost heap, or the slanting branch of the beech tree that stretches over the paddock, giving cool shade to the dappled stallion and the chestnut-brown mere with her loving eyes and mane full of victory ribbons – or any other sundry high-spots – and, what will he do?

He'll take a deep breath in, that's what he'll do.

Let us put it this way. Phoebus is sitting in his sky-scorching chariot with his feet up on the dash, idly reading a magazine. (Perhaps the pages smoulder as he turns them.) Chanticleer's voice reaches Phoebus; he sits up immediately, salutes, grabs the reins and kicks giddy-up, and suddenly the sun coach is rolling over the sky.

Not that Chanticleer particularly believes in Phoebus; there are a few strains of scepticism to his character, he believes in science, in fact he'd go as far as to say he's an empiricist – he believes what he sees. And his whole life the evidence has been there before him: Chanticleer's call is enough to summon the sun.

All that is to come. For now there is only darkness with patches of coloured light, and the smoke from his cigarette mingling with the predawn sky.

Or perhaps there *is* something else. If we look closer at Chanticleer, there's a glaze of sweat to his perfect face this morning, a certain fearfulness in his eyes. He's looking up into the sky as he usually does, but more to calm himself than survey his domain, as if he needs to ease the beating of his heart, and although he holds the cigarette as nonchalantly as ever, it's possible to see it tremble.

A fluting call comes from the entrance to the coop. 'Baby! What's the matter?'

The voice is full of concern, and soft steps bring Chanticleer company. He keeps on leaning heavily against the wall as she arrives, pulling again on the cigarette.

Her breathing comes audibly: she isn't used to sudden sprints at this hour. Her breath makes some fog that rises, intermingles with the smoke.

'You should go back to the hutch,' says Chanticleer. 'It's cold out yet.'

'Never mind that,' she says, her delicate voice full of concern. She pulls her white feather boa closer to her, though. 'You're upset about something. What's wrong?'

Her name is Pertolete – the farmyard's sleekest hen. Lounge singer, egg-layer, former competitive ice-skater, community organiser and card sharp, she's a vision as always in a pale satin nightdress, and with smokey make-up that outlines her dark eyes, and vivid red lipstick about her comb and wattle.

Chanticleer drops his cigarette to the floor and stubs it out by dragging his foot over it. 'It's nothing.'

'Don't say that. I can tell, you know. The way you moved in your sleep; and you were muttering something.'

Chanticleer looks up at her, lets his gaze become heavy and portentous. 'I had another nightmare tonight. The worst one yet.'

Pertolete shivers; the fan of white feathers in her wings flickers before him.

'The same image came to me again,' says Chanticleer. 'The monster with those terrible eyes. And this time I could not escape.'

'The monstrous eyes again,' says Pertolete in sympathy.

Chanticleer looks away from her. 'They looked deep into me,' he says. 'And the monster was all over me, and its eyes were wide and furious, it looked at me with glittering fury from within a coat of the most unnatural blue; a horrible blue it was, a poisonous blue; like cornflowers gone rancid.'

Pertolete nods and clucks sympathetically.

'I woke up just at the moment it was going to kill me. I came out here to settle my thoughts before...'

'Poor thing. But listen: you're awake now. It can't hurt you.'

'I can't tell the others this, but I can say it to you. The dream was so vivid I think...' Chanticleer swallows, contorting his long neck. 'I think today will be the day.'

'Oh dear,' says Pertolete, and she pushes her head against Chanticleer's body with affection. 'Look, dreams are dreams. When the day begins, the sun will banish these thoughts. You'll see.'

Chanticleer feels himself growing convinced. He does think of himself as sensible, after all, and Pertolete's company is calming and lovely. He gives her a peck on the cheek and saunters off in the direction of the old milk churn, a new potential high-point spot he's yet to try for the morning reveille. Pertolete watches him go, and the judgements of her husky-lidded eyes are ambiguous.

Chanticleer sings out and lo! summons the sun; the day breaks all over the farm, and soon the animals are out and scratching, and the whole place is alive with the sounds of bickering, chasing, laughing, lowing, joking and jumping. Everywhere are pails of milk and scatters of grain. And Chanticleer, sitting on top of one of the hay bales, leans back and enjoys the heat of the sun on him, watches the hens playing a game of cards near the grain store (Pertolete is dealing), takes a sip of very good whisky on the rocks and, the dark blue shapes of his dream forgotten, ponders the satisfaction of his life.

Pertolete flips a card over. 'Oh that *is* unfortunate,' she says, quickly collecting the deck to groans of disappointment from the hens. 'But you were very close. Shall we go again?'

A shadow falls over the group, and there is a gentle cough. The hens look up.

Framed by the bright sun is the outline of a tall figure in nice tailoring, and a head with a sprightly, bouncing shock of hair. Shades of blue ripple in the sunlight.

'Good morning,' says the new arrival, in a voice as smooth and deep as the sea.

He introduces himself to the hens by bowing deeply before them. The peacock's suit is sapphire-blue, with long billowing sleeves and the hint of frothy lace at the cuffs. His eyes are flecked with green and gold.

The hens all begin to coo, with the exception of Pertolete, who takes a subtle step backwards, her eyes narrowing in appraisal.

'Fascinating,' she murmurs.

'Excuse me,' says Chanticleer, entering the group. His chest is puffed out and his face is all smiles, he is the very picture of pomp and hospitality. 'To whom do I have the pleasure?'

'Sir!' The peacock bows again. 'You do me great honour by welcoming me personally: I can tell already you are an important fellow, with many commitments and responsibilities. I am but a humble traveller, seeking respite in your beautiful farm.'

'Is that so?' says Chanticleer.

The peacock tells them his story. Acquired by a hostelry establishment a few acres yonder, to increase the sense of classy leisured ambiance for their clientele, the peacock spent his formative years lounging about beside ornamental ponds and striding up and down neatly clipped lawns. But soon adventure called to him, and he had jumped and fluttered right over the wrought-iron gate and made a run for it. He wandered aimlessly for a while, begging nuts and seeds from besotted locals, until eventually he had gravitated towards the tall trees and promising rooftops and ochre colours beckoning him from Chanticleer's farm.

Chanticleer listens to all this with a friendly enough smile.

'And were there many hens in your previous innyard?' asks one of the hens.

'There were swans!' cries the peacock. 'Gorgeous creatures with their long necks and delicate plumage. They sailed along the pond to and fro in the most beautiful formation.'

'Ah that's tricky, I'm sorry for you; quite a temper on them, swans,' says Chanticleer. 'My grandfather once got into a fight with one and –'

'Only if you don't treat them right,' says the peacock, blithely. 'With me they were always the very model of grace.'

Chanticleer feels the grit in his stomach – swallowed earlier to help digest his food – begin to grind within him in a more intense manner than before.

The hens are flapping away cheerfully. They clearly enjoy the peacock's tales of travels through exotic climes. 'And what did you eat there?' they ask; it was inevitable they'd come to this subject, a topic foremost in their minds.

'Every meal was delicate and delicious! I was fed on grapes and the richest seeds and the most soft and lightest white bread you can imagine.' The peacock ruffles his feathers; the sun glints off gold and sapphire jewellery. 'Quite a decadent menu in all honesty, far too rich. I'm glad to be shot of it,' he adds, looking at the floor, where the hen's lunch of sunflower seeds and millet are still scattered about in the dust. 'I'm greatly looking forward to a simpler diet.'

'And do you sing?' asks Chanticleer, in a voice harsher than he had intended. The others all look over at him. 'We often sing and dance and make our own entertainment,' he adds. 'So it would be *wonderful* if you did.'

'Why yes, I do,' says the peacock, recovering quickly from his surprise. 'I was quite infamous in the tavern for my call, or at least I like to think so.'

'Let us hear it!' cries one of the hens, and the others all take up the line, jumping about and clucking eagerly. A cow, passing, stops to watch the action.

The peacock glances up to the sky, such an absurd display of faux modesty Chanticleer feels a tug of annoyance.

'I really shouldn't,' says the peacock. 'But all right.'

The peacock puts his head back and lets off a virtuosic turn of operatic trilling that sends the cow clopping off to the pasture to tell the others; the horses in the far-off field look up from the grass, impressed; in the farmyard the cats stretch out from their nap and dogs begin to bark and run around in circles. The hens are all silent, beaks open in shock.

Pertolete whistles softly.

And Chanticleer: he is struck stock-still, gone cold all over.

'That was without any warming up, of course, barely a ditty,' says the peacock, all bashfulness again. 'Please do not judge me on that performance alone. I do a much better job when the time is right!' He adjusts his cuffs, revealing a signet ring loaded with sapphires, and notices Pertolete clock it. 'This was a gift from the Queen of Turkeys,' he explains, 'from a pilgrimage I went on in my youth. I only intended a brief expedition, but so pleasant was my stay I remained a while in her court. She gave me this as a thank you for many a night's service of song.'

'You're quite the accomplished one,' says Pertolete. 'You'll be happy to know our Chanticleer here also has a glorious voice. Perhaps the two of you will give us a tune together sometime?'

'Sometime,' says Chanticleer, his voice quiet.

'I would adore that!' says the peacock. Then his face comes all over with mock annoyance. 'Oh bother, tripped over my tail again. This bloody thing,' he gestures to it. 'I do feel the load.

Must be a lovely lightfully tripped life for you, eh?' he says to Chanticleer.

'Worth it though, I expect?' says Pertolete. 'Must be quite a sight when you let it loose.'

'Well oh my, I don't know, don't ask me, ah-ha,' the peacock blushes and looks down at his feet – he wears impeccable shoes, by the way, turquoise boots up past the ankle, with white spats. 'I have received a lot of pleasant attentions about my plumage, but really, I don't know –'

And he raises his tail and ripples it open, shimmering it before them.

No sooner has the peacock's great feathers begun to rise but Chanticleer's whole body, already gone all over with ice, becomes damp and clammy with the cold sweat of panic.

'No!'

He backs away, his eyes and face fallen open with the terror of it.

'Get away!'

There in the peacock's tail, just as his nightmare had foretold: those monstrous dark eyes glaring from the vivid blue. The feathers ripple again, and in the distance Chanticleer thinks he can hear laughing, and the movement makes the eyes come alive and glitter at him, and the tail rolls inwards as if it would trap Chanticleer inside, and Chanticleer madly spins about but everywhere now, every way he turns are those monstrous eyes: a hell made of blue, the sky fallen in –

Chanticleer screams and races behind the barn, where he half buries himself in a pile of old straw and breathes heavily into the dry scratchy air. His heart is beating terribly in his body; he fancies it will burst then and there and drench his red suit with more of the same.

Before too long, he feels a friendly weight gently pressing onto his back. He raises himself from the straw enough to see the flash of Pertolete's feather boa.

'It's the monster,' he manages to say. 'I saw it.'

'Darling, you've lost all sense. That was simply our new friend's fascinating tail-dance. He's made quite an impression on everyone, no doubt there. He's talking now about going off to the coop for drinks and a few rounds of pluck poker with the hens.'

Chanticleer shakes his head. 'My dream tried to warn me, and just now was the proof. He'll be the death of me.' He gulps. 'I thought the dream meant a monster who would eat me. But I see now it is something far worse. I am going to be outdone, replaced and forgotten.'

Pertolete's voice comes harsher now. 'Stop this at once,' she says. Chanticleer looks up at her, surprised.

'You're jealous,' says Pertolete, 'that's what I think. So there's a chap in town with fancy tail-feathers. Pull yourself together. We owe it to him to be generous hosts, not rush off and hide behind the milk churns.'

'I am not jealous!' cries Chanticleer. 'I don't at all care for blue, I don't wish I'd done all that travelling –'

'Well then,' says Pertolete, and she falls silent, waiting. They sit together for a while, there in the straw.

'I'm simply experiencing a threat to my very sense of self,' says Chanticleer.

Pertolete gives him a squeeze, then stands up and adjusts her white gloves. 'Come and speak with him some more,' she says. 'Then you'll see this monstrous threat for what it really is.'

'And what is that?'

'Heavens if I know,' mutters Pertolete. 'I can't work out everything for you.' She turns and goes. Chanticleer follows her mopily back towards the farmyard.

When they arrive, the peacock is in the centre of a large group of all the animals, telling a thrilling story about a near run-in he had once with a weasel. Chanticleer sits on one of the hay bales in the back row, trying to ignore the fluttering fear of threat ever present in his stomach.

'His dreadful speed,' says the peacock, 'and his beady eyes. And his bushy tail! I feared for my life!'

He tells a tale of daring narrow escape and clever fast thinking, and at the end takes a small sip from the water trough while his audience applauds. Afterwards, when the rest of the farm animals are speaking among themselves, Chanticleer steps up to the peacock and bows his head.

'Sir,' he says, casting nervous eyes to Pertolete, who nods encouragingly at him between nibbles at the seed-box, 'Sir,' says Chanticleer, 'I would like to say that I... think you are very admirable. That tale of how you outwitted the weasel. It was... a *tour de force*.'

(For it had been a good yarn and grippingly told, and Chanticleer could not bring himself to be dishonest about anything to do with aesthetics.)

The peacock smiles, but much more bashfully than the sleek grin he had been performing earlier for the hens. 'The truth is... I feel the pressure sometimes, to always be "on" and at the centre of things. I should remember I am no longer the jewel of a tavern's pretentious gardening arrangements but a citizen of the farm, no? For then I could concentrate on my actual duties, and enjoy the important things in life.'

'Friendship and satisfaction?' asks Chanticleer, nodding along.

'Well yes, those. And the nightly duty, of course – but you'll know about that.'

Chanticleer's mind speeds through all the activities that go on in the coop through the nocturnal hours. 'Which nightly duty?' he asks.

'I mean the importance of my singing!' says the peacock. And he looks at Chanticleer expectantly. Chanticleer looks blankly back at him, and the two of them are held there for a moment, ruby eye to sapphire eye.

Chanticleer breaks first. 'I'm sorry?' he says, his face puzzled. 'I feel as if you expect me to know what you mean, but I'll confess I don't.'

'Every evening I ascend to the highest point and sing,' says the peacock. 'In order to bring up the moon and commence the night. You didn't know that? You're an experienced man of the world, I thought you must surely know about that... Oh well. Perhaps I shouldn't always assume my fame will precede me? There's a lesson for me there. Anyway. I have been meaning to discuss the question of my post with you. No doubt you'll appreciate the importance. I thought I might take the swooping one there, at the top-most corner of the cowshed?'

'I... am experienced,' manages Chanticleer. 'Know of the world, yes.'

'Then you'll understand how crucial this all is. Hence why I was nervous to sing for you earlier, in case something went awry and night came early. I would hate to do that to you all as soon as I arrive! For you never know. Sometimes I see the moon in the sky while the sky is still a bright daytime blue, and I wonder if it were my mistake, for singing during the day. After all, you never see the sun at night, do you? So, you see, it's a fair theory. But generally it tends to be all right, and I can sing during the day provided I am careful. But in the evening, well, I simply *must*.'

Chanticleer swallows, bristles, visibly struggles, then puts his face back into an expression of respectful interest. 'I understand you entirely,' he says. 'It is a grave responsibility you bear upon your gold-flecked shoulders.'

'Indeed. It would flummox a lesser peacock, I daresay.'

'Lucky for us we have a greater one, then!' says Chanticleer, his voice full of glee, feeling as if he were about to explode with joy and mirth. He leaves the peacock there and speeds quickly to Pertolete.

'You'll never believe what I just learned!' he cries. 'He only thinks he summons the moon!'

Pertolete smiles. 'Oh really? That's quaint of him.'

'You should have seen how sincerely he told me. What a fool, what an exquisite scholar of the ridiculous!' Chanticleer brushes tears from his eyes with one of his rust-red wings. 'I should have known there would be something. Oh ho, this fellow holds no fear for me at all!'

Flickers of amusement play about Pertolete's feathers as she watches Chanticleer shake with laughter.

'All the years we have been on the farm,' he says, spluttering to get the words out. 'Have we ever *not* had darkness fall? The night comes! It simply does! Oh-ho, I cannot wait to burst his bubble!'

Pertolete's face falls. 'You want to tell him?'

'He'll be so embarrassed. He'll go quite as red as me!'

'Darling, reconsider,' says Pertolete. 'You might bring his entire sense of self crashing down. Remember how awful that is?'

'Oh.' Chanticleer looks about and scratches his foot across the ground a little. 'It would be an unpleasant thing to do deliberately, that's true.'

'Perhaps there's no need to disabuse him of the notion?' suggests Pertolete gently. 'Look how much purpose and confidence it's given him all these years.'

'I suppose you're right. But secretly we can know, can't we? You and I may know. Ha-ha! I've realised I have no reason to worry, and that's the most important thing.'

Pertolete glances briefly at the sunset reflected in the water trough. 'Yes. I'm very proud of you,' she adds.

And so the farmyard carried on about its business, with a new pulse to the rhythm that measured the passage of time, the bright rooster crowing for the start of the day and the shining call of the peacock greeting the velvety night.

The Gunman Who Came in From the Door

The demand was for constant action; if you stopped to think you were lost. When in doubt, have a man come through the door with a gun in his hand.
— Raymond Chandler

It was a dull day, I wasn't doing very much. In theory I was working from home, but that theory wasn't working and neither was I. I tried looking out of the window but the sky was a smudged grey, like yesterday's make-up, and it didn't compel me out of doors or into better thoughts. I looked again at my work, but it could all wait a few more minutes. I didn't know what to write. I was waiting for inspiration, and starting to feel stood up. The phone was silent. The clock ticked. A man came through the door with a gun in his hand.

I stood immediately, with my hands up. I hate guns. I wanted to say: *who are you? why are you here? what are you doing with that gun?* or something stronger, but I found I couldn't speak. Anyway, it was his turn to say something. He had the gun.

We didn't speak for a few moments, just stared at each other. He had a hat as well as a gun. I had neither.

'I'm here about the case,' he said.

'What case?' I said.

'You know what case,' he said, and seemed content to leave it at that. I wasn't.

'I don't know what you're talking about,' I said. 'I'm not a detective. I'm an actor.'

He raised an eyebrow. 'An actor?'

He sounded unconvinced and I didn't like that. As if he thought actors didn't exist outside the theatre – like a school kid can't believe his teachers sometimes go to shops or restaurants? It wasn't my fault I was at home today. Let him walk into the theatre with a gun while I'm working, he wouldn't raise an eyebrow at me like that.

But he had a gun, so I kept it short. 'Yes,' I said. 'I'm a writer and an actor.'

'You in a play right now?' he said.

'I've just finished one,' I said.

'Get good reviews?' he said.

'I never read those things,' I said.

'Quit stalling,' he said – hypocritically, I thought. 'I'm here about the case.'

'I'm telling you,' I said (because I was), 'I don't know what you're talking about.' You hear stories about confused fans, practical jokes, that sort of thing – but I've never played a detective in anything, so this wasn't one of those stories. I didn't know what he wanted. 'Unless you mean, I don't know, do you mean an actual case? Are we talking lost luggage? Because apart from that I don't know what –'

He started to say, 'You know full well what I'm talking –' but he was interrupted.

A man came through the door with a gun in his hand.

'Oh, God,' I said, and stepped away until I reached the far wall. I thought this must be back-up, but the first man looked as surprised as I was.

The two men arranged themselves so they were evenly spaced. They pointed their guns at each other, which was a relief for me.

'Do you two know each other?' I said. They both shook their heads. 'Are you here about the case too?' I said to the new man.

'Aha! So you do know about it!' said the first man, pointing the gun at me. The second man kept pointing his gun at the first man.

'I don't know this man,' said the second man, 'but it sounds like you're the person I'm looking for.'

'Now look,' I said, 'I was just telling your colleague here: I know nothing about this.'

'She was saying that,' said the first man. 'But I think she's lying.'

A man came through the door with a gun in his hand.

'Is this where I can get some info on the Siddons Case?' he said.

The three men pointed their guns at each other.

'The Siddons Case?' said one of them. 'I'm here about the Terry Affair.'

'Look,' I said. I'd had enough of this. I went for a guaranteed tension-breaker: drinks. 'Does anyone want a cup of tea?' I had a feeling I should offer scotch or whisky, but I didn't have any. And I didn't want anyone to get drunk.

The men nodded. The second man said, 'Ooh, lovely.'

I went into the kitchen and put the kettle on.

As I returned, a man came through the door with a gun in his hand.

Without saying a word, I went back into the kitchen and put out another mug.

When I returned again, all four men were asking each other what they knew, and nobody was admitting to knowing anything. I watched for a while. After a few minutes, I started to suspect they'd forgotten about me. A man came through the door with a gun in his hand.

A man came through the door with a gun in his hand.

A couple of men sat on the sofa. One pulled up the footrest and sat on that.

A man came through the door with a gun in his hand.

A man came through the door with a gun in his hand.

A man came through the door with a gun in his hand.

I proposed a gun amnesty. Some of the men were reluctant at first, but eventually, they all agreed to put their guns in a pile in the corner. I don't know if there were any more guns hiding in socks or waistbands. I didn't want to check, I didn't look.

A man came through the door with a gun in his hand. He was immediately told about the amnesty by the other men, and complied with no trouble. The pile of guns grew by one gun.

I never made the tea. I didn't want to offer again, and anyway I didn't have enough mugs. By now it was standing room only.

A man came through the door with a gun in his hand. He added his gun to the pile of guns and looked around, was welcomed by the nearest group of men, and squeezed in. Multiple conversations were happening by now, and some of them sounded friendly. I saw handshakes, and some of the men were doing impressions of the other men. I thought about putting on some music. Then one man asked me where the bathroom was. That was it.

'All right,' I said. 'Everybody out.'

It took a while to get the men to go; eventually I had to move one of them off the sofa and stand on it to get their attention.

'I'm sorry,' I said, and I waved my arms until they were quiet. 'May I have your attention please?

'I think there has been a misunderstanding. I can't help any of you with any cases or mysteries you may have come here to investigate. I was sitting at my desk and I'd like to get back to it. I have a lot of work to do. Thank you.'

They took their guns with them as they went. I don't know where they are now, but last night I dreamt that a gun came through the door with a hand in his man.

The Modjeska Waltz

From the private papers of Irene Adler. Undated; from its tone, possibly intended for posthumous publication. It is in that hope, in any case, that we reproduce it here.

My first and most intriguing adventure with Professor Moriarty was – in more than one respect – an elaborate dance.

Shortly after the affair I note Dr Watson refers to as a 'scandal', although it had been nothing of the kind from my perspective, I found myself travelling the continent. It was a pleasure to do so, and enabled me to put the unfortunate fire in my London lodgings far in the past. On the occasion the Professor entered my awareness, I had dabbled in reprising my position at the Imperial Opera of Warsaw. Although I declared myself perfectly content with minor roles and chorus parts, I had been coaxed into accepting first a single solo aria, and then a full prima donna position. Indeed, by the time a lengthy tour took me back to London and Moriarty sought me out, it had become rather difficult to enter my dressing room for the sheer density of roses. Such is the life of a performer of my calibre.

It came to me via the usual routes for society gossip, tipping out of the opera boxes down to the 'merely players' on the stage below, the news that the King of B– was organising a ball for his son, to be held in the city; and it was perhaps due to my prominence as the Countess of *Figaro* that season that I was presented with a gilt-edged invitation. I make no claims on my vanity as an actress (or, indeed, as a dancer) as to why the Professor called upon me. Neither did he wish to accompany me to the ball for the chance to dabble in society. He hinted towards the fact that he and I were the only two minds ever to best our mutual friend, and that *this* was the reason for seeking me out, and not attempting to gain entry to the ball another way. This did flatter me, I confess. But I have reason to believe, in the cold mist of dawn, that even this was only a front for obtaining an invitation.

I was in my dressing room shortly after a performance of Mimi, given to great acclaim although *La bohème* does not, artistically, stretch me. A boy brought me a visitor's card – and although I have thought at length upon it since, I cannot now remember why I chose to pay attention to this card in particular, as so many came my way. Perhaps it was the lack of embarrassing praise, confessions of love, poetic follies, amateur drawings. No, only a request to meet, the naming of a respectable teahouse in a fashionable part of London quite far from the theatre, a table number (most intriguing!) and a time. And a coat of arms which I did not at first recognise. I was curious – perhaps the first moves of the dance between us were being felt out, even then. I told the boy to return to the giver of the card with the news that I agreed to the meeting. After that I was preoccupied with rehearsals and fending off would-be paramours until the appointed date.

The teahouse my mysterious companion had chosen was one known for its discretion. Young men hovered around the edges ready for any reason they might be needed, while remaining distant enough that the diners could maintain their privacy. I arrived approximately seven and a half minutes late (as is my wont) only to find the reserved table empty, but as soon as I had announced my name to the maître d and been seated by the window, a cream tea was set before me.

'I do apologise for the mistake,' I said, 'but I have not placed an order.' I did not wish to deprive the cream tea's true owners of their afternoon delicacy.

'No, 's definitely for this table, miss,' said the serving boy as he placed the jam and milk down. 'Sir says you are welcome to start, miss.' Only a slight quiver to his hands betrayed his nervousness; new to the role, perhaps. 'He said to say he'll b-be with you anon.' I recognised the stutter over a learnt line.

I thanked the boy – my companion's impudence was not his fault – and decided to pour my tea. A moment passed, which I spent gazing out of the window, before a silver-topped cane passed by my place and within another moment a gentleman was sitting opposite me.

He wore a topcoat whose slight shabbiness marred its original expense, and when he removed it I noticed that his grey suit, as fine as it was, had begun to fray at the edges. The chain of a pocketwatch glinted from his velvet waistcoat, and the silver-topped cane was placed gently down against his chair, frequently toyed with and never out of his reach. The overall impression was of a man who rarely attended such a social event as afternoon tea, although he could afford to do much more.

'Do I have the pleasure of sitting opposite the great Irene Adler?' he cried. I nodded, and any nervous tension he was carrying disappeared to be replaced by an eager courtesy that belied his years. 'It is an honour to make your acquaintance at last. I do beg your pardon for my lateness; a measure to determine that I would not be surprised by... any unexpected guests.' As I was not fully acquainted with the Professor's criminal reputation at this point, this struck me as only mildly eccentric – not justifiably cautious!

'And you are?'

'Oh! I do beg your pardon,' he stood and leaned over awkwardly to shake my hand across the table – thus compiling a baffling set of social inadequacies that marked him out as a Professor more readily than the chalk marks on his lapel ever would. 'James Moriarty, at your service,' he said.

'And what brings you to request the pleasure of a cream tea in this particular establishment?' I said. 'It is beyond the salary of a poor actress. I imagine also that it is outside of the usual range of experience for a scholar.'

'I am attempting to establish a social life,' he said, and gave a nervous laugh that showed he recognised – and respected – my correct deduction of his profession. (Although it was, of course, only half correct.) He then contradicted his stated desire for sociability: 'Madame, I shall get straight to the point.

'I have a great interest in the musico-social event that has been recently announced in honour of the Prince of B–. An impudent whelp, by my reckoning, to require his father to throw a ball so that he might reveal himself before everyone like a society debutante.' He checked his annoyance, and continued. 'In any case, the event is to be hosted by George Frederick St Clare, the King of B–, one month from today. I do not need to outline these facts to you, of course, as from what I have seen of the society pages, you will be gracing the occasion yourself.'

I nodded. It was a novelty for a man to be so forthright about the extent of his prior research.

He continued: 'I have invited you here, then, if I may put it bluntly, to beg you to attend with me as your guest.'

This surprised me – I have rarely known such bluntness, and was not expecting such an assertion from a man who seemed to be all elbows, and visibly desperate to return to his inkwells, or his abacus, or some such environment; not a ball for the highest of society. (I still had the man in mind as a shuffling, shy academic at this point, I confess.)

'I wish to attend the ball, Miss Adler, because I wish to gain a closer inspection of a specific gift the society pages inform us the Prince will be presenting to the Dowager Duchess of Croome.'

'A brooch,' I said, to show that I was as knowledgeable as he about this event, and did not need it explaining. 'We believe the Prince and his father have designs on arranging a marriage to one of the Duchess' many relatives. This gift is to sweeten the strength between the two families.'

I said *we believe* to make the Professor assume that we were still talking about information gleaned from the society pages and the gossip of chorus girls, but I had heard this from a very close source and knew it to be the case.

'Indeed,' he said, and continued to outline his plan. 'I must be absolutely honest with you, Miss Adler. If the timing is right, and I am able, and with your good assistance, I will be able to – I wish to obtain the brooch for myself. Merely to inspect it, nothing more. No damage shall be done to it, of course. The brooch is priceless, et cetera. But it is vital that it is in my capable hands by the end of the ball. The trick, as far as I can see, will be to take the brooch after it has been officially presented to the Duchess. The crowd will have seen it go to what is presumed to be its rightful home; and then we can get closer by means of strategic socialising – I leave this in your responsibility, as an actress – and remove it before we leave the ball.'

'Well,' I said, when he had finished. 'The plan you outline sounds foolish at best; criminal at worst.'

He merely nodded; clearly this much he already knew. So I continued.

'The chief problem, as *I* see it, sir, will be convincing the guests that you belong amongst their number. As respected as you may be in your field, this is a grand occasion. There will be few present who do not own, or lay claim to, at least two countries in the Commonwealth.'

He opened his mouth to interrupt, but I spoke over him. 'You are, no doubt, wondering how I myself achieved an invitation. Indeed, it is a question I have pondered. I believe it could be something to do with the desire of the host to add some culture to the affair; several singers, ballerinas, pianists – even a painter if the rumours I have heard are right – have been invited to attend. I fear I am primarily intended to be decorative.'

I did not mention the letters I owned from the prince, begging me to attend the party as the last chance he would have to see his 'true fair *Rosalind*' before the machinations of political marriage took him. I had barely considered the letters myself, and intended to take up his invitation in order to enjoy myself.

31

'So you see, Professor, it is not merely a question of behaving appropriately to the occasion. It is a question of clearly *belonging*.'

'You will be allowed to bring a guest, as you have an invitation,' he said, as if I had never spoken. 'Surely nobody will question your choice.'

'Sir!' I said. 'As a gift to the Prince, the King commissioned the composition of a new dance. All guests will be dancing the Modjeska Waltz. You could stumble once and give the game away.'

'What is the Modjeska Waltz?' he said.

'*Ah*,' I said. 'It is something that was not included in the society pages so as to weed out those who might attend without permission. It is a dance that the guests will know. I myself know enough of it to pass, but only because I am surrounded by chorus girls for my work at the opera. They are all experts in popular society dances and take pride in a comprehensive knowledge of the newest fashions. I can only imagine who is teaching the other decorative attendees.'

'Most interesting,' he said (and it was truly as if he did not know) — 'and the Modjeska Waltz will be a partner-changing dance, I suppose, in order to allow the illusion of social mingling without forcing the grander guests present to deign in actual conversation with the lower orders?'

I nodded, assuming that he regularly read the society pages as another point of professorial eccentricity.

'Fascinating. And who is Modjeska?'

'Oh, some snippet of an actress or a singer of some sort, that the prince feels pertinent to honour with a tune or two,' I said, and I sniffed to show that I had no interest in this matter.

'Very well,' said the Professor. 'In any case, you consider this to be a barrier to my entering the Ball?'

'I do indeed.'

He thought for another moment. I was considering adding cream to a scone when he changed tack.

'You are aware of my thesis, *The Dynamics of an Asteroid?*' said Moriarty.

I gave him a look that said *I am not.* I consider it irrelevant whether or not I really knew.

'It is my most renowned monograph,' said the Professor, and I guessed that he was not as confident as his words suggested. It was a forced boast.

'Indeed,' I said. 'I suppose your other writing is concerned with too niche and obscure a subject to warrant a large audience.'

'It is composed of such pure mathematics that no man can refute it!' he cried, knocking over his Earl Grey. A starched-apron'd boy ran to the table to wipe the mess.

'I am sure,' I said, once the boy had departed, 'that your thesis is highly renowned in the circles of those who speak, as you say, pure mathematics. However, my primary languages are those of the arts, Professor, and I cannot see why you wish to speak with me.'

Moriarty sighed, and commenced the story anew.

'Did you read in the newspapers last year, of the discovery of a fragment of asteroid in the Netherlands?'

'I cannot say it stuck in my mind, if I did,' I said. (And that was true; the latest scientific discoveries of the age were of some passing novelty interest, but of little use to me in any greater capacity.)

'Well, the news struck me with great force. For my experiments, it is vital that I have access to the stone.'

'It is for the Dowager Duchess of Croome,' I said, seeing now that his interest in the ball was nothing to do with the society pages. 'The Prince has had the stone embedded in a brooch, which he will present to her the ball.'

'It is *not* for the Duchess of Croome,' said Moriarty. I was put in mind of a child denied a sugar mouse.

'You seek to contradict royalty?' I said. 'Who – or what – do you suggest the stone is for?'

'It is for Mathematics!' he cried, and beat his fist upon the table so that the china rattled. I saw several of the staff turn at the sound, no doubt wondering if they would be required to mop up a further spillage.

Moriarty had, perhaps, even startled himself with his violence, and he spoke next with a more controlled voice. 'I need entrance to the Ball,' he said. 'You are invited.'

'I am,' I said.

'I need entrance. I need to get close enough to the Duchess to acquire the brooch. It is no use sending an agent in for this, I must do it myself.' I raised an eyebrow, and he explained. 'It is a matter of mathematics. I act in my professorial role; I do not propose to become a criminal.'

'You propose to steal.'

'It is the *King of B–* who has stolen!' he cried, and this time I feared for the teapot. 'Stolen a prime specimen from under the very eyes of Science! To reduce such a discovery of such importance to the modern age to a piece of… a piece of *costume jewellery*…!'

I let the jibe at costumes stand, and waited.

'I need to get to the Ball, Miss Adler, and I need to remain there long enough to acquire the brooch. I need to appear to *belong* at the ball. Miss Adler, I need to know the Modjeska Waltz.'

I waited for more, but he sat back, sipped his refilled cup, and waited.

Finally, the ha'penny dropped. 'Professor Moriarty,' I said, 'are you asking me for… *dancing lessons?*'

For the first time in this escapade – and, I wonder now, perhaps the only time – Moriarty seemed truly embarrassed. He pushed scone crumbs around his plate. 'Well,' he said, 'if that is what it will take to get me close enough to acquire the stone, then that it what it will take.'

I let him suffer as I pondered this.

'I must say, I do rather fancy the challenge.' I said. 'But first you must tell me, Professor. You claim to wish to accompany me to the dance in order to examine a brooch. Such a robbery would be tantamount to high treason; you do not seem to think I would quail at this. There is social danger, even if we are not caught in our designs, in our attending this event. There are better dancers than I, who would be able to instruct you in the Modjeska Waltz. And so I ask you, Professor Moriarty – why have you come to me?'

Now the embarrassment faded, and a sharp keenness flashed in the Professor's eyes like a stolen jewel in the wrong place. 'We are of one mind, Miss Adler,' he said. 'Or rather, we have both bested the same mind. I can think of nobody I would rather trust with such an important mission of personal and professional pride.'

'I know who you are thinking of,' I said. 'This is a case, I take it, of "my enemy's enemy"?'

If I have a fault, it is that, when poetic justice requires, I am also sometimes willing to put personal and professional pride above common sense. We shook hands and agreed on the date of the Professor's first lesson.

'This is nonsense! Why ever do people do this for fun and frivolity?'

'That is not for us to question. Let us begin again, Professor. And do *try* to not move your lips as you count.'

We were using the stage of the Opera House, a space that suggested the dimensions of a ballroom dance floor well enough. The manager of the theatre owed me a favour, which I was intending to call upon if ever a paramour caught my attention enough to warrant a moment of privacy about the stage-door; but I decided that this was a more exciting reason to call in my favour and take temporary ownership of the stage.

Moriarty stumbled through a passable imitation of the Modjeska Waltz – the complex patterning was simpler to his numerically inclined mind than the turns of the standard waltz and foxtrot. He placed his hands on his thighs, bending over slightly in a cruel parody of the gentlemanly bow with which the dance had begun, and breathed and wheezed out his hatred of the activity. I made no response to his complaining, and merely amused myself by making faces at the painted cherubim that decorated the opera boxes.

'So, ah, when,' he asked, between gulps of breath, 'we approach the Duchess –'

'I have heard enough criminal machinations,' I said. And, before he could take another gulp of air to protest my use of the word *criminal*, I continued, 'Let us run through the middle-turns twice more.' He made groans of protest which I ignored. 'This is the part where the partners change, Professor! It is the most important part of all to get right.'

The Professor grumbled his way through the rehearsal, and, following that, he suffered regularly for two lessons per week until the date of the ball. I confess, I was surprised that he committed to the full programme. After the first lesson I felt sure he would refuse the scheme, and had started to wonder if I had underestimated his desire to obtain the Duchess' brooch.

The ballroom was built to resemble a grand Orangery, or perhaps it *was* a grand Orangery once upon an era. Its glass domed ceiling was open to the sky, and we were blessed with a clear canopy of stars. The great space was lit on all sides with candles and framed with gleaming wood, silk and silver. The musicians played a selection of pieces arranged for strings and bassoon. The waiters moved with brisk efficiency around the samovars and between the great teetering settings of sweetmeats and jellies in the shape of castles. And the guests themselves were the prize jewels. Filling the great hall – although not, yet, approaching the dance floor – were dukes and barons, countesses and princesses, and everywhere glinted tiaras and medals.

I suppose the more excitable kind of reporter might have called it 'glittering'.

We approached the ballroom and my name was announced at the door but the Professor was not even asked his. I wonder now whether this might have been a deliberate move on his part, whether coins had changed hands at an earlier stage in order to bring about this cloak of anonymity. But I was occupied with making the necessary small-talk with the other guests as I deposited my furs with a porter (including a minor peer who claimed he had once sent a bouquet to my dressing room, and received no thanks; this was most likely true), and then it was time to descend the stairs to the ballroom. I had no time to quiz the Professor as to whether he had made any plans without informing me, and in any case it was soon put out of my mind. The Prince, I noticed, deliberately avoided my eye.

We had not been present long when the King had his crystal glass refilled with port, and he tapped on it with what looked like a golden letter opener.

'My fellow guests!' he cried, and the hubbub of high society quietened in deference and expectation.

'You are all most welcome,' said the King, and he barely concealed a hiccough. I could tell he needed to drink no more port this evening, and the ball had barely begun. 'We are gathered here to celebrate the coming-of-age of my son and heir, Prince –' and here he named his son, who I protect here with the same anonymity the Professor was currently enjoying by my side. There were several names and titles, and the King named them all. Finally we were encouraged to applaud the existence of this young man.

'Thank you, Father,' said the Prince, and at his voice the King sat down heavily, visibly confident in his son finishing the required address. (Perhaps the Prince had made deductions that matched my own regarding the King's capacity to speak with vast quantities of port and brandywine inside him.)

'I would like to thank you all for attending tonight,' he said. 'I am truly blessed to have so many excellent friends.' I fought the temptation to snort. 'In honour of the occasion, I have asked one of the nation's most skilled composers to create a dance for us. Thank you.' And he made a gesture at the conductor, and bowed for further applause. It was hardly a triumph of oratory.

I was surprised, furthermore, that the Prince had not presented the Dowager Duchess of Croome with the brooch. Professor Moriarty had been insistent that it would happen before we took to the floor, so that he might examine it during his twirl with the Duchess. His puzzled frown suggested that we had an accord of confusion.

The Conductor gestured for silence and the first, gentle strings of the new composition floated over our heads from the violas and cellos. It would have been pleasant, had I not been with a man plotting something akin to high treason in three-four time.

'That's the Modjeska Waltz,' said I. 'It is time, Professor, to prove that you belong here.'

'You mean,' said he, 'it is time to prove that *we* belong here.'

'No,' said I. 'You seem to be forgetting that I was already invited.'

'Ah! My mistake. You were always on the guest list, of course.' If the strings had not been soaring at that very moment, I might have thought more carefully about this remark. As it was, we had no time. We reached the floor, bowed and curtsied as required, and positioned ourselves ready to begin the dance.

The understanding reader will indulge me for a moment in a minor side note on the matter of ballroom dancing.

There are two roles in ballroom dance: he who leads, and she who follows. To he who leads, therefore, it follows that even the dance with the speediest and most frequent partner-changes will flow as smoothly as if he were dancing alone. To she who follows, each partner brings a host of potential dangers, embarrassing errors and awkward collisions, each new body the host of an unknown collection of possible faults, idiosyncrasies, potential tumbles and physical suffering. For the most part, at the manner of event we were enjoying, the men were, of course, highly practised and considerate partners. But she who follows can never truly relax during such an occasion, as she never knows what her next partner will do, or how she will need to adjust her own performance so that he who leads can continue to remain unaware of the challenges his dancing brings.

I mention all of this because, to wit, I wish it to be known, formally, dear reader, that I accomplished everything Professor Moriarty did, albeit I frequently found myself going backwards, and in a pair of stolen heels.

But I shall explain the latter in good time. Let us return to the ballroom.

We had successfully performed the first steps of the dance, and had made it beyond the first turn. Ballroom dances proceed in promenade, and I had made sure to begin in a position that gave us a long wall to travel down, to allow the good Professor as much time as possible to get into the rhythm of things before we were forced to turn a corner. But eventually, the necessity of moving about a finite space could not be avoided, and the first *chaînés en dedans* approached us.

The Professor's jaw was set firm, and there was fierce concentration in his eyes. Even the most casual onlooker would know that he was counting. I decided against reminding him of the need to smile, as I felt certain it wouldn't help his mood. We managed the corner thanks to my subtle steering – I dreaded to think how the Professor would get on without a guide. He was in the arms of fate, as were his partners.

I had a momentary respite when the first change arrived. The Professor positively had to be pushed away from me. I enjoyed the smalltalk of a friendly young man who claimed to be a writer and wit living in the city, who told me he had witnessed my Desdemona at the Royal and enjoyed it immensely.

Having not yet played Desdemona, I made do with giving him the ghost of a smile.

When Moriarty returned, he clutched my wrist as if it was the only thing keeping him on the floor.

'It is nonsense,' he said, already out of breath, 'to change on the two, when mathematically it is not at all expedient –' and, mercifully, he was whisked away again. It took another minute or two of rapid changing of partners – I enjoyed the solid steps of a considerate brigadier and suffered through a clumsy duke with far too loose a shoulder line, and damp hands – until we were together once again for the next quarter-turn.

'I despise this,' said the Professor.

'I am hardly having a debutante's delight,' I replied.

'Let us take the brooch now, and escape this infernal place.' The ordeal of dancing had made him anxious to commence the scheme and hasten our opportunity to leave. I sympathised, but it was far too soon, and I opened my mouth to protest. 'The Duchess is ahead,' he said. 'Let us –'

'Professor!' I hissed, 'the Prince has not yet presented –' but I was too late. After what followed, I feared I could never again spend time in polite society.

To describe the horror briefly: with the insistent strength of the Professor pulling me along, we danced out into a glittering tailspin, rocketed past the four couples ahead of us and stumbled directly into the Duchess as she danced with a dashing dragoon.

I heard a crack in my right foot, and braced myself for agonising pain. Fortunately – or perhaps unfortunately, given what happened after – it had come from my shoe, not my foot, and an examination revealed the heel had broken. I wanted to scream with frustration; damn the Professor and his entire expedition!

The Prince ran to the aid of the Duchess and continued to studiously ignore me as he helped her walk to the edge of the dance floor. In response, the Dragoon made a show of helping me arise and walk to safety. This was difficult, given the condition of my newly broken shoes, which I confess I allowed the Dragoon to assume was a limp borne of injury.

The biggest concern – and the focus of the rest of the guests – was directed at the Professor himself. He had performed his out-of-control waltz so well the ballroom was humming with worries about the frailty of the man. Eventually he had assured everyone of his health to their satisfaction, and he joined me. I was still sitting were the Dragoon had placed me, having bid him adieu so he might jostle with the Prince for care of the Duchess. All the attention was focused on that end of the ballroom, while at the other, the Professor approached the Actress.

'I have it!' said Moriarty, hissing at me through great excitement. He took out the pocketwatch from his waistcoat – and I saw the red glint of the ruby setting.

So the Prince *had* presented the Duchess with the brooch – presumably at an earlier, private moment, before the Ball began! I wondered, and the reader will forgive my vanity, whether this had something to do with my own RSVP.

'You have successfully committed a serious crime,' I said, 'but I fear we have greater problems. The stumble has damaged the heel of one of my shoes.'

'No matter!' he cried. 'Let us ask my good friend the porter whether he might find us any spares lying about the place.' And before he could protest I was being steered to this curious man's station, which through the whole evening had been maintained with military stillness and concentration by the door. They had a whispered conversation beyond my earshot, after which the porter swiftly disappeared.

(I have since wondered whether this mysterious porter fits descriptions I have heard of one Colonel Sebastian Moran. Although the porter does roughly match what I know of this dastardly gentleman's appearance, I would not feel comfortable confirming this as fact. For one, surely such a figure as the Colonel would be instantly recognisable to a great number of those present at the ball. Instead, I am afraid to say that the identity of the Professor's wicked assistant still eludes me. I understand he has many helpers spread throughout his home city and beyond.)

The porter brought me a box he assured me contained a pair of replacement shoes, and said 'the Prince was keeping these for just such an emergency.' Then he winked at me! After which he returned to his place by the door. I sighed, no longer able to contain my foreboding given the recent turn of events, and opened the box. The shoes beneath the crepe paper were very fine. They were shining with diamonds and decorated with a delicate filigree. Further inspection revealed the coat of arms on the sole – to my horror, I realised that these shoes belonged to none other than the Dowager Duchess of Croome!

I could not return the shoes without making it obvious to the whole ball that I knew the Dowager Duchess was keeping spare items of her wardrobe in the Prince's stores.

Moriarty smiled, and for the first time I felt I was able to see through the passionate mathematician and eccentric if harmless scholar. I saw an entirely different person lurking beneath. I felt I was looking into the eyes of the very devil.

'And now, my dear Miss Adler,' said the Professor, 'perhaps one more dance, or we might take a turn about the samovar, and I propose we leave the evening. I have had quite enough of high society, and, I assume, so have you. Waiter! Champagne!'

The robbery was discovered shortly before the last dance of the evening, when the Prince and Duchess came together and presumably attempted a secret look at the brooch that bound them. By that point the Professor had already bid me adieu, and the porter had opened the door for him, bowing him through it. We had made some more small talk with the various guests, and taken a few turns around the ballroom, but we did not dance again. When the time came to escape the evening, Moriarty was comfortable leaving me on my own, satisfied that putting me in a pair of stolen shoes would stop me from drawing any attention to myself. The Duchess' outcry at the discovery of the stolen brooch had set the ballroom alight, and the Prince (and the Dragoon) called for their pistols. Soon the Ball had dissipated into uproar, and if one listened carefully, one could already hear the newspapers preparing the story. *This* would not be limited to the society pages.

Moriarty had the reputation, among those who knew him as a criminal, of pulling off a stunning *coup de crime*. He had removed a priceless brooch from under the nose of the Prince of B–. (And the King, too, although he had been snoring in his chair since the welcome speeches.) News of the theft mingled in the air above the guests as they whispered and screamed, and shot up into the sky, spreading across London. Those listening out for tales of crime – perhaps in Baker Street, over the sound of their violin – would surely know instantly that Moriarty was responsible for such a terrible accomplishment.

But if I did contribute to the Professor's already formidable reputation in this city, let it be known that I did, at least, remove some of the satisfaction in this particular case. I may have aided Moriarty the master criminal, but I scuppered Moriarty the mathematician.

Even as the uproar began, I was leaving the Orangery. In the grounds, before I hailed a hansom, I paused by the box hedges and felt the side of my breast. I removed the brooch from an inner pocket of my coat. I had sewed the pocket in myself, and used it to store the trinkets of paramours I felt could afford to lose the weight. I looked at the stone. The Professor had not noticed my taking it from his waistcoat pocket as he beckoned a waiter to pour champagne, with which he toasted our success. To store it in my skirts I only required a split second loss of concentration from the good Professor; it came when he tipped the porter a salute and a wink.

The asteroid fragment itself was not stunning to look at; it was grey and did not sparkle. One could hardly countenance that it had dropped onto our humble orb from the depths of space, only to be locked into a ruby-studded mount for a dowager duchess, all to aid the politicking of a simple prince.

Still considering how best to use the stone to my own advantage, and with stolen shoes upon my feet, I hailed a cab to take me back to London, from where I would continue my own travels.

To this day I recall, looking back over the whole affair moment by moment, who was leading and who followed behind.

A Map to Camelot

On the Call to Adventure

It is not our place to ask why you have chosen to make this journey; if, of course, you made a choice at all. Some report a feeling of longing, urging them to set off and communicated from somewhere outside themselves in a language beyond words. Many travellers have more specific aims: glory or welfare or a change of scenery. Others, who might be the most unfortunate, have the journey thrust upon them, perhaps by a disgruntled wizard or by losing a bet, or both.

In any case, the likelihood of you reaching your destination is very low. We do not wish to adversely affect morale. On the contrary. Many travellers find the struggle against overwhelming odds to be a great stimulant.

On Saying Good-byes

There is no fixed method for this; we leave it to your discretion. Be aware that any last-minute pieces of advice offered in a whisper by friends, relations, tearful lovers, benign locals and/or anonymous passers-by are likely to be worth their weight in gold at some undefined point in the future.

It may be the case that you have no good-byes to say. If this is the situation, bid farewell to the trees. Again, we leave the exact wording and choice of bow, however formal, to you.

If you are setting off from a place with no visible trees, do not say good-bye to the wind or the rain or the clouds. They're all going with you.

On Packing

It is advisable that you only take what you need: food and water are essential, as are a pair of good dancing shoes for court. The judicious traveller may also wish to obtain/acquire/find themselves in possession of: a selection of favours, sleeves, and/or handkerchiefs (for bargaining with cowardly and/or lovesick knights); a full set of unicorn treats in assorted colours (should it be deemed necessary or desirable to gain the favour of such a beast while not disclosing private information regarding anyone's sex life); a working knowledge of local heraldry; a full set of wooden cutlery plus an additional bowl for guests; a quiver of arrows; a set of twine knots in different sizes; a back-up crossbow (for passing as an innocent hunting party should you be caught in Royal or otherwise privately owned woodland); spare verruca plasters (for acquiring Lake-based weaponry). Optional extra: a keen eye for the horizon.

On Compass Points

It is not necessary to be able to tell true north from magnetic north. The difference will not affect your journey.

On Starting Points

Begin where you are. Then go anywhere else.

This is an instruction many travellers find difficult to follow, but it is worth it if you can and will save a lot of back-tracking later. Think of the route as being drawn on tracing paper, able to be placed wherever you are, and then you can sort of go from there, if you see what we mean. Tracing paper is a far better and more charismatic material than, say, a humble piece of dirty old parchment like this one. Speaking of which: where did you get it? You must have found it in a relative's abandoned attic, or hidden at the back of a treasure chest in the library, or beneath the little windmill at the miniature golf course where your cousin's best friend gives the balls out on Wednesdays, or in the strongbox behind the tasteless painting in your boss' office, or wherever else you found it. Surely nobody actually gave this to you? See below: On Riddles & Paradoxes.

On Sidekicks & Fellowships

Whether it is necessary or desirable to have an acquaintance for this journey or whether it is better to travel alone is a matter much discussed. Really it depends on your aims. If you foster dreams of glittering knighthood it is always good to have a retinue who can stand nearby and clap, but if you want to draw on uncanny associations when you get there it will be much more dramatic to turn up alone. Remember, though, that not everyone gets to be a knight, and fear and suspicion go along with wonder and can easily be turned against you.

Larger travelling parties make for fun and relaxing questing experiences if you can keep a lid on the endless storytelling, but it is sometimes difficult to resolve who is in charge.

On Setting Off

Start early.

A nocturnal getaway may harbour some romantic attraction: you are not the first traveller to fantasise about stealing away in the dead of night. But in the dark it is all too easy to mistake every second shadow for a troupe of bandits or a night constable or a dragon with a headache or a sorcerer with a grudge or an enchanted tree with a face. It is dangerous to be walking at night, along hazardous roads, especially when you're shaky with adrenaline from the buzz of getting going. We recommend your party be en route shortly before dawn.

We realise that to some extent this suggestion is moot, since you have no doubt set off already.

On Disguises

Do not be ashamed or embarrassed to hide beneath the appearance of another. You might find it necessary to perform as somebody above or below your own social station, and may be required to continue this deception for many years. Sir Bandolever is our example of choice here.

Sir Bandolever is not included in many of the greatest poem cycles about your destination, but it is still a good idea to know a few facts of the history.

Sir Bandolever was a champion at the joust, mace, and sword, and put in a decent effort at fencing, squash, and cabaret acts as well. Arriving at Camelot without any warning, it is no surprise they proceeded to make themselves indispensable. Sir Bandolever never gained immortality for questing, quest planning, or ad-hoc quest admin, but they were wise, or at least acquired a reputation for wisdom which is nine-tenths of the battle. It is rumoured that even Sir Galahad sought them out for advice. They say it was only because of Sir Bandolever's hints that Sir Gawain was able to capture a ruddy great crow/bat everyone thought had put a curse on the trellis in the herb garden. And so on.

However, on occasions when Sir Bandolever was without armour, people saw only a squire. Take heart from this story, and know that in Camelot it is entirely acceptable to live a way that many outsiders wouldn't dare.

On Navigating Forest, Desert, and Sword Bridge

The Great Forest is where you are most likely to meet any unicorns and/or dragons. Although it is (understandably) tempting to call a unicorn to you, generally speaking it is never quite as useful or glamorous as you think it's going to be. On no account interrupt a boar hunt.

The desert will not last as long as you think it will. Keep drinking water in small sips. Search discarded armour for jewellery, money, or anything else you may be able to trade at She'spire Village. Although the view looks barren, harsh and empty, take time to appreciate these qualities. They long for stories of lonely sunsets at court, where due to all the light pollution the stars do not twinkle half as much.

Since it has been designated an Official Quest Point following Lancelot's Comeback Victory Tour, there is likely be a long queue to cross the Sword Bridge. Place a token or hire a squire to stand in your place, and take the opportunity to explore the surroundings. Be sure to collect the watercolourist's likeness of yourself crossing the bridge to prove you did it, should any sceptical maidens or (on a nautical route) cynical pirates question your claim to this achievement. If you do not cross the Sword Bridge, cynical pirates can be placated by being beaten in a game of chess. If you can't play chess, cynical pirates also enjoy operatic duets along the themes of unrequited love, tragic romance, and misspent youth. Strangely, neither opera nor chess will placate a sceptical maiden.

When it is your turn to cross the Sword Bridge, don't try to saunter over on foot in the manner you will see naive young scallywags attempting. Kneel and shuffle. There's no shame in it.

She'spire Village

It may become necessary to seek employment during your stay in She'spire, depending on whether you reach this village at the beginning of your journey or when you're nearly at your destination. Many enjoy their visit to She'spire so much they choose to stay. This is an entirely valid decision.

Be sure to ask for Kate at the corner shop as she is always willing to extend the deadline for buy-one-get-one-free offers – although note that she turns a blind eye to best-before dates, claiming they are all for show anyway.

Left at the Crakshaw Mountains

This item has been placed here deliberately to catch out those who would merely scan the main points of our argument, just as a devious cartographer will introduce a deliberate error into their work to prevent plagiarism by lazier mapmakers. We must make it clear, then, to those who are reading this carefully, that it is imperative you do *not* go left at the Crakshaw Mountains. Going any other way will result in your eventually reaching the Broken Road, around the Wobbly Mirage, and thence directly to the suburbs by the castle grounds. Taking a left, however, will lead you through the mountain pass and along the remains of an avalanche and into a non-gobackable dead end with mould on, by which time you will have realised your mistake but it will be too late, and you will find yourself left at the Crakshaw Mountains.

On Duplicitous Castles

Castles look foreboding in the distance – especially if they are well fortified and prone to boiling-oil-based business. But if you seek warmth, shelter, entertainment or directions (we hope you will not by this stage in your perusal want for directions, but we understand that you may wish to seek out a second opinion from time to time) it is always worth knocking. But be wary of Castles that merely perform hospitality while actually impeding your progress. Remember your ultimate destination and try not to be waylaid. See below, A Handy Metric for Gauging the Duplicity of Castles, including: Sprinkling of Seductive Lies, The; Tools Abetting Procrastination, Know Your; Fear Factor, The; and Leaps into the Unknown (Temptation to Avoid), Making Your First.

A good rule of thumb: if too many people say they're so glad you're staying, look for the exit. But don't tell anyone you're doing that. This is an occasion where it is advisable to steal away under cover of night.

Give ruins a chance. They have much to teach you. See if you can identify the cause of the ruin. If you discover any individual responsible, consider becoming friends.

On Achieving Success at The Fisher King's Arms Pub Quiz

It is forbidden to place a list of the answers here, but we can offer some advice: be on the lookout for double-, triple-, and quintuple-bluffs; multiple choice questions may favour the second-least obvious; the circumference of the Round Table is to be given in imperial measures via the usual algebra; hawks and handsaws have the same collective noun; page thirty-four of the *Livre de chasse*; nobody knows; it was there all along; *wheelbarrow*.

Although The Fisher King's Arms is one of the few places in the kingdom with access to broadband rather than the dial-up ynternet under which most of the populace suffers, it is vital that you do not cheat. Spies will report you to the ombudsman whereby you'll be put in the stocks, and the quest will be for nothing.

And next time you visit the pub, it will be completely empty.

On Fighting Dragons

Keep a gold coin in the bottom of your shoe, or in the bottom of a friend's shoe; in most places this will be enough to hire someone to do the fighting for you. Or else, run. This is why it is best that the heavy coin is not in your own shoe.

On Breaking Curses

In the unlikely event that you find yourself cursed, above all do not panic. Take deep, steady breaths and consider your options. Ask yourself: do you *really* feel cursed, or are you merely succumbing to a placebo? There are plenty of fraudulent sorcerers out there. Ask yourself if the magickal effect(s) you think you saw might not have been concocted manually: perhaps involving an intricate rope and pulley system; an accomplice hiding in the trees; a partially inflated balloon full of coloured dust; a secreted knitting needle; a dove or sparrow let loose at the operative moment from an overly embroidered sleeve; a cunning mishmash of various obsolete and sinister-sounding languages and a simple *abcb* rhyme scheme; centuries of superstition; or just having the confidence. Ask yourself how you might recreate a similar curse effect to frighten and disorientate your own enemies. Ask yourself: wasn't there something just a little bit, you know, *off* about the way they swooped their cape like that, almost as if there were strings attached or something?

These sorts of questions will serve to distract you while the curse takes full effect and you sink into oblivion.

On Not Getting Involved in Grail Quests

When the knight first puts it to you, this may seem like a great opportunity: an acknowledgement of your skills, a useful means to get you in with the Round Table crowd. However, remember that these quests only ever lead *away* from your destination.

Once the negative answer has been given, do not rise to anything the disgruntled knight may consequently declare about chivalry being dead or dying.

On Dinner and Miracles

Perhaps the most commonly known fact about your destination is that it is impermissible to begin dining until a miracle occurs. Many travellers decide, therefore, that the best way to obtain entrance into the Great Hall is to take on the responsibility of supplying the miracle themselves. The rest of the guests will certainly be glad to see you, especially those of the lower orders who are not even able to fill up on bread in the meantime.

See below, A Taxonomy of Miracles, to help determine which activities, apparitions, and appearances are designated Miracles and which are merely classed as Marvels, Events, Excitements, Interruptions, Troubles, Bothersomes, and Get That Imposter Out of Heres. If you do decide to get into the Great Hall this way, you don't want to waste your time concocting something that will fall into one of these unfortunate categories.

On Love Triangles, Parallelograms & Other Geometric Shapes

Should you find yourself faced with the heady politics of the Arthur and Lancelot situation, we can only suggest that you do your best not to get involved. We realise that sometimes this will not be possible. Therefore, a primer: the system of meritocracy (which names Lancelot the best) and the fact of divine right (which names Arthur the best) are in conflict over who is therefore truly, really, *actually* the best, and this, as you can imagine, casts great precarity over the respect, seating plan, and love life that are consequently due to these gentlemen. Don't be fooled by the apparent democracy of a circular dining surface. It's war out there. A good rule of thumb is to do whatever Sir Galahad does, but if he is out questing and/or otherwise unavailable, Guinevere is your best guess. But try to keep your head down. It's advantageous not to rock the Round Table on this particular issue. It'll sort itself out. You've only just arrived.

Should you find Guinevere herself is asking your advice in this regard, it doesn't really matter what you say. You are already in trouble.

On the Episodic Nature of the Great Poem Cycles & How to Navigate It
This structural conceit is why it is difficult for us to inform you of the exact order in which you might encounter various landmarks, crossroads, allies, enemies, obstacles, and personal crises (both existential and food-based). No two journeys to Camelot are the same. However, you will find that wherever you go first provides vital information and/or items to help you succeed against whatever you face at the next destination, and so on. The problem is knowing which objects to keep and which to leave behind. A further complication: sometimes leaving an object behind is the very thing you need to do to make the best use of it. Overall it is best to take the nature of your excursion in your *stride*, as it were. The mindset will suit you well at court in any case.

You may even find that once you reach your destination the adventure, if we might use so grand a term, has only just begun.

On Major-to-Minor Character Dissonance & How to Avoid It
The problem crucially is one of authorship. Depending variously upon historical agenda, political agenda, religious agenda, patriotic agenda, gender agenda, or confirmation bias; depending variously upon how one feels about the verse/prose binary (if,

indeed, one accepts such a binary at all); depending variously upon what one deems necessary in terms of plot complications, rising action, Grail questing and its conflicts (both internal and external), familial strife and the intricate mechanics of blackmail and/or betrayal within those dynamics, the status of any pair (or trio) of lovers (star-crossed, unrequited, or Other) – not to mention symbolism, which there's no time to go into – all these points of interest will affect the landscape in which you find yourself. The point we are making here is that you may meet a great and brave and mighty knight one moment, and, in the time it takes a lion to walk the perimeter, find yourself confronting the same person as a meek and mewling guttersnipe the next.

For example, you may find Sir Bandolever is spoken of once in passing, as, say, someone who was present at a jousting tournament or sitting at the war council, and then they're never mentioned again: not so much a cameo appearance as a possible proofing error. Or they might be at the centre of everything. Do you see?

On the Heavy Burden of Protagonism
It falls to you, we're afraid.

The Ghost of Cock Lane

There's going to be another séance! And you cannot move for people crammed together in that narrow road, the crushing of shoulders as they shove, seeking to peer in at the windows. These people stand in the snow-slush without a care in the world for the chill creeping up their legs, soaking around the edges of their skirts, and some enterprising soul has set up a stall to sell them roasted nuts.

It is the year of our Lord (*my* Lord, the Light-bringer) 1762: we are five minutes' walk from St Paul's and scandalously close to Gin Lane. To prevent ambiguity let me declare that your narrator is dead, and a ghost (though not resident in Cock Lane); but be assured this will in no way encumber our tale, and know that every word is true.

Voices can be made out through the bustle: 'If you want *my* opinion we shouldn't be having another séance at all.' That's a young woman wearing her fair share of powder, leaning nonchalantly against the dark brick wall. She underscores her point by spitting into a puddle.

'I agree,' says a woman in a ragged shawl, tapping her foot impatiently. 'Why speak to the ghost yet *again*? She's already been quite clear.'

Jostling to the front, closer to the house, a pair of fellows with canes give their input.

'Aye, the ghost has spoken, therefore they should hang him and be done with it!'

A newly arrived woman, panting for breath, worried she might have missed it, says: 'Hanging's too good for a wife-poisoner!'

Everyone joins in, except me.

'I hear this house is alive with the horror of that ghastly scratching!'

'I heard the daughter never sleeps these days, for the horror of the wailing!'

'Aye well, it's her who's *doing* the wailing, ain't it.'

The reply is given suspiciously through narrowed eyes: 'Be that as it may…'

'Have you heard who is attending today?'

'Who's that then?'

'It's that pedantic bloke that knows about spellings.'

'Says he's going to put a stop to it!'

'They always say that.'

'Any nuts left, Mary?'

'Oh, yes please!'

The crowds fill almost the whole of Cock Lane but their attentions are centred on only one residence. It's been a palpable frustration to be one of the neighbours, these past few months.

From the dusty window of the narrowest room on the top floor of the thin tall house standing spindly in the middle of Cock Lane – from up on high it's possible to make out the felt hats and woollen scarves of the onlookers, to chart their dance through the sodden streets. Shouts and calls rise above the general din.

'*Hang William Kent!*' is the cry to be heard the most by now.

A bit of explanation for you, since you're here. This house in the middle of Cock Lane is owned by a man called Richard Parsons, his wife Carrots (as she is known most affectionately by all, on account of her hair colour) and their little daughter Elizabeth. Until recently, the landlord has been renting out the house to two of your upstanding tenants, the Kents: William and Fanny… but that was until poor Fanny died of the smallpox. William tried to cope however he could, however you can – but however he coped, the fact remains that shortly after and not even before poor Fanny's funeral could occur, there began to come a-scratching on the walls and the doors of the house in

Cock Lane, and a series of dreadful knocks, and the little girl Elizabeth began to have difficulty sleeping.

The day William and Fanny moved in to the house on Cock Lane – only a matter of months ago, how things change – they had been sitting shivering at the kitchen table, while the landlord leaned forwards most helpfully and enthusiastically stated his case for hospitality. The child Elizabeth stood in the corner of the room, sucking her fingers and dangling a rag doll by one leg, watching these strangers negotiate the details of where they would live.

The landlord threw his empty bottle into the basket by the fire and said:

'Well, never mind that your previous landlord threw you out, or why – I'm sure that's none of my business!'

Just as they grow unsure of where exactly he's going with this, his face widens into a generous smile.

'I can tell from here you're upstanding citizens, no doubt in m'mind. Elizabeth!'

He turns to his daughter. 'Take Fanny upstairs and show her the rooms.' He spreads his arms wide. 'Welcome!'

The landlord waits for the footsteps to take them all the way up the rickety staircases, until they are safely away at the top of the house. He swills a sentence around in his mouth, then casually speaks into the air:

'I've a thought for you.'

'A thought?'

'A little one. By which I mean nothing so urgent as to become a *question*. It's a matter concerning money.'

'Of course,' says William earnestly. 'Rest assured we've enough for a few months in advance.'

'All for the good,' says the landlord. He takes a moment to gently drum his fingers on his thighs.

'Can I ask: do you happen to have any more besides?'

William looks up and for a moment the gaze between them sticks.

'I'm sorry?'

'It's a money matter.'

William nods in agreement, confused.

'Merely a few guineas, that's all I'm talking about.'

William's mouth moves without sound, as if counting what could be bought with these few guineas.

'Can you lend me twelve guineas?'

The landlord's expression is placid.

'What?'

The landlord sits back, as if the matter were already agreed. 'We'll call it a loan. Imagine: you'll be in the loaning game!'

William rouses himself. 'Now just a moment –'

'I know, I know,' the landlord waves his hand about as if performing a magic spell to eliminate all troubles. I'm aware it makes the first payment feel a little heavier.'

'That's certainly a concern –'

'Come now, William,' he says, softly holding his hand between both of his. 'I'll pay you back regular as clocks. A guinea a month.'

And the landlord breaks off and wanders freely around the kitchen, eventually coming in close to throw his arm over William's shoulder.

'I can see this is going to work out for us both. You seem like my kind of fellow. Who'd've thought you'd be looking to move into a lovely new set of lodgings – in a nice house – with your lovely family? And it's so convenient because I was really scratching my head about sorting out that loan, and the fact that the two situations can work together couldn't be any neater, could it? Well that's just fantastic. I'm glad you agree. It's lovely to have you both moving in.'

So William Kent loans money to his landlord.

*

Back to the bustling street, then. And you're just in time, because the séance party is about to arrive. In the throng of people, as the new arrivals – in their dark coats with buttons of silver – push through the waiting onlookers, you must try to keep an eye out for three figures in particular: the priest; the great and famous man of letters brought in to aid proceedings; and the tragic, tensely striding figure of the accused man, William Kent, whom you've just met.

The priest is highly esteemed in this part of town, since he has been conducting the séance at Cock Lane for several weeks now. Each one draws a larger crowd.

There is a reason for the repeated séances. This is because there can be no mistakes. This is a city of reason, and of utmost reasonableness; and as people of reason the investigation must be conducted in the most logical manner, and please no one get overexcited, as is explained in the priest's new pamphlet.

The first thing a person of reason should do is try to establish what the ghost actually wants.

Through a slow and scientific method, the priest has developed a means of impressive communication with the ghost, and found that the spirit of Cock Lane is none other than Fanny herself: that she is newly dead but not of smallpox; that she seeks vengeance for her foul and most unnatural murder. The spirit of Fanny claims her widower William poisoned her with arsenic in her broth, and seeks revenge, naturally. So you can see why everybody in the street is calling for the hangman.

Back to the road – Cock Lane close-pushed with eager onlookers. More arriving, fresh flecks of snow arching past the gas lamps as another cloud opens. And there's the carriage pulling up, there's the grand buckled shoes getting out. It's Dr Johnson! There's the first people to notice his approach; the increase in the general intensity of the buzzing. He is not alone, of course, he is surrounded by folk of near-to-close social standing, a small clump of darkly dressed respectable gentlemen of this parish, including the priest himself who will be communicating with the ghost – but really it is *he*, Samuel Johnson, the people are excited to see – esteemed composer of the Dictionary and occasional call-upon for civic matters, it's *he* they've heard of, mostly for the former – and now he strides through the Cock Lane crowds chest forward, eyes on the peeling paint door on the wooden front entrance to the house he seeks, the knocker glowing before him like the end of the alphabet – pushing open the door and standing confidently in the parlour of the haunted house, his eyes gazing briefly about the rafters before coming to rest with the heaviness of a millstone in the soft superstitions of the masses; it's the man himself, the very definition.

'We've a hoax to expose, let us hurry up and get about it,' says Dr Johnson.

The priest pinkens about the cheeks as they all go upstairs.

The understanding that had somehow been keeping the crowd outside is abandoned, and people spill in through the entranceway, bringing the snow-chill in with them. Since the house is smaller than the street, soon people are squashed in the doorway.

There's a sudden surge in the shouts from below.

Dr Johnson interprets. 'That must be our final participant.'

The crowd jeers at the accused, William, as they part to let him by – from the front door all the way up to the top bedroom. There's really not a lot of space.

A stately woman in brocade speaks from the crowd: 'We'll have answers to-day, Mr Kent. No more guesswork, no more approximation.'

The whole party ascends to the top of the house and soon the whole building is filled to the rafters. Much of the occupation goes to groups of friends who always look to do their catching up at the Cock Lane séances, due to the social ambience.

The smallest room, right up in the dusty attic-space of the house, contains a small bed with crumpled sheets. In the bed sits Elizabeth, the daughter of the landlord of the house, looking pale and resolute. This whole thing by now is an accustomed ritual. Above her bed towers the landlord, an image of concern and haggardness.

A row of chairs line the walls and Dr Johnson sits in the centremost, facing the occupied bed. The priest looks around for support, aggrieved at the new seating arrangements. He eventually perches on a chair at the far end – opposite to William.

There is a moment of heavy, full silence, as if they all sit within a giant ball of snow. I look from one face to another, and observe the airs of concentration and anticipation. Johnson is looking quizzically at the door lintels.

The priest leans forwards slightly on his chair and clears his throat. It resonates in that thickly quiet room.

He closes his eyes, and everyone holds their breath.

'Remember the system, O spirit; please knock once for yes, twice for no.' He raises his arms slightly. 'As per the usual.'

This news is echoed in excited whispers all the way down the stairs.

The girl screws her eyes closed and tosses her head around a bit.

Someone hollers: 'It's Fanny – she's with us!'

The priest catches the moment and launches into his first question, his knuckles clasped.

'Are you the ghost of the wife of Mr William Kent here – by which I mean, do we address the spirit of Fanny Lynes?'

One knock.

The crowd gasps.

'And did you die naturally?'

Knock. Knock.

'By poison?'

Knock.

The crowd hiss, newly riled. William looks irritated.

'And do you know which poison?'

Knock…

Knock.

'I see. Would you be willing to hazard a guess?'

Knock.

'Arsenic?'

Knock.

The crowd whoops. The priest looks serious.

'And was this poison administered, without your knowledge or desire, by Mr William Kent here?'

Konckhm.

That's the simultaneous sound of the knock in response to the priest's question and William rising angrily from his chair where it bangs heavily against the wall.

'I will not have this go on any further!' he cries. 'This is slander upon my life and I shan't sit idly by!'

'Your life is exactly what's at *stake*, sir – pray calm yourself and sit down!' The priest's eyes are starting to glaze over with the stress of an interruption.

'I'm telling you this is ridiculous, I didn't kill her,' says William. 'I don't want to be back in Cock Lane. I'd be away grieving if you hadn't dragged me here.'

The landlord rises from his chair: he and William now stare at each other across the room. It's a game of tennis and contempt is the ball. 'Ridiculous, sir? Are we wasting your time?' says the landlord. His voice is as thick as coffee house dregs. 'It's making my daughter suffer, sir, and I don't find *that* ridiculous at all.'

They turn to Elizabeth, who shrugs and does a little cough.

William concedes. 'Of course not.'

The landlord's hands are fists by his sides. 'So let the ghost say what she has to say!'

'Kind words, I'd hope!' cries William. 'I loved Fanny and she me. For what reasons would I poison her?'

'If you were so in love, sir, why weren't you married?'

A gasp sweeps through the crowd.

'Mr Kent,' says the priest, his voice level. 'Is this true?'

William Kent looks down at his shoes. 'Not through any lack of will. But through difficult circumstances.'

'Oh yes, you heard what I said,' continues the landlord, looking around at the shocked company. 'Drummed out of their previous lodgings for ungodly behaviours. I didn't judge though, did I? Took 'em in out of my own charity, and get repaid with a murder under my own roof and a daughter forever channelling spooks.'

William points to his landlord with his full arm. 'You, sir, are horrendous.'

The landlord points to himself, innocently. 'Am I on a murder charge?'

'Neither am I!'

'*They* all think you are.' A round gesture, taking in the audience. The priest mutters something vague about jurisprudence.

'His first wife even had the same name as my little girl!' cries the landlord. 'Perhaps we are dealing with a serial wife-poisoner!'

'What?' William looks around indignantly. 'That hasn't even anything to do with this. She died in childbirth!'

'Interesting,' he mutters.

William's mouth moves but no sounds emerge. The priest takes the opportunity to jump back in. He claps his hands together and rubs them.

'Shall we carry on?' he says brightly, as if everyone has just returned from taking a break for lunch. 'To be honest I do think we are nearly finished.'

Without turning to look at his daughter in the bed the landlord speaks. 'Bring her back to us, Elizabeth.' He looks again at William, standing there seething by the wall. 'This'll be the final chat we'll need, I have a *very* good feeling.'

Silence settles again as the company turns its attentions to the girl in the bed, and she closes her eyes to channel the ghost. It's irrelevant now, anyway, whether William and Fanny shared the surname Kent; what's in question is solely whether William will live to mourn her.

Silence once more descends, and the reverend opens his mouth to speak.

He is interrupted by someone else. This time it's the renowned composer of the English Dictionary.

Dr Johnson holds up his hand.

'I have a thought,' he says.

The priest throws both his arms up at the interruption. 'Is it necessary to declare your thought *right now?*'

Dr Johnson raises both hands before him as if in surrender and looks around, making sure everybody observes his apparent humility. Instead of lowering them, he addresses the room: 'This is my gesture.' Everyone looks at him bemused. He continues: 'With my arms in this position I am saying: *I will not intervene, I will not interrupt, I surrender to whatever comes.* And I would like everyone on these chairs to do it with me.'

The priest hits his thighs with his hands several times. 'Will you stop it, sir! You are making mischief with my spirit. This matter is incredibly serious. Pray desist!'

Another thought strikes him.

'And added to that, this motion of yours not to disturb proceedings is indeed an utmost hypocrisy, as it is in itself an interruption!'

Dr Johnson remains placid, hands gently wiggling in the air.

After a brief standoff the priest is surprised to find himself mirroring the gesture.

The collective of séance-followers look to the priest for guidance. He looks back at them, pasting an expression of wisdom over his face like a poster for the circus.

'Let us all follow along with Dr Johnson's idea,' he says. His face registers serene calm, but there is a slight waver to his voice that indicates Dictionary Johnson has taken him a few miles beyond the end of his tether.

The people standing together in the door frame immediately raise their hands, then turn to check everyone behind them is doing the same.

The gesture travels down the stairwell and across the rooms, resulting in the rustling of hundreds of arms taking on their new positions. In no time, hands are raised all through the house in solemn promise. Hands of various shapes and sizes, all pleased to be in the air.

The landlord tries to protest, but his objections are already stale as old beer. 'Can't we just continue on without any of this sort of nonsense?' But the social pressure is too much as he looks around at all the forest of excited fingers, and eventually he too raises his arms with a laboured sigh.

Dr Johnson turns his gaze to the small child in the bed. His eyes twinkle with kindliness as he waggles his raised hands at her.

The landlord glares at Dr Johnson and addresses his daughter. '*You* don't have to,' he says. 'You're the one suffering here, don't let him boss you around.'

The priest, having now given himself fully over to the sense of community Dr Johnson's instruction has instigated, is positively jolly. His hands wave about enthusiastically in the air. 'Oh let's not leave anybody out! It's all about demonstrating our commitment to getting to the bottom of this whole issue. Good idea, Johnson.'

The girl looks towards her father. He looks back at her and she slowly begins to slide her hands out from under the bedsheet; the landlord follows the movement, whilst willing the hands backwards with his eyes. Reality wins and the hands eventually come up over the sheet and are raised slowly up either side of her concerned face.

The landlord looks about the place, his eyes flicking from door to windows and back, over and over, perhaps wondering which route would provide the least difficult escape. The only swift route is out the window; but at what angle is the drainpipe? Too high to leave it to chance… certainty slips away from him as he realises that, unfortunately, while he remains the owner of the property, he is pitifully unaware of his own floorplan.

The priest clears his throat, finally ready to begin again with the ghost. But then a strange thing happens and it would appear Dr Johnson is now leading the proceedings.

'O spirit,' he says, 'sorry for the wait. Please do speak with us again.'

A look flashes across the priest's face, the briefest of protests, but no one else seems to mind Dr Johnson's takeover.

'We're all wanting to know if you're here to see justice done for your murder?'

No knock comes.

'Do you wish William Kent to be disgraced and surely hanged for the crime of your murder?'

No knock.

'Are you still there?'

Nothing.

'O spirit?'

Nothing at all.

Looks are thrown around at this unusual development.

'Right,' says Dr Johnson. He is already tidying his personals into his bag. 'I trust this settles the matter. Do you think that carriage will still be outside?'

Reader, I am *so* tempted to deliver a single *knock* at this point I cannot tell you.

The priest pays keen attention to the frost gathering in the corners of the window frame.

'Elizabeth?' he says, innocently, not looking at her. 'Is there anything you would like to share with the group?'

Wincing a little, the girl reveals a small wooden block from about her skirts. The priest takes it from her hand, getting a sense of its heaviness, and attempts a few trial knockings 'pon the bedframe. The ghost's voice, exactly.

With the look of a man who has just guessed someone's card in a pack, the priest glances excitedly around the room, as if to say, *Ooooh.*

'Well that's a result,' says William.

66

The crowd all drop their hands down again, and let out a collective despondent groan followed by tuts and scuffing shoes as they make their way back down the stairs.

In truth I feel despondent myself, as if we've all been taken round the bloody houses.

The priest stands fully upright. 'I for one am glad,' he says, looking around the assembled company, 'for we have uncovered an act of utmost deception using approaches of reason and fact. It seems clear to me now –' he raises his voice to shout over the sound of droves of people leaving – 'that this is the real crook, here.'

He points at the landlord. 'Shame on you, sir, for inducing your daughter to act the ghost for you. It's a blasphemy to go about imitating the presence of spirits.'

Dr Johnson has pulled on a pair of dark brown gloves and is already at the door. 'Call trial on the landlord and let's get out of here.'

The priest is fastening his collar. 'I think this has gone smoothly, considering various factors, interruptions and so on,' he says. 'Well done everyone.'

Dr Johnson nods politely in receipt of varying acknowledgments, then addresses the newly uncondemned man.

'You must be feeling suitably relieved. I do hope you have a good afternoon.'

'Thank you. I suppose I shouldn't expect him to ever return my twelve guineas.'

Dr Johnson raises an eyebrow.

'In future, William Kent, I would advise against loaning money to your own landlord. Most unconventional a direction for debt to flow.'

And he leads the party out of the house.

And Dr Johnson and the others stand triumphant in the front doorway, framed by a rectangle of light, the glare of winter sun on half-melted snow; and he cries to the awaiting crowds that the so-called Ghost of Cock Lane has finally been revealed as a dreadful hoax, and now to get out of his way please – for they'll have their chance to read about it in the papers and pour over the etchings and see it enacted in the popular dramas… and in time, of course, there go the crowds: disappointed in truth, realising what they really preferred was speculation; and there goes the landlord in the grip of the constables, which is just as well, because Fanny's tragic story of arsenic before marriage was in danger of blossoming into a cautionary tale against indulging in the old pre-marital. But now we know it was never Fanny scratching there, only a small girl with a block of wood, enlisted through pressure and persuasion by a man who was a sort of block of wood himself in his own way, who'd rather see an innocent man hang than give up any of his money owed. It's all property and the exchanging of coin, in the end.

Beware landlords!

The New Woman

The final days of the nineteenth century may appear to have been dormant, the hours steadily passing over the snow-covered rooftops: the remains of an exhausted century, lying dead on a slab. But throughout those last days crackles a steady current of activity that it is possible to feel – if one concentrates – in the back of the teeth. This hissing spark of life goes deeper than the city's usual rat-fights in underground dens, it shines brighter than its riotous cabarets, flashes stronger than its bouts of bareknuckle boxing; and it is more than the pouring of absinthe and the adjusting of hat-pins, although such things will occur, those green and sharp things. The week is going to rise up against itself, claim a strange new life of its own.

But not much of this is known, yet, on the evening of Christmas Day, eighteen ninety-nine: and, as the bells ring out from the churches, a spirit of revelry and warm laughter pushes against the ceiling and presses against the tapestry wall-hangings of a grand house in a respectable district, the house of a famous actress and philanthropist, who is currently entertaining in her dining room.

Mrs Stella Moore enjoys the status of artistic genius and eccentric national treasure: in a glittering career, long-established, she has played every romantic, tragic, and comic lead in every great play upon every prestigious stage in the world. The press and adoring public know her fondly as Mrs Stella, and she describes herself to the periodicals, fans and love-letter writers as 'a keen collector of people'. This year she has surpassed herself in the bohemian assemblage seated around her table, pushing their forks across their Christmas puddings. Mrs Stella finds her people in the coffee-houses, backstage of the theatres; selling their canvasses or standing bored to tears behind the counters of perfume shops, longing for anything in life but scents by the ounce. Those who sit around her table – there are five, this year – are without any other family. Mrs Stella will give them a pension; rooms, should they need (although not *quite* in Bloomsbury); and, most precious of all, an audience for their work.

Mrs Stella is holding court at the head of the table, as she always does on Christmas Day. (There was, once, a Mr Stella, but Mrs Stella never mentions him.)

She claps her hands together. The conversations that had begun to rumble around the dining table give way to an expectant silence.

'While we finish our pudding,' says Mrs Stella, 'let us return to our earlier conversation, upon the relationship between life art and life. Who shall start us off?'

She takes a sip of her coffee.

The china cups are white and paper-thin, decorated with filigree patterns picked out in green, highlighted with gold. The room is the height of fashionable style. The polished tables and cabinets are laid with delicate lace cloths and long-runners, topped with pieces of pottery; vases and statues imitating ancient sculptures of Greece and Rome. Tall rubber plants stand in porcelain vases, their thick waxy leaves casting shadows upon the wallpaper, which bears an intricate design of winding vines. Atop the brandy cabinet are spider plants and Venus flytraps.

It being Christmas, there is additional decoration: the table is clustered with gleaming candlesticks. Garlands of spruce, picked out with silver bells and velvet ribbons, loop across the ceiling in great glittering ropes, criss-crossing the chandelier, shuddering in the air as if taking breath, demanding to be given more space. Wreaths of ivy and holly droop from the walls and ornament the table, as candles dripping pale yellow wax make the whole room flicker. Mrs Stella has given the servants the day off, and so the table has been steadily filling throughout the evening; a great goose carcass remains in the centre on a large silver plate. Its bones and torn flesh, along with a few leftover roast potatoes and slimy scraps of cabbage, glisten in the candlelight.

A French lilt across the table: 'Of course, for us writers, such things as art and life, they are always of greatest interest.'

Jacques-Louis le Page. His mother was a chorus girl in the least reputable theatres of France; his father a distinguished member of the aristocracy. (He won't tell anybody *which* distinguished member of the aristocracy, although Mrs Stella, of course, has her ideas.) Jacques makes his way through the world primarily by producing reams of waspish journalism and devastating theatrical criticism; but he has dabbled in writing a play or two of his own – under a pseudonym, naturally – and he dreams of someday composing the libretto for a great opera. Perhaps the gentleman to his right will dance in it.

Edwin Turner. Principle ballerino in London's proudest opera houses. Of all of them, Edwin could choose to spend Christmas elsewhere, with any of the corps du ballet who would see him; but it is only here, at Mrs Stella's, he feels free to be himself.

Edwin clasps Jacques-Louis' thigh beneath the table. 'And for us, too,' he says; 'you could say that art *is* life, for dancers, because we dedicate our whole bodies to it.'

'You mean you *ruin* them,' comes another voice from the opposite end of the table. The voice is as proud and shining as a silver button. The speaker proudly cleans a monocle with a silk handkerchief. It is Oliver Allbright – wit, flaneur, occasional producer of oil paintings. His trousers are silk, his shirt is embroidered, and his velvet smoking jacket is edged with fur. 'The leotards make you look pretty enough,' he says, 'but underneath, your bodies are soon unfit for purpose, and where's the beauty in that?'

Edwin looks at Oliver, wearing an exaggerated expression of shock. He knows what Oliver is like. 'We retire young, it's true,' he says. 'No flame can burn at its brightest forever.'

Oliver examines the pearl handle of his dessert fork. 'In my opinion, it is far better,' he says, 'to dedicate your art to life, than to sacrifice your life to art.'

Mrs Stella laughs. Jacques bangs his fist on the table.

'Stop doing aphorisms! For Christ's sake, it's just saying something you don't really mean!'

There are some dull chuckles around the table, not least from Edwin, pleased by Jacques' quick defence.

Mrs Stella sits very still, her head flicking like a bird between the three of them. Oliver gazes at Jacques steadily through his monocle.

Mrs Stella wrinkles her nose and, to create a diversion, stands and levers open the glass door of the drinks cabinet. 'It seems to me,' she says, pulling out a bottle of brandy, 'that the boundaries between art and life are becoming ever more porous. Perhaps *that* is what our friend Oliver means. For you, of course, Oliver, your life *is* a work of art, isn't it?'

'I should hope so,' mutters Jacques, 'in *those* trousers.'

Oliver smiles. 'Just so,' he says. 'I greatly admire our friend Edwin's embodiment of the balletic ideal, and of course I enjoy Jacques' commitment to drama.' He addresses his closing remark to the whole table. 'Far better to say something you don't mean, than to mean something terribly badly but never get to say it.'

Jacques throws up his hands as if to say, *there's another one!* but the party does not take him up on it, and instead falls into silence while the brandy is poured. Mrs Stella goes around the table, tipping a heavy golden measure into everybody's glass. One of the Venus flytraps moves a toothed head, grabbing at something.

'I think it is time,' says Mrs Stella, resuming her seat, 'to hear from our friend Christine about the newest scientific advances! I think you will find much of interest here, friends.' She leaves the bottle on the table, clustered among the silver gravy jug and a pile of crumpled napkins. 'Tell them, Christine, what you were saying to me earlier.'

Christine Sparks.

At first, Oliver had objected to the inclusion of a medical student in the party; he had voiced his doubts over the third cup of Earl Grey when visiting Mrs Stella a month or so prior. Surely the hard, rational approach of the sciences, he suggested, crumbling his scone to pieces in his fingers, had little to do with the higher ideals of art. And wasn't *that* what Mrs Stella wished to patronise? If she started bringing *medical students* into her parlour, where would it end?

Mrs Stella's eyes had shone as she advised Oliver to consider the practice of medicine as *the* quintessential art of the human body. And besides, she added, Christine is quite the catch.

'She is one of the finest minds in her field,' she had said. 'Or fields; since she has recently been pursuing astronomy and electricity in addition to medicine and chemistry. She has several prizes, a good chance of coming first in the Tripos; scholarships to continue her learning abroad.'

Recently, she had told Oliver, as a sort of crowning fact, Christine has been studying on the Continent – and wouldn't he like to know what people are getting up to out there?

Christine pushes her dark curls away from her face. She wears a smart blue jacket with brass buttons, and a pair of trousers, wide-cut enough to resemble a skirt at first glance, but infinitely more convenient for attending lectures by bicycle. Even Oliver nodded briefly when she first arrived at the table, forced to concede that Christine possesses both aesthetic sensibilities, and the salary to exercise them.

'Tell us something wonderful, Miss Sparks,' says Mrs Stella, taking up her spoon again to serve up a second helping of Christmas pudding from its silver bowl.

Christine nods, full of enthusiasm.

'If this decade becomes known for anything, as far as science is concerned,' she says, 'it will be for the way it treats cadavers.'

'You see,' murmurs Mrs Stella, cake dropping from the spoon. 'In discussing art we are only a shade away from contemplating death.'

'The last few years have seen spectacular advances in the use of a particular substance,' says Christine, 'to keep a body looking much – almost exactly – as it did in life. *Formaldehyde* is a method of embalming a cadaver, uniquely, from the inside out, rather than from the outside in as our present techniques attempt. It is still in the experimental stages.'

'Where do you find the bodies to practise upon?' Edwin asks, then looks sharply towards Jacques with a pained expression, as if he has just been kicked under the table. 'I want to know!' he hisses.

'They are donated to the college from those who would be part of the great journey of science even after death,' says Christine, smoothly, as if speaking by rote. 'They are not obtained by any malevolent means.' She clears her throat, and returns to her explanation. 'It works by passing the vapours of wood spirit, in the presence of air, over copper heated to redness…'

'Speaking personally, I prefer the thought of being preserved in alcohol,' says Oliver. 'One should always die surrounded by what one loved in life. The old pharaohs had it right.'

Christine nods; her face expresses that she has heard this sentiment often, and understands where it comes from.

'Formaldehyde is much cheaper, though, than alcohol; and easier to carry in the field.'

'But surely you would need too much?' Edwin twirls his hair around his hand, abstractly waving his fingers through it. 'However can you carry enough?'

'You are imagining a body lying in a bathtub's worth of green liquid,' says Christine. 'Far less is needed. That is what I mean by embalming from the inside out. The fluid is injected directly into the body; the resulting effect is of blood passing through living veins.'

'Good grief,' mutters Jacques.

Mrs Stella leans forwards, her elbows resting on the table. 'I just want to make sure everyone is holding up in the face of the present topic?'

Opposite Christine, someone is sitting very still, listening properly for the first time all night. They barely hear Mrs Stella speak. Mrs Stella notices this, passes over it for now.

Mrs Stella turns her sympathetic gaze towards Jacques-Louis.

Jacques looks down at his pudding. The raisins clustered densely within the heavy sponge appear to have a very particular texture, now; the whole thing resembles an exposed cranium, shiny and wet. The wrinkled currents flicker in the light of the candle, seeming to shrink and pulse and breathe and move. The thick yellow custard has taken on a teal-green pallor and has begun to set, a skin slowly forming, trapping the sponge pudding in the centre of the bowl. The still-setting custard wobbles grotesquely. He throws his spoon onto the table with a clatter and sits back with an air of surrender.

'You may as well carry on, now,' he says.

After a pause to check he means it – with no clear answer – Christine does so.

'And the wood spirit is volatised, mixed with the forced air… anyway, how it is made is less important than the effect it has. Which is: the moment of death can be perfectly captured. The body looks just as it did. Although it does bleach slightly, since it lacks any actual blood.'

A heavy silence descends over the table as the diners consider what they have been invited to imagine. Only Allbright and Mrs Stella seem to have retained their appetites enough to spoon more pudding onto their plates. Edwin and Jacques-Louis wrap their hands around their brandies and coffees as if clinging to a life raft upon the open ocean. Christine sits back, thinking about her studies; she is due to present a lecture upon the treatment of cadavers in the New Year.

And the fifth guest is staring straight ahead, not seeing the candle flame before her. Her mind is racing with possibilities, a series of vivid images having come to life in her mind.

Mrs Stella leans forward, resting her chin on her hands. She directs her gaze towards her silent guest. 'And how fairs our sculptor?' she says. 'You've hardly said a word tonight.' Her manner is polite, but the words are a challenge. The others see it as clearly as if she'd thrown a glove down on the table.

The sculptor understands. She licks her lips, forces out a rushed idea. 'I was thinking, Mrs Stella, about Christine's comments, and – ah – the remainder of the goose.'

'You've an eye for animals, haven't you,' says Mrs Stella, not knowing where the sculptor is going, whether she needs to provide friendly encouragement or a witty obstacle.

'I was wondering: if it's perfectly acceptable, as the aristocracy do, to stuff a quail inside a goose, inside a turkey, inside a swan, and so on, could you not create your own previously undiscovered festive beast by stitching several different parts of various animals together?'

There is silence around the table. Jacques' mouth opens and closes to no avail; instead he settles for running his fingers idly around one of the table's holly-and-ivy adornments. Perhaps hoping a sharp spike from the leaves might draw blood across his fingers, providing a distraction from this grim company. Christine comes to the sculptor's aid, laughing in an embarrassment. 'I wouldn't want to try that,' she says. 'You'd create an abomination, most likely.'

Mrs Stella clears her throat. 'Promise me you won't attempt it,' she says. There is some lightness in her tone, but an undercurrent of disapproval pulls strongly too. 'What I admire about your work is its beauty. I cannot abide ugliness.'

'And such a thing would be ugly indeed,' puts in Oliver. He must always have a say on whether or not something might be beautiful.

'Of course!' says the sculptor, relieved to have made a contribution to the conversation, however it was received. She casts her gaze towards the ceiling, not seeing the confused looks that pass between the rest of the collective. In truth, Christine's talk led her down a different path of thought, and she threw out the animal creation as a distraction.

Mrs Stella stands and swoops around the table, gathering her guests' pudding plates and piling them up with loud pottery scrapes. 'Typical of you, Frances,' she says as she passes, her voice ringing across the coffee and shortbread, though she spoke softly. 'Going down the morbids. I do prefer it when you see the beauty in things.'

At the door she says: 'When I return I will bring everybody's Christmas presents, and inform you of my plans for the New Year. Perhaps a parlour game or two! I rather fancy a round of Exquisite Corpse.' She leaves, and the collective breathes out as one. Christine desperately tries to catch Frances' eye, but Frances is still distracted.

Frances does see the beauty in things. Or rather, she sees beauty she herself can create. Mrs Stella's collective think of her as a sculptor, and this is true in a sense: she has made ceramic things: delicate vases, glistening sugar bowls. Mrs Stella has one of her plates displayed upon the sideboard even now.

But Frances has been experimenting recently in making sculptures out of once-living things. Mrs Stella approves, as long as the things are beautiful. A stuffed magpie, treated by Frances, stands in Mrs Stella's front parlour, looking over her visitors with a glistening jet eye.

Next, Frances had worked for weeks on a fox she found dead beside the cobbled road, and discovered an aesthetic sense she did not know she had. She replaced the eye with a shining diamond, and woven strands of gold thread with the fox's fur, which she treated until it shone. She wove decorative knots through the fox's tail. The fever with which she worked on these animals made her barely notice that she did not, at any point, feel revulsion or disgust as she worked with the hollow carcasses, pinning silver spikes to replace bones, teasing out papery flesh into the shapes of the once again living.

Frances considers herself a sculptor of dead things, these days. And Christine's description of human preservative has set her mind afire.

Mrs Stella reappears in the dining room laden with parcels.

'Time for presents!' she cries. 'And then let us sing some carols.'

As the twenty-fifth of December melts away and the next day arrives to take its place, Christine leans over in bed and gently touches Fran on the shoulder.

'What is distracting you?' she says. 'You've hardly said a word since we came home, but your eyes are so alive – you seem far away.'

Fran smiles and rubs her eyes. 'I'm sorry,' she says. 'I've been thinking over the day. I didn't mean to worry you.'

Christine might not be completely convinced, but she takes it as reassurance that nothing serious is wrong. It is usual for either of them to become quiet during a new project, or (in Christine's case) in the approach to examinations.

Her breathing soon becomes deep and regular. Fran does not manage to sleep for a long time.

On the twenty-sixth of December, the bohemians meet at a local cafe to gaze out at the already fading light of the early afternoon and drink away the flat greyness that accrues after any celebration. Mrs Stella does not join them; she is away, pursuing the many other demands filling her social calendar: entertaining, visiting, generally sparkling. Mrs Stella is interested in everyone, and highly desired by the public; as such, she is constantly busy. She never sends an invitation without accepting at least two.

And so the group cluster around a table in the corner of the Wine & Roses, a cheap, familiar drinking den in the centre of Soho. They huddle together, nursing strong liquors. Oliver Allbright is busy adding sugar to his absinthe.

'How did you get on with your family this morning, Edwin?' He means the ballet school.

Edwin smiles. 'I'm to play Romeo again in the new season.'

Jacques-Louis puts an arm across Edwin's shoulders and squeezes. 'Glad to hear it; I wouldn't wish you cast any other way,' he says. 'And with the roles taken care of, we can all look forward to Mrs Stella's New Year's party. It'll be a field day for the dreadfuls. They'll want more gossip inches than even I can provide.'

Oliver nods. He is no stranger to such publications, and broadly encourages their inaccurate reporting of his own activities. He turns to the others. 'And have you been doing any more of your hideous anatomy preparations?'

Both Christine and Fran go to answer, which makes Oliver laugh.

A door disguised as a dusty bookshelf, hidden in the far wall, swings open: a group of people come out with red, watery eyes; they are giggling uncontrollably and slapping each other on the back. They leave the door ajar, and from the back room comes a sweet-smelling, heavy fog. It is intoxicating to breathe.

'I meant Miss Sparks, of course,' says Oliver, removing his monocle to wipe it with his handkerchief, 'but has Miss Clayton returned to the taxidermy table?'

'And over the festive season, too!' says Jacques-Louis in not quite mock-disgust.

'Stuffing a goose, were you?' says Edwin. The table erupts into laughter.

A waiter has seen the opened door, and rushes to close it. Frances' head is already swimming with the sweet-smelling fog. And it is *this* that brings her to decide, once and for all, that she will go ahead with what she has been considering ever since the Christmas dinner.

She *will*, she thinks. She will suggest it to Christine.

And so it is late on the twenty-sixth of December, the sky outside the colour of old snow, when Frances breaks her silence. The whole group has joined Oliver in the drinking of absinthe, and everyone is involved in another heavy discussion – as is their wont – about the nature of art.

'I'm telling you,' Oliver is saying, 'this naturalism stuff is but a blip. We shall soon tire of its exhausting, *quasi-scientific* method of analysing human behaviour – gazing down upon ourselves as if our parlours are only so many dirty petri dishes – and return to enjoying art for the sake of the sheer *pleasure* it provides.'

'I hope you're right,' says Edwin. 'If I am required to dance naturalistic ballet, I shall no doubt pull a muscle.'

'And if we writers must stick to things that have *actually* occurred,' says Jacques-Louis, clutching his absinthe with an evil leer, 'the gossip columns of London will be as blank as a map of the Arctic.'

Frances leans towards Christine. Her mind is still foggy with the cloud of poppy-smoke; she notices the shine on the dark blue of Christine's velvet coat.

'I can contain myself no more,' she says. 'I have something to propose.'

Christine's eyebrow arches. "Propose'? What about?'

'The things you said yesterday: about the preservation of a body.'

'And?'

'It made my mind come alive!'

'What do you mean?'

Christine leans her head over her absinthe, clutches her fingers around the glass as if afraid Frances will put something in it.

Frances gabbles her words; if she stops now, she may never start again. 'I make bodies beautiful; you know of my work on dead things,' she says. 'Why don't we work together?'

'Together?'

'For your medical exams. I'll make the body beautiful; I'll treat it with my instruments the way you treat it with yours – the scalpel and the syringe and so on. And, in return, *you* preserve it as best you can; we will make it look positively alive.'

Christine drinks the whole of her absinthe down in one. Ignoring the shouts of congratulation from Edwin, Oliver and Jacques, who immediately set about ordering more for everyone.

'There's something I discovered,' she says to Frances, slurring slightly. Frances nods, waiting. She recognises Christine's energy, which mirrors her own, and realises Christine has been wanting desperately to suggest something, too.

Christine peers into her empty glass, runs a finger around the rim and licks it.

'We can do more than make her *look* alive,' she says. 'I think I've found something better.'

Back in their lodgings, not a long walk from the Wine & Roses – Frances and Christine live in a cramped set of rooms, in a high building squeezed thinner by its neighbours, where mould grows on the crumbling bricks and the gas lamps flicker through the dirty windows from the street – Frances has been pestering Christine all night for more information. Every other step she tugs her sleeve, whispers, 'What did you mean?' But Christine hasn't dared go further, beyond her first utterance. It is as if it took all her energy to announce the theme, and she has lost all energy for the details.

It was Mrs Stella's idea that Frances and Christine live together. It is perfectly natural for young ladies to share accommodation in the capital. To bring a man into the scenario would be to teeter on the edge of immorality; but two young women together and no mischief, of course. In any case, Christine is often away pursuing her studies, leaving Frances to litter the tables with the hollow carcasses of flattened rodents, scatters of gemstones, gold thread and plucked feathers.

They climb the stairs with a clatter of boots on wood, and Frances pleads again as they enter the dingy parlour. Christine finally gives in.

'I made some discoveries,' she says, hanging her coat on the hook, 'while working – alongside the usual anatomy – on the physical properties of electricity. A delirious account of a controversy at Newgate, half a century ago; rumours of an affair on the Orkneys, years before. Things began to link together. It isn't a single method,' she adds, for Frances' eyes are lighting up as she imagines turning a body on at the flick of a switch. Christine shakes her head. 'I wish I had a simple recipe to show you. No; I had to compile different materials to reach my current theory. The method I have in mind, I put together myself, pulling pieces from dead or dying ideas. It's a little of everything. It's a mixture of the believed-to-be-obsolete, the known-to-be-arcane and the who-knows-how-it-works. It's a forgotten ancient alchemy in the veins; electric tendrils in the brain; a new chemistry in the heart.'

'So let's try it!'

Christine's shoulders sag. She was hoping to put Frances off; but instead Frances is thrilled, inflamed. She takes Christine's face between her hands. 'We must experiment,' she says. 'If it doesn't work, nothing is lost. If it does work – why, *death* will be lost!'

Christine smiles – humouring rather than humoured – and reaches up to gently take Frances' hands away. 'It's a collection of scrappy theories, pulled from ancient books scattered across the continent.' She squeezes Frances' hands, tenderly, putting the issue, as she sees it, to bed. 'It won't work.'

'Think of Mrs Stella's face,' says Frances, 'when we tell her. And Allbright! We can make art and life one and the same thing, on a level never before accomplished.'

Christine looks over the parlour table, the plates scattered about with the remnants of bread crusts and cheese crumbs. Mrs Stella's patronage added to Christine's income would stretch to employing someone to clean for them, but they prefer their living to be private. It means more things become acceptable, unremarked; like kissing the other on the back of the neck while she is reading, or lacing each other's fingers as they pass towards the door, or eating quickly in the parlour before going out, without thought to good manners. Or keeping a human body on the table in the back room.

Christine thinks. 'We cannot damage the body,' she says. 'We must think of this as being for the greater good of science.'

Frances is beaming. 'With this 'formaldehyde,' we won't damage anything! It will only become better; *more* like a work of art. That's part one. Then we apply your mysterious theories, see if they work.'

'And you'll be able to cope with the process? This isn't like one of your taxidermied squirrels.'

Frances' hands become fists, press to her sides amidst her skirts. She stands to attention. 'I will perform to the best of my abilities,' she says.

Christine's eyes blaze with a new vitality. 'Let's do it, then.'

The reason there is a body in the back room, instead of where it should be – in the anatomy halls of the medical college – is mostly down to fortune. Whether good or bad fortune depends primarily upon one's perspective.

The body was not donated by a patron. It was found, days before, backstage in one of the district's many burlesque houses. One of the dancers, the owner said, had been jilted by her lover and fallen down in a faint. The others, presuming she was being her usual melodramatic self, had ignored her; only when she missed her cue to perform did anyone examine her closely, to discover that she would never high-kick again.

The dancer's bad fortune became Christine's good. The owner, who knew Christine through Frances – the sculptor had undertaken commissions for the establishment's decor – told Christine about it, insisting the club could not handle any public fuss. And so the body was delivered in the dead of night, providing Christine an unprecedented opportunity to get ahead in her studies.

It was initially an inconvenience for Frances, who likes to spread her taxidermy projects over that table; now, of course, she realises it is a gift.

Christine takes the first shift with the body. She begins by reapplying the preservative, to replenish, as it were, the body's stores. Frances watches from the corner with her hands knitted tightly together, hardly daring to breathe.

The syringe is cold, made of tarnished silver and thick glass, and it weighs heavily in Christine's hand. She fills it with a bubbling green liquid, prepares the dosage, jetting a short burst from the pointed tip of the needle. The sickly fluid splashes her cheek and she wipes it away absently, before brushing the hair away from the body's eyes.

'There, there,' she says.

She injects the formaldehyde into the chest, pushing the needle in as steadily as if she were behind the counter in The Black Cat, plunging down the brass handle of a cafetière. She injects the preservative again, into the arms, the legs, between the shoulders, then turning the syringe sideways and pressing it into the temple.

The body's delicate hands seem to move imperceptibly as the chemical powers through the veins. Slowly, the body takes on the illusion of pale life.

Christine leaves on a midnight errand to the medical college, leaving Frances to take the next shift alone. This occupies the majority of the night.

The instruments of taxidermy, in this era, are not dissimilar to the tools found in Christine's medical chest. Frances uses them with equal, if not greater, care.

The nails on the hands she shapes and paints; and she adds fine, barely noticeable patterns to the soles of the feet, and colours the toenails so they glow gold. She sews rich aquamarine jewels onto the backs of the hands, and, with a rich turquoise powder – the lead-based paste she might normally use to enrich the tail of a peacock – she paints the eyelids. She adds rows of glass beads through the hair. She threads metal wire through the inside of the lips, shaping the mouth into a beguiling smile. Using a sharp device that resembles a hooked scalpel, she scrapes the teeth until they shine white, reshaping them until they sit uniform inside the pink gums. She adds a beauty spot made of jet just above the corner of the mouth, a stone she might otherwise have set into the eye of a freshly mounted sparrow.

The sensation is curious, as she works; the arms of the body are cold, undoubtedly unliving; yet they are soft, and the formaldehyde in the veins gives the illusion of pliability. If she gets it wrong a bruise will, she suspects, slowly form on the skin, mottled like dead leaves and black at the edges. She applies subtle powders of gold and bronze to the flesh. She wants the final product to appear artificially beautiful – treated, unnatural: symbolic of her art – but the effect must be subtle.

Using a needle so thin it is barely visible, she sews threads of gold into the eyelashes and eyebrows. She has some left over, and threads it delicately through the hair between the legs.

Christine re-enters the room, having snatched a quarter-hour of sleep, and they hook the body up to a collection of devices Christine has brought from the college. Frances feels her heart beating; she is certain it must be audible across the room.

Christine presses the switch.

The electricity is silent, coursing through the body on an invisible network of arteries and nervous clusters. Once, an eyelid flickers and Frances clasps Christine's hand so tightly she is surprised Christine doesn't cry out.

Christine only shakes her head. 'It is the power of the electricity,' she says, 'coursing through the skull, affecting the eyeball. Proof of nothing at all.'

As morning light breaks and brings to the city the twenty-seventh of December, Frances and Christine stand, their breath coming deep and snagged, as if they have been running for hours, nervous sweat turning their hair to ropes. They gaze down together at the supine body. The pale light of morning is beginning to push through the windows, outlining the thin curtains with a border of grey light.

'Her pallor,' says Frances, 'is not what I was expecting.'

'I did say bleaching would occur,' says Christine.

'Yes – but this is such an extreme case. I feel that I'm looking at her through fog.'

'Well then, perhaps it is just as well she isn't sitting up to speak with us.'

They wait a few more moments.

'It didn't work,' says Christine. Her voice is as flat as the table on which the body lies. 'Fool that I am. Of course it didn't.'

Frances takes her hand. 'She's beautiful, though. We can display her at the New Year's party; nobody will think it a real body. She looks like a fine marble sculpture.'

Christine shakes her head. 'I'm going to get some more sleep,' she says, and goes to their bedroom, leaving Frances with the body.

Frances watches their creation for a few moments more. She focuses on one of the hands, willing it to tremble so much that, when it finally does, she believes she must have fallen asleep too and is only dreaming. It is not until the fingers twitch all together, slowly tapping upon the table as if remembering a tune for the pianoforte, that Frances knows she is seeing something real. Her gaze moves over the body's stomach and breasts and lands with a gasp upon the body's face just as the eyes flick open.

Both parties in the room register equal amounts of shock. The silence is thick, as if Frances and the body are buried together under six feet of cold soil.

The shining lips move, stiffly, as they navigate their wiry frame.

Frances holds out a finger. 'Stay there,' she says, and within a moment the door to the back room is open and her feet are falling heavily along the floorboards.

Christine is sitting at the writing-desk in their bedroom, running her pen over an anatomic drawing, craning to use the little light that filters in through the dusty window from the street lamps. She looks up at Frances, standing breathlessly in the doorway.

'I couldn't sleep,' she explains.

Frances shakes her head; she feels she will never need sleep again. 'You've got to come back in.'

Christine holds her gaze. 'What is it?' Her pen drops ink onto the carefully drawn diagram. The body she is drawing has a black splatter for a heart.

Frances taps on the doorframe. Impatient. 'What do you *think*?'

And so the clock ticks through the early morning of the twenty-seventh of December. Frances and Christine have gone from their bedroom to the back room, to the bedroom, to the parlour, to the back room and back again into the bedroom – travelling between disbelief, horror, exhilaration; hugging, crying out; racing from one room to another. Finally they stand in the small room where the body still lies on the table, blinking and – newly, extraordinarily – slowly sitting up.

'What shall we call her?' Frances follows the curving slope of the body's shoulders and neck. The throat trembles with the new pulse.

Christine taps her foot on the floor. 'It ought to be something of magnitude,' she says. 'Something that signifies what we have achieved here.'

The body is sitting up fully, now, her feet dangling over the edge of the table. She is looking down at her toes, wiggling them.

'One name springs to mind.' A smile plays about Frances' face. 'How about Eve?'

Christine's eyes widen at the audacity. 'Just how many blasphemies do you propose we commit in one day?'

But Eve does seem to fit, and it is decided.

They complete the christening by clinking two high-stemmed glasses together and downing the contents. They kiss, tasting wine on each other's mouths.

Christine is immediately busy; the main body of Christmas being over, she is obliged to return to her studies and thus, while it is still dark with the freshness of the twenty-seventh of December, she leaves the house to commence once again the business of crossing the city for lectures, practical examinations, discussions. Frances, under the patronage of Mrs Stella, is able to remain at home to proceed on her sculptural work. She has a taxidermy commission. The parlour table is a tangle of hollow skin, scraps of fur, glass vials of tanning oil, and the scattered gemstones that will become eyes. A full scene; a selection of dormice mounted to recreate the revelry of a dancehall. The door to the back room remains open, and Frances sits so she can face it, utterly unable to concentrate. The presence of Eve sits squarely across her thoughts like bars on a window.

She discovers Eve can speak when Eve comes into the parlour, standing unsteadily in the doorway. She looks at Frances for a few long moments, then asks for a picture.

'A picture?' Frances is careful.

'A pattern,' says Eve. Her voice has a lilt to it – Christine delicately aligned every vocal cord, finely tuned it like a concert violin. 'I want to look like that.' She raises an arm and points to one of the decorated pieces of fabric piled in a rough square on the table. (It will eventually be sewn into intricate ruffles for the dancing mice.)

Frances goes into the back room and paints a delicate pattern over Eve's back and shoulders, piercing it through Eve's skin with a needle. She uses black and green, outlines it with gold. A beautiful bruise.

Christine comes home early; the twenty-seventh of December has been a half-day for her. A professor, still recovering from the fine port and sherry of the season, cancelled his lecture on the anatomy of the stomach.

Frances does not greet Christine properly, but stands and immediately says: 'We shouldn't tell anyone about Eve.'

Christine is pulling off her gloves. The fierce, alcoholic smell of anaesthetic hangs around her like an invisible fog. 'What do you mean?'

'We should keep her a secret,' says Frances. 'I've changed my mind; about telling Mrs Stella. I don't think we ought to tell anyone.'

Christine arches a sceptical eyebrow. 'She's a medical marvel!' she says. 'And an artistic one. I could barely stop myself shouting out about her to the entire lecture theatre. Of course we must show her. What's got into you?'

Their rooms are filled with a sulky silence for the next few hours. Offended at Frances' abrupt change of heart, Christine does not tell her she has already sent a letter of invitation.

The afternoon light is waning in Soho, and the air is damp, as are the buildings. The streets are lined with melting snow, most of which has long since turned to sludge. Sure-footed as ever, Mrs Stella makes her way across the cobbles from a hansom cab; her umbrella hangs on her arm. Christine is peering out of the window to watch for her arrival, and Mrs Stella has barely rapped upon the door before she breathlessly lets her in.

'I received your missive, dear,' says Mrs Stella, 'and came directly. This is something to do with the New Year's festivities, I take it?'

Frances is sitting at the table when Christine rushes past, unwinding an old Yule wreath she found abandoned in the street. It was half-trampled by horses, but still salvageable. She pulls the branches apart, separating them out; the stronger twigs will do for modelling dormice poses and she can use the holly leaves for something. Perhaps a hairpiece for Eve. Her fingers are covered in red scratches. On hearing Mrs Stella's voice she immediately stands, and her fingers press down onto the hard wood.

'No,' she mutters, but Mrs Stella is already breezing inside, raising her arms towards her. Christine follows behind, her face slightly sheepish.

'Drab old day, isn't it?' says Mrs Stella. 'I was summoned,' she adds, seeing the faraway glance in Frances' eyes. 'I gather you have something to show me?'

Frances nods, unable to speak.

'It's through here, Mrs Stella,' says Christine. The great actress adjusts her hat with a murmur of, 'Marvellous,' and leads the way into the parlour.

Frances marches to Christine, takes her wrist.

'I said we shouldn't,' she says. 'We didn't agree. What are you doing?'

'Mrs Stella needs to see her,' says Christine. 'It was for her benefit we went ahead with the experiment at all.'

'You didn't *tell me*,' says Frances. 'What if I don't *want* –?'

Mrs Stella's voice ripples into the room. 'My dears?'

'Coming!' calls Christine. She lowers her voice to an urgent whisper. 'We will *have* to show her sometime, Frances. Are we supposed to keep it a secret for ever?'

'Perhaps!'

Christine laughs and pulls Frances' arms away. 'I'd rather Eve's first sight of humanity beyond the two of us was Mrs Stella, not some ring of anonymous professors in a viewing gallery.'

Frances wants to tell Christine that neither option particularly appeals, but she is unable to swallow the hard lump filling her throat. In any case, Christine has already disappeared into the next room.

'You recall, Mrs Stella, my conversation on Christmas Day, regarding the technologies of formaldehyde?'

'Of course! How could I forget them?' Mrs Stella is seated grandly, her gloves in one hand and her umbrella in the other. 'I daresay poor Jacques is still experiencing nightmares.'

'Frances and I –' Christine glances at Frances, who is standing, arms folded, in the doorway. She smiles: an olive branch extended. 'We have been working on a project together. And, thanks to your inspiration, we have succeeded in something I doubt you have encountered before.'

'I wouldn't be too sure about *that*, my dear,' says Mrs Stella, 'I've seen some things. In eighteen-eighty-two I toured Europe for an entire year playing Rosalind.'

'Nevertheless,' Christine's eyes glisten, 'I believe this will surprise you. You'll see what Frances and I made together.' At this, Frances takes the olive branch, smiling back at Christine.

Christine opens the door into the back room, beckoning Frances to follow.

Inside, Eve is standing by the window. She frowns at them as if displaced, thrown off course by the new voice.

Frances wrinkles her nose. The room smells of burnt lavender, and overpoweringly of basil; Christine has endeavoured to mask the chemical odour that follows Eve everywhere.

Eve nods towards the door that leads through into the parlour, clearly wondering what is happening, who is there.

'It's a good friend of ours,' says Christine. 'We'd be honoured to introduce you.'

She holds out her hand. Eve looks down at it, unsure: and, with a flicker of her eyes Christine cannot help but notice, her gaze moves to Frances, and waits there until Frances gives the smallest of nods. Then Eve turns her gaze back to Christine, and allows her to take her hand.

Christine looks at Frances as they turn towards the door. Her look is odd, as if she is trying to place where something began.

Christine leads Eve into the room. They walk together in silence until they are by the window, where Christine leaves Eve standing alone. Christine stands beside Mrs Stella's chair; Frances remains in the doorway. She has a better view of Mrs Stella's face from there.

Mrs Stella sits forward on the wicker chair, leaning her weight into the floor, pressing onto the handle of her umbrella.

'Oh, my dears,' she says, 'what on earth have you done?'

Frances and Christine share a nervous glance.

'It's the new formaldehyde,' says Christine, quietly. 'As you see, she looks as she did in life. Better, even.'

'Quite extraordinary,' she mutters. 'And how do you get it to move?'

'The precise method would be difficult to explain,' says Christine, as she slowly reclaims her confidence, 'but it involved electricity. Needless to say, I don't believe anyone has achieved such a thing as this,' she adds, with pride.

'And it... thinks, and feels, and so on?' Mrs Stella's face is held taut. 'It is alive in the same sense that we are?'

'Perhaps *more* alive,' says Christine. 'In a sense. She required a lot of power.'

Mrs Stella frowns and looks down at her umbrella, slowly rotating it on the spot. Dirty water accrues on the floor beneath its tip. 'I must confess this development worries me slightly,' she says.

She looks up again and examines Eve with the keen precision of a fine art collector, examining the fall of Eve's hair, her stomach, her fingertips.

After a time none of them can measure, Mrs Stella seems to relax.

'Very well,' she says. 'Your enthusiasm, and, I confess, the sheer *beauty* of your creation, has convinced me. I shall suppress my doubts. I love it!' She stands. 'It's darling. In fact, I've an idea. You must exhibit it at the New Year's party!'

Frances leaves the doorway: she finds her voice again. 'We thought that at first,' she says, 'but now we don't –'

'It would be an honour,' says Christine.

'I've got it!' Mrs Stella is already pulling on her gloves.

'She can perform. A *tableau vivant;* that's the ticket! We'll do a beauteous display upon the stage, half undressed and completely still; in a classical attitude, so they know it isn't smut. Give her a vase to hold.' She re-pins her hat into place with a sharp stab. Eve remains, standing silently, her arms by her sides. Forgotten.

Mrs Stella fluffs the feathered plume of her hat with a careless hand. 'You've *made* the New Year's party, my dears. It will be as your creation is: perfect. Heartiest of congratulations.'

As soon as Mrs Stella is gone, Frances and Christine are at loggerheads.

'There you are, you see,' says Christine, 'What were you so worried about?'

'That wasn't an introduction,' hisses Frances. 'That was a demonstration. You didn't address one word to Eve, neither of you.'

'What's got into you?' says Christine. 'We'll present her at the party and become the toast of the city! I'll be a certified doctor within weeks, I'll bet, and we can move into a grand house like Mrs Stella's. What's the problem?'

Frances doesn't know. She is filled with emotion, but no tears. She feels too on edge to cry. She feels as if every nerve in her body is raw.

'I don't like the way it's going,' she says, 'that's all.'

Christine's face softens, and so does her voice. She takes Frances' hand and gently stokes it. 'We've always trusted in each other,' she says.

Frances leans her face against Christine's chest. 'Yes,' she says.

But in the red-blackness of her half-closed eyes, she sees Eve glance her way, checking that everything is still all right. With a further burning feeling in the back of her eyes, Frances realises with a jolt: Eve *trusts* her, more than she trusts Christine.

Christine is out again – sitting through lectures and attending demonstrations of the latest anatomical discoveries. She may be preparing for a great presentation in the New Year, the reveal of Eve; Frances cannot bring herself to ask. It is the twenty-eighth of December and they have barely spoken, so enraptured have they been in their own activities. As soon as Christine leaves, Frances goes to the back room to sit with Eve, the ghost of Christine's farewell kiss still lingering on her cheek. Frances finds that she and Eve can go for hours without speaking. So can Frances and Christine, of course; but that is a silence of mutual busyness, of the contentment that arises between two people pursuing separate but simultaneous activity. The silences between Frances and Eve are more companionable: it is the silence of two people thinking and feeling along the same lines. Unopened post piles up beneath the letterbox.

Mid-afternoon, Mrs Stella pays another visit. She does not ask about Eve and remains in the entrance, refusing even the offer of a drink of Lady Grey.

'I mustn't stay,' says Mrs Stella. Her hat is new; its ostrich feathers threaten to scrape the ceiling. 'I just wanted to pop in, see how you are. Oliver tells me you are never to be seen in the café-theatres now. He expected you to dine with him last night, spend an evening chatting throughout the applause – not that I approve of those behaviours, but there you are – but he tells me you never replied to his letter. Are you quite all right? You're not ill?'

In Frances' mind she sees Eve's tattoo, follows the delicate pattern along her shoulderblades. She has spent the morning making it more ornate, spreading interlocking patterns over Eve's body. She shakes her head. 'Everything is fine. It's only been a day or so, hasn't it – two days? How can Oliver say he never sees me?'

Mrs Stella holds her gaze a moment. Unconvinced. Then she blinks, and the moment snaps, and she rummages around in her carpet bag.

'I've brought you something to read, anyway. These are Jacques-Louis' old copies; sadly discontinued, of course, all of them. But he thought they might be of interest anyway. I think he wants you to get a new hobby, my dear!'

She holds aloft a thick pile of pages, brown parchment with greasy wax-covers in green, grey and garish yellow. Lurid brush-strokes outline bodies and landscapes on the front pages. Periodicals of Bohemia, best in the city.

Frances takes them, deposits them heavily by the hat stand without looking at them properly. She pushes a lock of hair out of her eyes. 'To tell you the truth, Mrs Stella, I've clean lost track of what day it is.'

Mrs Stella hooks her umbrella over her arm and adjusts her hat. 'Oh, I shouldn't worry,' she says, turning to leave. 'That's perfectly normal for this time of year.'

When Mrs Stella has gone, Frances finds she is utterly uninterested in the gossip, doodlings and apocalyptic predictions of the magazines. She totters to the bedroom, lies on her back upon the bed and stares out of the featureless window. Her fingers play with the embroidery upon her bodice, and she pulls a thread loose, barely noticing as she does it. Her eyes wander from the blank sky across the walls of the room, and her gaze snags on a dilapidated patch in the corner of the ceiling. Here the cold and damp have combined to rot away one corner of the beams, revealing, among the splintering wood and clouded knots of the old webs of spiders, some scraps of the previous occupant's yellow wallpaper, which has become dulled with time and peels away at the edges.

Frances sighs deeply. She feels time is an exhausting tunnel she must pass through; the week is a scatter of grey days, lacking life, all badly stitched together. She rises to go into the back room, to sit longer with Eve.

A papery sound drops through the front door, and an envelope lands heavily on all the others. This time, Frances musters the energy to open it. It is an invitation to stroll in Green Park and, not seeing why Christine should have all the fresh air, she goes.

Oliver Allbright is already there, standing by a bench, wearing green-and-yellow-check trousers, a viridian velvet waistcoat and a dark brown jacket with long tails. He is holding a pipe, and Frances knows better than to enquire what is in it. She takes his arm and they stroll down the path. The sky is pale and watery, the path slushed with old snow. Not many people are out in this weather. A few children play about, wearing muddied, torn scraps.

'Mrs Stella tells me you have been distracted of late,' he says. 'I hope it's not this absurd project with Christine I heard you talking about?'

Frances starts. 'How did you know about that?'

'It is my business,' says Oliver, 'to hear things that are whispered urgently in the corner of an absinthe bar. I promise neither Edwin, nor Jacques-Louis, nor anyone else in the Wine & Roses heard what you were saying. Only myself. Hence, my taking the liberty of inviting you out.'

Frances looks down at her feet. Her grey shoes kick lightly over old leaves that have turned to blackish slime.

'It's an artistic project,' she says, 'and it's overtaken my imagination. Apologies for my absence. It really feels as if it has a life of its own. I can't concentrate on anything else.'

'Now that, I can understand. I certainly have been lost to artistic endeavours in my time. Do you know, there's at least a few months of this year I have completely forgotten? It is all a haze, and it's not even aesthetically pleasing. At least you have Christine to comfort you. You'll give my regards when you see her tonight?'

'No. She's out. Again. Some keynote lecture, I think, on the ethics of preservation.'

'I see,' says Oliver. But Frances is not quite sure *what* he sees.

They walk on a little more. A flustered nanny passes them, pushing a squeaky-wheeled pram, desperately making shushing noises into the whimpering bundle. Two boys kneel by the side of the path in a puddle of murky water, muddied to their knees, tormenting a frog.

'Will you be glad to see the year out?' says Oliver.

Frances contemplates a rotting oak leaf lying by her shoe. 'A few days ago, perhaps. But now everything feels… upended, and yet the same. Let the century die, I feel I will hardly notice.'

Oliver nods. 'Of course, there are those who insist the century is not actually about to end. That might be why it's all the same to you. Supposedly, we ought to hold off until 1900 turns into 1901. We're a year early.'

More dead leaves. Their walking breaks the leaves up, causing them to merge into an indistinct wet shape. Frances shakes her head. 'Does it matter?'

Oliver smiles. 'Not in the least. Ninety-nine growing into a new hundred *feels* so much more satisfying, does it not? And feelings are everything. And if this year's revelry proves unsatisfactory, we can always consider it a dry run, do it over.'

A breeze comes through the bare tree branches, finds its way into every buttonhole. Frances shivers. 'I couldn't bear it happening again,' she says. Oliver squeezes her arm.

Darkness descends as they walk.

Winter days being what they are, it is long dark by the time Frances returns. Even as she approaches the door, something tells her that things are wrong, and her step falters; she gazes for a long moment at the tarnished door-knocker and she feels the heavy, fat presence of something waiting for her beyond the entrance. She shakes her head slightly, closing her eyes to brush off the sensation, and grasps the door handle in her gloved hand.

The rooms seem the same as when she left them, only darker with the onset of an early winter's night; from the far bedroom comes the dull yellow glow of a candle. Somebody is in, but it is not Christine; her coat, hat and boots are absent from the hat stand. Frances lets her umbrella drop to the floor, and it lands with a heavy sound that makes Frances jump, sending electric prickles across the back of her neck. She finds her thoughts cycling rapidly: *Nothing to worry about. Christine must be on a late call.* Yet those very thoughts make Frances' heart beat faster: why does she feel the need to conjure reassuring thoughts?

Her mind races as she peels off her gloves. There is nothing inherently unusual in the candle. Eve has revealed a tendency to stay awake late, just as Frances and Christine do, stretching out the final hours of the century staring at the black square of the window, the candle's glow a comfort in the dark. Eve may well have lit the flame. Yet, as Frances paces towards the bedroom, some deep dread sends a shiver up her back. Her feet make louder creaks on the floorboards than she is accustomed to, or wants.

As her hand reaches out to push open the bedroom door, a memory from a second earlier rises to the forefront of her vision. She realises that, as she passed the table, the stack of empty plates remained upon it, bearing crusts and crumbles of cheese; and that the plates have sat that way for far too long, and the bread has become dotted with dark mould. She feels ill.

The bedroom door swings open and her gaze skips first to the bed – tangled sheets, unmade – and then, in the dim light of the single candle by the window, her eyes adjust to the lumpen shape sitting in the biggest chair, facing away from her, leaning forwards, legs stretched out towards the empty fireplace.

She breathes a sigh of relief.

'You had me worried!' she says, and her voice bounces off the thick silence. Instantly she sees that something is very different; the body in the chair does not turn around to face her. She feels a movement to her right, and looks that way.

Eve, tallow-yellow in the candlelight, her face a rictus. She is pressed up against the wall and her eyes blaze in the darkness, glittering more in their fear than the jewels on her skin.

'You said I was the only one!' she says. 'I heard you!'

'What...?' says Frances. Her attention switches back to the fireplace.

The being in the chair sits up and begins to turn around.

Frances backs against the bedroom door, her hand to her mouth. She does not scream.

It pushes itself out of the chair.

Frances' eyes take in the lumpen boots, caked with old mud, the dirty trousers, torn jerkin; fashions from an unfathomable time. The creature's arms are roped with muscle and streaked with dark, dried grazes and scars of old wounds. He takes a heavy stride up, heaving his weight from the chair, until he stands, back to the fireplace, looking almost polite.

'What?' says Frances.

'He claims to be like me,' says Eve from behind her. 'He says we're the same.'

His face is a death-mask. In the light of the candle his skin is ghastly and worn and his eyes are filmed over, milky and bloodshot with old, dead blood. He stares at Frances. He opens his mouth again and a black tongue flickers out, licks his dry lips. His hair is like dirty straw, falling loosely across his face.

'Good evening,' he says.

'You're *not* the same!' Frances presses her hands to the door, feeling the flat of the heavy wood against her sweating palms. The room smells thick, she realises, like sour milk or rotting hay. The mould on the bread. 'How dare you!'

'We are – similar, then.' His voice comes from somewhere deep, beyond his throat; it rises like a bucket of sludge from an old well. When the noise reaches his throat it grates and splinters; by the time it reaches his lips, forming into words for Frances, it is a dull crackling moan, full of old pain and long-boiling anger. Every utterance, Frances sees, causes this monster a great deal of physical strife. He will not waste words.

'He came through the window,' says Eve.

Frances imagines him, sitting all afternoon by her fireplace. 'How did you find us?'

The monster raises his shoulders, slowly, with a popping of rotten cartilage, and lets them fall again. A shrug. 'I sensed.'

'And what do you want?'

'He wants us to go away together,' says Eve.

Frances' head presses on the side of the wall, her eyes rolling to their whites with the effort of looking at Eve as well as trying to keep watch on the interloper. 'He *what?*'

'He says the world is dangerous,' says Eve. She looks down at her body, runs her fingers across herself, holds her arms there in a light hug. Frances realises she has become conscious of her nudity. 'Not just dangerous for me. For us both. For the *likes* of us. He says people will not understand us, so I should go with him, and all the sooner.'

'You want to take her *away?*' Frances can feel cold sweat down her back, dragging at the fabric against her body; it trickles down her neck, across her face.

Dark creases form in the monster's neck as he nods.

Frances barely resists the urge to scream. 'Why?'

'Safety,' he says. 'Companionship...' His eyes bulge at Frances; a trickle of dark brown liquid leaks out of one tear duct – too dark to be a tear, too thick to be blood. His materials cannot be categorised. 'We belong together,' he says. 'Do you understand?'

Frances understands enough.

She races to the writing desk beneath the window, flinging out her hand, her fingers flexing for anything she can reach. Eve cries out in anguish, causing Frances to adjust her movements by sudden instinct, as if ducking out of the way of an attack. She flings her arm out again, upends the candle, and the room is thrown into darkness.

Her fingers grasp something cold and sharp: Christine's brass letter opener. She holds it out at the full stretch of her arm.

The room fills with a new odour, the ashy scratch of the extinguished candle.

The lumpen silhouette takes a heavy step closer to Frances, and Eve lets out another faint cry. Frances tightens her grip on the letter opener. Her eyes adjust to the moonlight, which catches its edge with a golden glow, and Frances wonders what on earth she imagines she can achieve with such a narrow blade.

Nevertheless, she grips it until her knuckles go white.

As he reaches the window, it is clear the monster can see the blade too, and that he also wonders at Frances' strategy. His face splits into a wide smile, more terrible than his sterner face; his mouth surely contains more teeth than it should.

His voice takes on a new quality. Softer, like wet mud. Trying another angle. 'We will eventually both need... companionship,' he says.

Her hand shakes. 'You, sir, are making *many* assumptions,' she says,

The monster throws his head back with a faint popping of vertebrae, and the tone of his voice returns to gravel-pit anger.

'She will see reason. I can teach you how to get by in this world, better than these people can. They will turn against you. I will not.'

'We will not *turn*,' says Frances. She feels Eve take some steps behind her, coming closer, and her breath catches. Her heart is squeezing into the top of her chest, pressing down on her lungs and windpipe, stopping her airflow.

'I don't need you,' says Eve, and for an appalling moment Frances thinks she is talking to her. But the monster lets out a roar of frustration and leaps up onto the writing table.

Frances and Eve step back, together. Frances reaches out a hand and Eve clasps it. Eve's fingers are cold; Frances' are flattened red from her grip on the knife handle.

He is in a crouch on the table, rocking slightly on his heels. He is looking towards them, his outline not quite human; an appalling shape in the darkness. Frances has not yet taken a breath; any moment now, the table will surely collapse beneath his weight. Some pale light reaches the window from the gas lamps that line the street, illuminating his greasy hair and picking out the grey-green of the skin on his shoulders and arms.

The monster's head moves a fraction and, even though she cannot make out any of his features, Frances knows he is speaking directly to her. 'Just wait,' he says. 'If you do not turn, *she* will.'

And, with a smooth elegance she would not have expected, in a single movement he has opened the window, swung himself out across the casement, and let go, flinging both hands out with splayed fingers. For a moment he is fully framed by the window, his hair streaming behind him, as he sails silently through the night, cutting the air like a blade. He disappears and there is no sound of his landing.

Frances and Eve remain in the darkness of the bedroom for some time. Frances places her hands over her knees, leaning over with the effort to catch her breath, taking it in deep, heavy, gasping sobs, while the remaining adrenalin pounds through her mind and spins itself out between her shoulders. Quicker to compose herself, Eve steadies and relights the candle. Its new light shines on her skin and its gemstones, showing the curve of her stomach, clinging to her breasts and thighs. Her arms are covered in gooseflesh and she rubs her hands over them, crossing her arms over herself.

She steps towards Frances. Frances stands and takes Eve's hands in hers.

'I promise,' she says.

Eve's face is entirely open, trusting. Before Frances realises what she is doing, she has bent her face towards Eve and touched Eve's mouth with her own.

Eve's lips are soft, with a fullness revealing the hard copper wires that shape them. Their kiss becomes harder, and Frances raises her arms to clasp Eve around the shoulders. Eve's hands, in turn, take Frances around the waist, and her white, straight teeth gently bite her tongue. It sends a pulse of electricity across

Frances' body, spinning the adrenalin of fear into a new kind of rush. She looks deeply into Eve's eyes. They shine like emeralds.

They move to the bed. Eve's body shudders as Frances' hands explore. Her caresses draw on the experiences between Christine and herself, of course; but partly they are expressions of a craftswoman surveying her handiwork. Frances knows Eve's body well. She strokes her fingers lightly down Eve's stomach, teases across her golden hair, and down her thighs. Eve's breathing becomes heavy and thick. Frances feels the movement of Eve's chest with wonder, matches her quick breathing as they kiss again.

Eve pushes herself up and holds the back of Frances' neck. Frances shudders as Eve's moist lips tenderly press down onto her neck, over her shoulders: Eve's gentle tongue reaches her breasts, and Frances leans her head to the ceiling and arches her back against the bed. Her eyes catch, once again, the yellow wallpaper in the corner near the ceiling; the beams seem to have rotted even further since she last looked. In the flickering of the lone candle the decay seems almost to move.

Her attention leaves the wall as Eve stops kissing her and leaves the bed. She goes to the corner where Christine's medical bag sits, squatting heavily on a wooden stool. Eve reaches inside and pulls out a large, silver wand-like instrument, and for a moment Frances fears some divine retribution, a kind of electric revenge.

But, of course, she realises what it is.

It is a relatively new medical technique. The vibrations are intended to bring about an ease of anxiety, massaging the tenseness from hard-working shoulders.

Eve brings the tool back into the bed, places one hand upon the small of Frances' back, and with the other, switches on the device.

Bright sparks of electricity zip through the inside of the machine. Frances' eyes widen.

'What are you going to do?' she whispers.

Eve places her arms above her head, holding her wrists together. Frances wiggles and pretends to struggle, pressing her weight into the tangled sheets of the bed. She finds she cannot move. Even a light touch from Eve is able to pin her, totally, to the bed. For a moment Frances feels a spike of fear, a thrill of the unknown; in an instant, it is unclear who has more power. Eve notices and lets go.

'Are you all right?' she asks.

'You're very strong,' says Frances, rubbing her wrist.

Eve looks down at her arms, considering. 'I don't *feel* strong,' she says. 'He told me – before you arrived. He said I would be able to withstand most anything. That the world is dangerous because of what I can withstand. Perhaps that's what he meant. That I'm stronger than... than I ought to be.'

'That's interesting to know,' mutters Frances. A faint thought passes over her mind, like a wispy cloud crossing the moon: Christine would like to know that.

'I'll have to be gentle,' says Eve, and she moves the instrument closer to Frances, gently places it upon her skin.

Frances arches her back again as the pleasure rises. Her first orgasm is swift, building rapidly and peaking with electric efficiency. It happens quickly, opens her appetite rather than fulfilling it, and she is left gasping for breath and renewed with energy.

The instrument glows, a living silvery-blue, and Frances still hungers. She rises, propping her body on her elbows, shaking.

'Give it to me,' she says, and she pulls Eve onto the bed and straddles her, taking the silver wand into her own hands. They take it in turns, building and slowing, rising and falling, gasping for joy and losing their breath.

Night falling, the twenty-eighth of December. Mrs Stella, seated at her writing-desk, her pen flying across the paper.

She is following up her invitations to the New Year's party. She writes to those who initially sent their apologies, as well as those who have already confirmed their attendance.

She writes that she has a magnificent surprise in store for the guests; a piece of entertainment never before seen in this city. She acknowledges the feelings of hopelessness or despair that the addressed may be feeling as the century dies, but explains that her planned event is sure to bring it back to life, just for a moment, before it leaves forever. She signs off with love and the fondest of wishes, and finally, just the once more, repeats how much, and how earnestly, she hopes the addressed will be in attendance. If they have already informed her that they must keep to other plans, she begs them to reconsider. She remains, sir, madam, your most gracious, obedient, and humble, servant.

When a thin jade-and-white cup is placed beside her, she barely looks up from her work. The tea grows cold as she begins the next letter.

In the middle of the night, the darkest part of witching hour; the twenty-eighth of December has passed into the twenty-ninth, and Frances wakes in the pitch-black bed. The covers are tangled over her legs, and the pillow has a fold in it; her neck is pained, stretched at an awkward angle. She feels the weight of Eve beside her, the cold heaviness of her arm resting across her chest. She strokes Eve's arm lightly; it feels smooth, like living marble.

She's wide awake.

'Eve?' she says.

Eve does not reply in words, but her other hand begins to gently stroke her hair.

'I feel extraordinary,' says Frances. A red hot fire is burning between her legs, smouldering low in her stomach. She feels wet, awake, all over. 'I feel as though a thirst has opened up in me that can never be quenched,' she says. 'All I can think is: I want to do this again, and again, and again, and again.'

'So why don't we?' murmurs Eve, and she leans over to pick something up. In the quiet dark of the bedroom there is a metallic switch, followed by a gentle, insistent hum.

Christine is growing tired of Frances' distracted state. On the thirtieth of December – early in the afternoon – she cracks, and says so.

She is in the bedroom, unpacking her satchel of papers scribbled with diagrams and formulae. 'You haven't touched those dormice,' she says, striking a match and putting it to the candle. 'Am I the only one pursuing any work?'

Frances shakes her head. The room smells of dying lilies, with an undercurrent of ozone. Eve's scent. 'I *am* working,' she says. 'I can't be blamed if you're never here to see me!'

Christine comes towards her, offers a brief kiss of apology, and rummages through her bag, motioning that she has something exciting to share. Frances wonders that Christine can't smell Eve on the bedsheets, or even taste Eve on her tongue; but Christine is visibly exhausted. She pulls out a bottle from her bag and brandishes it aloft.

'It's a medicinal bitter,' she says. 'I was given it today. It was invented to combat malaria, but turns out it's *incredible* with gin. Go and get the bottle.'

The drink they make is dry like black pepper, with a tang of bitter orange that burns the back of the throat. The quinine in the bitter reminds Frances of a doctor's surgery, but it isn't unpleasant. She looks at Christine as they clink their glasses together. They don't kiss again, and after the first sip Christine goes immediately back to her papers. Frances feels she is watching her work from behind glass.

Edwin Turner looks out over the city from the high windows of the dance school, temporarily distracted from the swishing of tulle and the wheeling of limbs.

'What you looking at?' asks a young woman in pale pink who has just pirouetted into his vicinity. She stretches out a leg on the barre, pretending to deal with a sudden attack of cramp, cocking her head to gaze keenly at Edwin. Her sash is an odd shade of green, which jars with the pink in a way he finds troubling. He feels a strange pulsing at the back of his mind; perhaps the beginnings of a headache.

'I'm looking out at the city,' he says. 'Doesn't it make you feel dizzy?'

She follows his gaze. 'What, the view? Same as always, isn't it?'

'The *date*,' says Edwin. 'The end of the century.'

'Speaking of which.' She points at something. 'That's where *I'm* going tomorrow night. Reckon I can sneak in. Madame says it'll be the best party in the whole city. Won't stop going on about her invitation, smug old sow. Wish she'd take me with her.'

Edwin thinks it would be cruel to admit that he is also invited. Instead he smiles sadly and nods, and together they look out towards the district where, even from here, a distinctive light can be seen sweeping over the houses and the church spires.

The dull winter weather being what it is, the hands of the great clock tower have only just drifted past the hour of noon on the thirty-first of December, and already the day has begun to grow dark. Christine performs some cursory work, revising from a lecture on the structure of bones, and after an equally cursory meal – some old beef, cutting off those parts which are going green at the edges – Frances and Christine dress for the party. Frances is borrowing Christine's medical coat and leather bag. She adds a stethoscope, hanging it heavily around her neck.

'Very professional, my dear Doctor Jekyll,' says Christine, with a wink. She – as Hyde, in a shabby blouse and long skirt they slashed with a knife – back-combs her hair, deposits some twigs in it, and paints shapes around her eyes. They grin at each other, pleased with the effect. Before they leave, they look again at Eve's mask, slightly adjust the angle. Eve wears a black dress trimmed with lace and subtle beads of jet (the dress is usually reserved for mourning); her Venetian mask is painted green and yellow, shot through with dramatic intersecting lines.

And so, arms linked, with Eve in the middle, the three leave their lodgings and make their way on foot through the freezing streets of Soho, occasionally stopping to stamp their feet to warm them. Once Frances does this in the wrong spot, upending a loose piece of pavement; Christine laughs at the muddy splashes it leaves over her skirts, as well as soaking Frances' shoes. By some luck of angle, or quirk of timing, Eve remains untouched by any smudges of dirt and mud, and she does not seem bothered by the cold in spite of her bared shoulders. Eventually, the three join the crowds greeting each other – a mix of formal coats and flamboyant masks and headdresses. They are all heading towards the most notorious dancehall in the city, drawn by its famous absinthe glow.

The great blades of the windmill, as they sweep around and around, add a sense of urgency, of inevitability, to the crowds passing along the sludgy street. They enter the mill with the sense they may simply be chewed up and spat out again; it seems appropriate to Frances that this is a place where a whole century will pass by in seconds. The blades themselves are picked out in glass globes that send an eerie light across the street. The Viridian Windmill has a reputation that towers over Soho. Mrs Stella would host a New Year's gathering nowhere else.

The three stop a moment outside the main doors, a steady stream of people passing inside. Frances and Christine exchange excited looks, then turn to Eve. She raises a hand to adjust her mask, leaning back a little, intimidated by the great sweeping blades. Frances squeezes her arm.

'You'll be all right,' she says. And they go in.

Inside is a glittering cavalcade of large mirrors, sparkling crystal and polished wood. The spicy, earthy colours of the walls and furniture shine elegantly in carefully arranged light. Great chandeliers pour from the ceiling, elegant waterfalls of diamond, picking out the dancers and glinting off the champagne bottles. Round tables decorated with potted ferns cluster at the edges of the great hall and surround the dancehall's centrepiece – and the true key to the its success – a large, open, *public* dance floor. A glistening platform of polished oak, it is already filled with people. Above it are the upper galleries, where it is possible to sit and drink and watch the dancing from a happy multiplicity of angles. People fan themselves, jostle for best position, lean over the rails to stare.

There is a stage at one end shrouded in a velvet curtain, olive edged with gold; but the centre of attention is only rarely to be found there. The public dance floor, and the people upon it, are what's really on display.

Frances immediately loses sense of herself among the crowds, as their route to the dance floor must navigate tables, sprawling chairs and secret alcoves, all of which seem full to bursting already. They pass groups of cheering drinkers, their tables filled with wine bottles and liquor glasses, their hairpieces lopsided with great feathers that dance through the air. Gleaming beads line the puffed sleeves of ballgowns; the tasteful light from the chandeliers wink bronze upon costumes of velvet, silk and fur the air is filled with roaring cheers, the clink of glasses, the clatter of dice.

'There!' cries Christine, pointing. A recognisable flash from the centre of the dance floor. The three navigate their way towards Mrs Stella.

Mrs Stella's costume comprises strips of golden silk, dripping with and pearls. In one hand, instead of a corsage, she carries a disembodied head crudely stuffed with feathers. Several strands of red ribbon trail from its spongy neck. Its eyes are painted white, as if the pupils have rolled up out of sight. It swings absurdly as Mrs Stella raises her hands in greeting.

'Let me introduce you to Salome!' she cries. 'I would dance for you, my dears, but I shan't be held responsible for the consequences.'

She adopts a pose from her performance in the role, a half dance with delicate arms and lurid suggestions of falling cloth. Just as suddenly, she drops her arms. 'I'm so glad you could come. And to you,' she adds, curtseying to Eve.

Eve says nothing. She remains standing, still and silent. She is holding herself tight, almost shivering, as if she were caught in a cold breeze. Frances supposes she is overwhelmed with the bustle of the event; imagines it will pass.

'What a party!' Frances says to Mrs Stella, to get the conversation going again.

'Oh yes! And I must speak to you about the entertainment, later – the *tableau vivant*. I haven't forgotten. Oh! Hello!'

A black cloak swoops into the throng, held by a crooked arm over the wearer's face.

Mrs Stella shrieks with delight. 'What have we here?' he says.

The arm is lowered to reveal the painted face of Oliver Allbright.

'Count Dracula, at your service,' he says. It is unusual to see Oliver in black. His suit is as sharp as a knife, its high collar wrapped with a blood-red cravat and fastened with a crystal pin. He spreads his arms dramatically, to reveal the inner linings of his cloak. The puckered silk recalls the inside of a coffin.

Eve is trembling beneath the soft touch of Frances' arm.

'You look *divine*, Oliver. And have you brought the young man you've been telling me about?' All mention of the tableau has stopped – Mrs Stella's eyes flash a brief a warning to Frances and Christine. It is clearly to remain a secret until the moment of unveiling. Mrs Stella places her hand affectionately on Oliver's shoulder. 'I had hoped to meet that fine gentleman tonight – a poet, wasn't he?'

'Oh, *him*,' says Oliver. 'He shan't be coming.'

Mrs Stella's face collapses. 'What happened?'

Christine leans forwards, craning her neck to hear the gossip. Frances checks Eve, who is still quiet.

'I had no choice but to end it,' says Oliver. 'I discovered a fatal incompatibility of opinion.'

'Which was?' A smile plays around Mrs Stella's mouth, matching Oliver's expression. They have both coloured their lips with smudged red paint; their smiles do not resemble the sharing of a friendly in-joke so much as the bloody ecstasy of Dionysian revellers.

Oliver performs an exaggerated sigh.

'I am an atheist,' he says. 'And tragically, so was he. I couldn't possibly agree with a lover on something so important.'

Christine and Mrs Stella throw their heads back and laugh; Eve does not move. Frances feels caught between them.

'Outrageous! Mr Allbright, you are a *one*,' says Mrs Stella, wiping her eyes.

Oliver nods. 'But I have met a wonderful *new* person,' he says, 'who may be along later. She is quite lovely; studying fine art. I hope to bring her to your next dinner, in fact.'

'That would be wonderful,' says Mrs Stella, and Oliver bows and departs with a swirl of cape. She turns back to the others.

'So sorry about that interruption – now, where were we? Oh! Whatever's wrong, Frances?'

On finding Christine's gaze upon her, and Eve's too, Frances suddenly realises she is frowning, and that her jaw is clenched. She tries to release the pressure; she can feel her teeth grinding with the effort. 'If I may speak honestly, I feel Allbright was disrespectful of Eve just now, he didn't acknowledge her once.'

'Well of course; he won't address a young woman in a mask he hasn't been introduced to. You should have made the effort yourself.'

Frances is unconvinced, but a thought occurs: if Oliver had lavished Eve with attentions, she wouldn't have much liked that either.

But there is no time to think on it further, for they are assailed once again by a pair of party guests, clinging to each other as if for dear life, with the aniseed stickiness of absinthe already upon them.

'You two look the perfect picture,' says Mrs Stella. Her role as hostess is her favourite to play; she is practically glowing. Frances smiles in recognition, but Christine frowns.

'Who are you supposed to be?' she says to Jaques.

'Who do you imagine?' he replies. Beneath a tweed cape he wears a smoking jacket, grey trousers and a pair of slippers. On top of his head is a tweed deerstalker, pulled down to a rakish angle. He holds up a bulbous magnifying glass on a long brass handle, and peers at the others through it.

'I'm Sherlock Holmes, the world's greatest detective,' he says, and through the glass one enormous eye closes and opens in a grotesquely lopsided wink.

'And I'm Irene Adler,' says Edwin, tossing his feathered scarf anew around his neck. He wears a costume borrowed from a member of the corps of swans at the ballet school. He grabs Jacques-Louis' arm and kicks up a leg as if trying to climb up to steal the deerstalker hat. 'I'm outsmarting him at every turn.'

Together they merge back into the dance floor.

Mrs Stella claps her hands, visibly overjoyed. 'The libraries must be empty, for all its devils are here!' she cries. Frances and Christine look at each other, and then, together, at Eve. Eve is, by now, visibly shaking.

Christine makes a decision. Frances is grateful for it. 'We're going to sit for a moment,' she tells Mrs Stella. Their host nods, and spins around to greet another dear friend she has just that moment spotted, while Frances and Christine cling tightly to Eve and lead her away from the dance floor, in a futile search for a less crowded corner. (Mrs Stella's voice comes after them: 'Darling! Such a delicate lace dress: who might you be –? Ah, of course you're Edna Pontellier! Mind you steer clear of the water feature…')

They make their way along the walls of the great hall, and eventually push through a door to emerge into the landscaped pleasure gardens. The air is cold and sharp out here, but the music is quieter – muffled by the ornate doors – and they manage to find an empty table. The trees send long shadows over the grass.

'What's the matter?' says Frances.

'I'm not comfortable here,' says Eve.

Christine jolts back in her chair, and Frances realises she is hearing Eve's voice for the first time. Christine's eyebrows knit together. Analysing.

An attempted diagnosis: 'It's too cold for you?'

'She means *here*,' hisses Frances. 'The whole place. She doesn't want to be the entertainment at this godforsaken party. And I don't want her to either.'

Christine relaxes, as if that is nothing that cannot be dealt with. Frances feels a quirk of irritation in her stomach. 'Well – tough!' says Christine. 'It's all been arranged. Half the people here have come especially to see her.'

A passing group of revellers, some in white robes and wigs and delicate pearl-coloured masks, and others in angular make-up with strips of mottled fur bulging through their waistcoats a group costume, a tribe of Morlocks and Eloi – squeeze by their table, reaching out and waving at everyone, twirling and laughing. One offers Christine a cigar as they pass, and she takes it, drawing in deeply and blowing the smoke out into the air.

Eve puts a hand beneath her mask to wipe her eyes.

'I can't believe you're ganging up on me like this,' says Christine.

Frances holds Eve's other hand beneath the table. It is difficult to know whose fingers are colder.

The Viridian Windmill is growing more raucous. Mrs Stella darts to and fro, trying to be in every corner of the party at once: she vaguely snatches at Frances' arm, reiterates that she wants the performance by Eve to commence soon – but then she is gone again, to pour more champagne; to show people around the pleasure gardens; to sign autographs; to admire the flowers; to dance with everybody in the room. The hours pass.

Christine and Frances stand in the middle of the drunken bustling crowd on the dance floor, jostled by bodies, shouting at the top of their lungs.

'You said she would be safe here!' cries Frances.

'She's not supposed to go wandering off!' says Christine. 'And if she takes it upon herself to do so that's her look-out, not mine.'

Frances bites her lip, looks around the dance floor at the blur of stockings, raised skirts and half-masks, distorted faces. She feels herself coming apart, separating into lots of little pieces. 'She's strong enough.'

'Excuse me?' Christine leans back as a pair of madly waltzing revellers in animal masks spin about them, knocking their wine over her tatty Hyde blouse. 'In fact; never mind. I don't need to know. I've got to tell you something,' she says. 'About next year.'

Frances' gaze snaps back to Christine. 'What is it?'

'Things have become different,' says Christine. 'Since Eve, I mean. Things are changing between us and it's too much for me.'

Frances' mouth moves. Nothing comes out.

Christine scrapes her hand through her back-combed hair, releasing twigs and dead leaves that drift down to the floor.

'I've been offered a new scholarship,' she says. 'The train leaves in the morning. From thence, a ferry, and maybe even a balloon. I'll be gone. You and... *her* can hide away together. Do whatever you want.' She turns on her heel, and heads towards a group of people who appear to be attempting a human pyramid, reaching them just as it topples.

Frances thinks about going after her, but Christine has already disappeared into the throng. Frances spins about, trying to discover the quickest exit, or catch a glimpse of Eve's graceful walk. But she recognises nothing. The world has turned into a smudge of dim colour, and she can feel her spirit leaking out to join it; she is unsure where her panicked grief starts and stops. With a deep, difficult breath she lets Christine go: but she must continue to look for Eve.

A few seconds until midnight.

Frances cries out with a noise that sounds like a high-pitched whine, and, her heart thumping against the bone cave of her chest, she races through The Viridian Windmill and out into the street, the vision blurring through her salt tears.

'No!' she cries. The retreating figure of Eve does not turn, does not answer. Cold stars look down over the city.

And the bell tolls: and one drunken actor in a green suit raises his glass to begin cheering for the New Year; and two dancers cling together on the balcony, oblivious to the chaos down below as their legs wind together; and three, three empty absinthe glasses roll from the table as Allbright's head lands unconscious in his hands, spilling drops of green liquid over shattered fragments of glass; and four horses, pulling carriages, rear up on their hind legs to avoid the woman in the road, her gaze blank as if unseeing, as she walks through the streets and away; and five is the number of people Mrs Stella is trying to dance with at the same time when the clock strikes, her hair flying as she twirls her veils around her body, her own head thrown back in the reverie of the dance, the head of feathers long lost in the corner of the dancehall and forgotten; and six musicians continue to play brightly upon the dancehall stage, sending rhythms across the bouncing, crowded dance floor; and seven pipes of opium send out billows of smoke into the air above the pleasure gardens; and eight layers of fabric create an effective dancehall skirt, thrown up into the air and tossed about as dancers high-kick on, knocking champagne glasses out of the hands of the patrons, to roars of joy and the thundering of applause; and nine cries of 'get out of the way!' and 'watch it now!' follow Frances as she sprints away from The Viridian Windmill, her breath coming as clouds of steam that rise into the indifferent air, shaded green by the great sweeping blades; and ten gas lamps stand along the street, hissing and spitting, sending pools of pallor across the snow, melting to sludge, as Frances runs along the street, losing a shoe in a cold puddle and tripping, tearing the skin over her arms as she falls; and eleven streets away by now, moving fast as a spider, goes Eve, heading out of the city, and beyond, to a coastal town, to steal passage out of the country on a rusty vessel churning smoke behind it; and, as the final toll of the bell fades into silence, her hearing is filled with a dull roar, which she recognises as the onrush of despair: and she lies in the gutter, helpless and trembling, looking up at the stars, but between her tears and the fireworks bursting over the city it is impossible to see them.

Miss Scarlett

There's been another murder, *yet another murder*, and your presence is required, again, and you know full well where you're going, no need to RSVP to the glittering black-edged invitation, you'll be there: Miss Scarlett sighs and drops her cigarette to the ground, crushes the ash under the heel of her satin shoe and looks about for the nearest exit. As usual, there isn't one.

As for the victim, there's only a chalk outline on the ground. A heavily marked absence and an instruction: solve this. The suspects will also be required to act as detective, witness, cross-examiner, judge, jury, courtroom stenographer… and they can trust no one, not even themselves. Place of death: huge crumbling great sprawling ancient manor house on a stormy darkened night. That much, at least, everyone can agree on.

Miss Scarlett is the first to arrive. She lets herself in: she no longer bothers with the ritual of banging on the door and waiting a great stretch of rain-sodden time for nobody to come and open it. The great brass doorknocker has long since rusted into place anyway. So, Miss Scarlett opens the heavy door herself and steps inside, high heels tapping on the neatly tiled floor.

She calls out a greeting, simply for the pleasure of hearing her voice travel down the empty hallway. The door slams behind her, and that echoes too. For a moment she stands there, breathing the familiar smell of must, rotting wood, mystery.

Miss Scarlett: a woman of secrets. A woman *for* secrets. Highly visible and at the same time utterly unknowable. Can you look at her directly? In the darkened manor house hallway she blazes like a flame, a chilli pepper in red-hot satin and lipstick to match. In a red dress, always a red dress, she simply won't be imagined any other way: whether in something revealing or, alluringly, not *yet* revealing, Miss Scarlett is a wearer only of the bespokest of pieces. Off the shoulder but never off the peg: no, Miss Scarlett favours high fashion, skyscraper-high, designed and created and sewn up especially. Honestly, it's the only way to get dresses that fit like that. On hearing news of the murder, it's easy to imagine Miss Scarlett looking languidly over her wardrobe before doing anything else, running a hand across all those fabrics, all that red, ignoring the more dazzling items spangled with sequins or edged with fringe to eventually choose the number she's in now, in which it's easier to visit a film premiere than explore a crumbling old mansion house in the dark. Miss Scarlett, holding her favourite red dress up against herself and looking into the mirror, examining her divine vision reflected in the antique glass. She sighs as if asking herself: *has it come to this?* (And does she mean murder? Well, she might. There's no relying on Miss Scarlett, suspect number one.)

There are others, though, and Miss Scarlett knows they're coming. Soon there will be six in the house, and one of them did this: that much they know. Distrust will permeate the house like fog, only to be lifted when there is some degree of certainty. And so Miss Scarlett and the others creep through the otherwise empty building, seeking to learn the secrets of the crime that drew them here, looking to recreate the chain of events that ended with the chalk outline of the body there midway up the stairs; which, like some ghastly hidden treasure, is marked with an X.

There's nothing Miss Scarlett can know for sure, although, that's just a theory. As is the question of her relationship to the deceased. One can only imagine adoration coming her way, but that's based on our own response to the sight of her in the red dress. Infatuation we may take as a given, then, but remember: that needn't lead to anything further, dangerous or otherwise. Or perhaps infatuation is being too flippant. None of this is incompatible with her being suspect number one, of course. Look at her, in that lipstick: no doubt she could love and kill the same person on the same night. If anyone could…

She enters the library, in an already quiet house, the hush insulated by all the mouldering books stacked two or three volumes deep along the shelves. It's one of the warmer rooms, too: Reverend Green has got the fire going, and the light flickering away from the fireplace reflects golden shapes over the gilt spines of the books. There is an antique revolver on top of the drinks cabinet. Miss Scarlett knows a thing or two about firearms and moves towards it for a closer look.

There's a sound behind her, something like paper rustling. A leather-bound book falls from the shelf, lands with a dull thunk on the floor.

'I didn't touch it,' says the Reverend, a soft-spoken man it's difficult to imagine telling lies. He's backing away from the fallen book, pointing: 'Look at the dust: those books haven't been moved for years. It must be the wind getting in from an open window.'

Miss Scarlett goes to investigate, but before she can reach for the book, there is another soft sound behind her. She turns; the Reverend is gone.

This is not a house you can relax in.

Even if there wasn't a chalk outline on the floor to remind everyone of the deadly truth among them, the house is too big, too grand to be comfy. It's never been welcoming, even in its heyday of flung-open doors, hearty greetings, a string quartet playing in the corner as guests mill about: even in those days this house was intimidating, cold. It's exceedingly draughty due to the huge spaces between each room, made of long empty stretches of hallway. The lamps are low, so shadows are always thick, and every footstep echoes, and there is hardly any brandy left. The conservatory has not been tended for many years, and most of the glass panels are broken so a lot of the outside gets in these days. Ivy strains its fingers into this old hothouse and rain often batters the few remaining tropical plants. Sometimes, someone declares they are going to the conservatory for fresh air, but they never stay long. An abandoned hosepipe is tied in a way that hints, shudderingly, at something sinister; is that rust or worse on the secateurs? The conservatory might be the true memento mori in this place, never mind the chalk outline of a body out in the stairway.

Miss Scarlett has someone in a headlock. They gasp for breath as she tugs them across the room, their feet scrabbling uselessly to get purchase, the Persian rug bunching up under them, aiding Miss Scarlett's efforts to get her opponent into the corner to immobilise them, somehow, quickly, any way she can. Her breath comes heavily with the strain of a sudden vicious ambush. Adrenalin makes her vision shake and everything slows down: she times the seconds through the pumping of her own heart, the sound resonating in her ears. There's blood in her mouth and a new cut across her cheek.

The job done, Miss Scarlett dusts her hands and locks the door behind her when she leaves.

Just outside the dining room, Miss Scarlett hears a conversation:
   'Found anything?'

'Only this.'

There's a metallic rattle, followed by the thump of something heavy. Miss Scarlett, hardly daring to breathe, inches closer to the open door.

Their voices are urgent, the words come quickly. 'Well, what do you make of it?'

'On the whole, as a piece of evidence, I think it's convincing.'

'How so?'

'Easier, more straightforward: these things are all over the house, you'd just have to pick one up. Much less messy.'

'Having your skull bashed in is *less* messy, in your opinion?'

'You know what I mean. Less messy to organise beforehand: just grabbing the candlestick and the job's done, right there on the spot.' There's another heavy sound, as if it's being demonstrated against some old furniture. 'I say, if it's the candlestick, we're talking something emotional. Nothing premeditated. Crime of passion, if you like.'

The response to this is full of sneering scepticism. '*That's* your theory?'

'Well, I...' There is a clatter, as if a candlestick has been dropped to the floor.

'Enough of this nonsense. I'm getting out of here.' Footsteps approach the door and Miss Scarlett quickly ducks behind an old tapestry. As the figure stalks by she hears their further contemptuous muttering. '*Crime of passion* my arse.'

Miss Scarlett understands the frustration. Someone always ends up getting bogged down in the question of motive. They attempt to learn things that would shine light onto the history between victim, suspects and killer, things that might begin to unlock what may have led to the murder. But Miss Scarlett knows there's no use thinking that way. It's far too late for *why*.

Miss Scarlett has known these people for years, that's the tragedy of all this. In other circumstances, they would have come to know each other more intimately by now. But hoping to reach any level of understanding is folly. *Why* is an unknowable black hole around which the suspects all spin, pulled along by its gravity, unable to reach a centre. They can never know each other that way. Miss Scarlett accepts there's no use getting sentimental about all this: in fact, there isn't time to, and it would be dangerous to try. She cannot risk the vulnerability it would require. And so, she finds herself, like the others, surrounded only and always by potential enemies. The six of them dance around each other, forever bristling with distrust and double-bluffs, lying to each other and lying about lying, they are a company wracked with paranoia and suspicion and doubt.

For this reason, Miss Scarlett has taken to wearing a Glock at her upper thigh.

Colonel Mustard! Now there's a chap, a true man-about-the-place and no mistake and definitely one to keep an eye on; you mustn't ever trust anyone who wears a pith helmet indoors. Or outdoors, for that matter: wearing a pith helmet at all might safely be considered a warning. We can at least hope that, when the body was discovered, he temporarily removed the pith helmet as a sign of respect, but there's no way to be sure. (Assuming he was there, which we can't yet.) Even when he doesn't wear the pith helmet the faded yellow of his clothing implies one. Here's a man with a past, with experiences, more inflicted than endured. This is a man who has pulled off some shady business, who has cast some insidious orders. No doubt there are many noble statues of him to be found in his hometown, and/or any towns he has made himself at home in through the years; equally we may be sure those statues are regularly defaced with graffiti and a series of strategically placed traffic cones. Upright, ever upright, military bearing, stunning moustache. What a hero.

Miss Scarlett avoids him when she can. Here he comes, there's no mistaking the regularity of his footsteps.

He stops, standing to attention as he always does. 'Looking about here, are we?'

'Who's *we*? You can help me look, if you like.' Miss Scarlett rises from examining footprints in the dust and leans against the doorframe. She winks at him.

He bristles at that. She does have the power to wrong-foot him, sometimes. They all do: the colonel underestimates everyone, so it's a hobby they all share, wrong-footing him. Except for Reverend Green, who's far too nervous for that sort of thing.

The Colonel taps his foot, looks from his own foot to the markings in the dust. 'I've got my eye on you,' he says, sounding unsure. 'Just you remember that.'

Miss Scarlett could do all this in her sleep. She replies, 'I will. And I bet you do.'

You'd think, from the job description, anyone going by the moniker "Professor Plum" would be an old, jolly sort, exceedingly well-read from decades of thinking, debating, taking ideas out for a walk (while remaining sitting down, of course, no dedication to exercise in this one), not to mention possessing smiling cheeks exceedingly well-red from happiness and beer. A bushy beard and a home-knitted jumper in warm, welcoming purple, stretched over a huggable stomach. You may think all this but Professor Plum clawed through the education system like a young wolf, and now looks at you with hungry eyes from the peak of the scholarly clifftop. You can barely imagine him without a prestigious position: it must have been no more than a week before he landed the plum job (ahem) at a top university. Yes, he's working on his next book; and yes, the grants came through, and oh, in the meantime, he has a few comments on *your* latest efforts…? Long in the tooth, he is, to take sharp bites with. There is a damson tint to his polo-neck jumper but the royal tone does not imply happiness or warmth, and certainly nothing like mercy. No, this professor's purple puts you more in mind of a Roman emperor, swathed in the colour no commoner may wear on pain of death, and like a bloodthirsty voyeur at the gladiator games he casts a casual eye over your bibliography, laughs at the sight, and loosely throws out an arm to give the whole thing thumbs-down.

So much for the professor. But murder?

It seems unlikely he would need to employ a messy and attention-grabbing technique like *murder* to get anyone out of his way. Surely he has access to cleaner, smoother methods to destroy someone: ways that are quieter, more devastating, tactfully eloquent, perhaps involving passages in Latin. Far easier to imagine someone setting out to get rid of *him*, and the poor victim outlined on the mansion cobbles is only an accidental crossfire-catch, a third party striding innocently into the wrong place at the wrong time just at the moment one of his long-suffering colleagues *finally* gets their own back. Still, you never know, maybe the messy and attention-grabbing technique of murder was the best way for him to achieve his very precise and particular research aims this time around. Best keep an eye on him.

As is often the case, Colonel Mustard and Miss Scarlett are, quite by accident, in the ballroom together. The varnish on the dance floor has faded to dullness, while the chandelier has long since been taken down and now sits bulbously in the corner, half packed into a bag. The crystal drops that are still visible swing slightly in the draught of the house. Sometimes music plays and when it does they usually dance, taking turns to lead.

'Do you ever imagine this place filled with people, all happily dancing?' Miss Scarlett asks. (It's something she imagines often.)

He shakes his head. 'I don't much care for social gatherings.'

Miss Scarlett laughs, resists the temptation to bury her face into his shoulder. 'I'm not saying you'd be *invited*. But can you imagine it going on?'

His face falls into a sadder shape. 'To be honest with you, I can't.'

'I know what you mean. I can't imagine life happening here.'

'Everything's so wretched; the sadness is worn in.'

'Careful, you're getting romantic.'

They reach the corner of the ballroom, perform a perfectly executed turn. These moments are the closest thing to a truce between the two of them. They've had all arguments possible. *Let's agree to disagree*, says the Colonel, and Miss Scarlett allows it, because after all, he's the only passable dance partner in the place.

Miss Scarlett sighs, feels the press of the pistol beneath the satin fabric of her dress. 'I suppose *our* lives are happening here.'

Thinking about it, it's never going to be Mrs White, is it? She's safe and dependable. Her name isn't even a colour; it's the soothing calmness of a fresh tablecloth, the richness of whole milk, the thick sweetness of royal icing. Mrs White whipping past you in her starched apron to get to the stove before something boils over. The metallic clattering of pans, the soft sprinkling of sugar, the breaking of eggs, her presence brings all these sounds with her and a sense of calm with it: a reassurance that the most important things in life are being taken care of, somewhere. Fine dust of flour on her cheeks and hands, even though she isn't actually baking anything; she's no murderer. When it's Mrs White, it's a fluke.

Miss Scarlett knows this, and that's why she and Mrs White, out of all of them, have the strongest enmity. Absolutely hate each other, these two. You'd think Miss Scarlett would reserve her strongest anger and resentment for Mrs Peacock, that louche widow dripping with sapphires – a vision, we might suppose, of what Miss Scarlett will become in a few decades' time, so a mutual hatred would arise from the vanity of small differences. But no, Miss Scarlett's biggest rage is reserved for that fucking baker!

In one way this is easy to understand, for they embody pure opposites: one is the bringer of the feast, chief creamer off the top of the harvest, while the other would have you believe she never eats. One was made to host and manage night after night of joyful communal gathering. The other remains fiercely individual, destined for a life of clandestine meetings in darkened alleyways even outside this particular murder case, a life riding roughshod over any concern of dinner schedules, a life swapping betrayals for secrets, a life spent trading deadly knowledge for deadlier certainties. But in another way, the rivalry between them is a great shame. They have more in common than they'd like to admit and naturally they both wish, secretly, that they could be each other, if only for a little while.

'Quick game, while we're here?'

The billiard room is the most fun room in the house. Although admittedly this is not a house that prioritises fun, this room is where you at least have a chance. It feels somehow doubly antiquated: an entire space dedicated to games feels luxurious enough these days, and this game in particular is evocative of things our own age has left behind. Kitchen, dining room: fair enough. We have those too, even if they're smaller or combined. Even the notion of a ballroom survives in part (we've all danced about indoors), and if you don't have space for a conservatory you might manage a few plant pots. But an entire room – for *billiards*? We can only dream. Thus, we gravitate to that room, and wonder at the sheer novelty of it.

Naturally Miss Scarlett often lingers in here. It's not uncommon for a game to be played while the case ticks over through the rest of the house, not to mention the fact that the soft baize covering of the table has seen other kinds of action: energies grow intense in the presence of death, and during a mystery investigation there are stretches of time when there is nothing to do. It cannot be a surprise that the felt has been rubbed raw. But, you know what they say. What happens in the billiard room…

Miss Scarlett runs a finger along the table. 'I don't want to play,' she says, noticing the blue chalk dust newly over her fingers. 'Thanks for asking.'

'None of us do,' says Mrs Peacock, her tone betraying a state of utter exhaustion. 'Why don't you tell me what you were whispering to the Reverend just now?'

'Oh, don't try it.' Miss Scarlett rolls her eyes. 'I would have nothing to say to him.'

Mrs Peacock narrows her eyes, presenting an expression of absolute distrust. It gives Miss Scarlett an opportunity to examine her refined acquaintance more closely. Mrs Peacock is ever distinguished, even when she's clearly bone-tired… blue eyeshadow! Miss Scarlett looks down at her fingers. Same shade. Maybe *that's* why Mrs Peacock is out of breath. The Colonel was leaving this room earlier, and didn't he have a bit of a spring in his step? Mrs White, too, left here looking rather jolly. But then Mrs White always looks jolly. So maybe it's nothing sordid, and Mrs Peacock is simply tired the same way they are all tired, and has taken to retouching her make-up with the cue chalk.

The secret passages beckon with dark charisma. They're perfectly positioned in each corner of the house. They imply a journey of great length but there's also, it would seem, hardly any travel involved. Reappearance at the other end of the house is instantaneous. This structural secrecy is part of the appeal: for most, there's an ongoing question of what traversing these passages actually entails.

Miss Scarlett knows. She travels through here often, picking a careful way across the treacherous terrain, treading over the gaps in the floor, the uneven wood, the slippery patches of mould. Her eyes slowly adjust to the darkness, and eventually she can pick out the brass pipes here and there (duck to get under them), a few splinters of old furniture (turn and contort to get past them), the air thick with dust and silence, everything cobweb-shrouded and untouched for years. Once, to Miss Scarlett's utmost surprise, Mrs White's old catering trolley. So *that's* how she serves up so promptly.

A shadow moves before her, at the far end of the passage. Miss Scarlett whips the gun from her thigh and holds it out. 'Who's there?'

The shadow moves, slowly and gradually: both arms being raised. 'Only a friend.'

She wants to laugh. 'That tells me nothing. You can't be a friend of *mine*, so are you a friend of the *killer's?*'

'I could be both. Not to mention that you could be the killer.'

Miss Scarlett says nothing to that. She continues to aim the gun.

A gentle sound, like a sigh. 'If you fire that down here you'll blast through something structural.' They sound weary.

'If it makes you answer me. What are you doing down here?'

'Oh, making my way about. Searching.'

'What for?'

'I don't know yet.'

There's a particular quality to their voice: it takes Miss Scarlett a moment to place it and when she does, surprise makes her tremble, and her aim wavers. She remembers the headlock, and the painful fight as they battled over the Persian rug. 'How did you get out of there?'

The figure gestures broadly to the secret passage that surrounds them both. Then they take a step: Miss Scarlett's finger tightens on the trigger, but too late.

'Damn it,' she says. Subtle changes in the acoustics confirm she is now alone.

Miss Scarlett leans against the wall. From above comes a high whistle, which within moments, even down through the stone, grows in volume to a piercing shriek. It's the sound of Plum bringing the old kettle back to life to make himself a coffee, so she must be below the kitchen.

Pity Miss Scarlett. It's hard work, being the alluring figure of danger in the red dress all the time. Come towards me, back off, come closer, stay away – it's difficult to constantly put out such contradictory messages. She'd let the act drop if she could, but she's forgotten how, and she doesn't know who she'd be if she did. Not to mention the fact she might be a killer: in this much, she can still surprise herself.

It's true for all of them, trapped in a house of nightmares, voyaging into the darkness that pervades these ancient rooms, groping towards an answer – *any* answer. Miss Scarlett knows she'll never be the one holding all the cards, of course, but it runs deeper than that; she knows they'll never solve the true mystery that runs through this place, the fact of death itself, and that's the real pull: what really draws them here, regardless of the chalk outline and who's responsible for it this time, *who* did it and *where* and *how?* The best they can do is to leap once more into the impossible and try again, straining towards the promise of an answer but knowing, deep down, that any answer would be insufficient, Miss Scarlett's red dress screaming danger to herself as much as to anyone else – but all this is yet to happen. Miss Scarlett sighs, and goes back to polishing her gun. With a shiver, she knows it's time to play again. She receives a black-edged invitation.

A Game Proposition

Well, now.

There's a hostelry in Port Royal, or there was; little to no point in going there these days, unless you've a fondness for charred things. Were you to go there yourself you'd see some old posts and a plaque but once, oh once, once there were people and games and frolics and what fun we had – until there wasn't any more fun to be had, if you understand me, you pretty thing.

The little cherubs you see pouting away in the corners of the map, they were free to fly and they are still, if they want to; our wings, though, they were clipped one night, clipped good and proper. I'm to tell you how it came to pass.

Can you picture a tavern? A bustling one. A hubbub of excesses, picture it for me now. With barrels and spillages and pistols cocked on whims and a violently low tolerance for lack of payment, whatever you're buying. Do you have it? No, no you can't quite picture it, not correctly, not yet. Mucky it about a bit. Add more dirt. This wasn't a high-end place, and it would never pretend to be one. And for Port Royal at this time, 'twas a piece of pride to be able to boast so. Vicars used to run away from Port Royal, hankies over their mouths. Fair enough. But this place? Some of the saltiest knave dogs that ever sailed the South Seas avoided this place.

And this place was where we would attend. Me and my girls, my fellow ladies; and whatever picture of us you've got, you might as well mucky that up a fair bit too. We didn't stand on ceremony. We didn't stand at all, hardly. Well, we would if that's what was wanted. Nan in particular was a great one for doing it standing, or leaning up against walls. No-Conscience Nan would lean up against anything you wanted. Gravestones. Peg preferred to lie, but she'd sit at a push, or a pull. Jenny was 18 for kneeling. And I – what was it that charming lad said of me – *'as common as a barber's chair: no sooner was one out, but another was in.'*

His ship sank on the way home.

Look, there were worse ways to earn five hundred pieces of eight, in those days. And we weren't even in it for those pieces. We were in it for what I'm to tell you about. We were in it for the fun that follows.

So picture it, this tavern in a part of Port Royal, just afore the turn of the seventeenth into eighteenth. And picture us four, the four of us. Strumpets wenches harlots all four. Having a veritable holiday.

I rolled the dice and turned over a card. 'Full flush,' I said, and Nan got a blush in her cheeks to match. And not much made old No-Conscience blush, so I knew I'd made a fair move.

'Aye,' said she, 'you've won that for a daring go, have you or have you not,' and with reluctant fingers she pushed her counter back over the Caribbean swells. She'd wanted to go further.

'Two points forfeit,' said Peg, 'and I'll be having an easterly trade-wind as yet, come cyclone, come as not.'

More picturing for you to do. A board, as with your trictrac or your backgammon. Overlay 'pon it a map of the world – all of it, the whole world, the most comprehensive cartography yet, says I – then overlay that with a grid, and counters, and wooden posts, and pegs, and cards, and dice. Do you see it? You haven't got it quite right, my friend, but hold on to what you do have. You shan't get closer. This was our game. I say was, because we don't play it any more.

'Three cards to you, Salt-Beef, and I'll be finishing a new round at whatever latitude!' Nan rolled the dice and cackled at the result. 'A-ha! I'll place my prime counter facing westwards, methinks. More than a breeze rippling along that clime, then.'

Now don't get ahead of yourselves; I can see you thinking, you might be wondering if No-Conscience Nan was calling herself Nan for N for North, yes? True she liked to sit in the north-facing chair but we'd ne'er be so predictable. Although there were four of us, we couldn't be divided as easily as all that.

'Indeed, Nan,' said Salt-Beef, 'You're playing without mercy over that coast, no mistake of mine.' She moved her own counter. 'In fact, I'll take three score off the degree of tempest at that latitude, if you'll barter me for half a counter on the next turn-up of cards.'

Nan grunted. 'I'll consider it over a little,' she said, as Jenny prepared to take her turn.

You'll know very well by now that there were four of us. We were well known in this tavern – although not for what we really were, of course. Only for what we seemed to be. Corsets and rouge and tankards of gunpowder rum – you can picture it sweet, it's all right, t'aint forbidden today – and my point is that in this drinking place they all knew us by name. We hadn't started out with our nicknames. We were once Nan, Peg, Jenny and me. Now we were known as something much more salty around the mouth.

No-Conscience Nan, they called her. And Salt-Beef Peg, who was there too, this night as every night. As for the third of us, she had earned her nickname proud: but you'd be a fool to ask Buttock-de-Clink Jenny anything if you weren't prepared to pay well for the answer.

And then there was myself. And those were the names the folks of Port Royal called us. A joy for it. Four of us, as I say. Enough to play 'pon the whole world until this particular evening, darling.

'Three cards,' said Jenny. 'And I'll wager rapids along the Thames.'

'Upstream?'

'Of course.'

'Then – snap!' said Peg.

'Damn you through the blasted hemisphere,' said Nan, who had to miss a go now.

Once a month we would meet, and you ought to know that we would meet when the Moon was full, so that she was at her strongest and able to take over the business of the tides for us. And we would retire to the back room of the place, this tavern, the one we called ours, and there would be no business today no matter who asked for us; and we got asked for by name oftentimes enough. On game night there would only be this. The board, the counters, the dice.

'I think old Salt-Beef's bluffing,' said Jenny. 'I'd move your counter up the next Tropic, Nan.'

'I'd agree,' said Nan, 'apart from the way you're moving your own along the Great Dead. You can't fool me for a fool, and I'll take two of your precious Navy shipwrecks for that.'

High stakes, did we play for? None higher.

And now I'm to tell you, though I can't think you deserve it, but as I said before, I've got clipped wings now, and I'm to tell you about the last game we truly played.

Jenny was counting her cards. 'I'm afore the equatorial, I believe, my sweets,' she said, reaching to take up the dice. 'And if I can square it with a circular, I'll take two wrecks off the Madagascar coast.'

'You bloody won't!' said Peg. 'I'm to pass a current up along there and sink a frigate and if you go denying me that I'll pull your hair out.'

'Listen here, you trollop,' said Jenny, preparing to roll. 'You counted already –'

Then a man's voice said, 'How goes the game?' and Nan nearly fell off her chair.

We glared at the intruder; Jenny stood up to stare and I tell ye, my sweet, she could loom when she wanted.

Men weren't meant to come here. Once a month was the wenches' back room for games, and all the barkeeps knew that was sacred. We four looked to each other, deciding to try words a little afore commencing violence. 'Get gone,' said Jenny; and Peg, she growled.

The man bowed, which was a gentlemanly enough act, but he didn't go like we were asking which marked him out as a rogue to me. Nan had got her composure back and was fiddling with her hair and, if I weren't mistaken, preparing to bat her eyelashes at him, No-Conscience to the end. I could see it myself, the man had dark hair that was pleasant enough, and knowledgeable eyes and a smile that was interesting. And that's as complimentary as can be got out of me. He wasn't swaying on his feet; nor, I noted, was his jerkin completely covered in a drunkard's dribble; and so it seemed he was, if not sober, surely able-brained enough to know what he was getting himself into. Well, by that I mean us as a quart of angry ladies; nothing else. Nothing *more*.

'Might I not join you, madams?' he said. Peg took her turn to stand up now. She'd turned a shade of red she had, my lady Salt-Beef, and she was cursing fit to make the northern breezes blush.

'We don't invite anyone to play with us,' said Jenny, fierce old Buttock-de-Clink. 'It's a game for four, with dire consequences. Get you out.'

The man looked at our board, the pieces strewn about mid-game. 'I'm new in Port Royal,' he said. 'I sail aboard the *Roebuck*. Before that I'm from London. From England.' At our ignoring him he bloody well kept on, did he not know wiser? The next thing he said gave his wherefroms away even if he hadn't just told us: he was truly an Englishman no matter how far flung he would ever travel, for as a conversational gambit he disparaged his home weather. 'Plenty worse than these climes, the weather in England. Damn rain and the drizzle.'

That did it. We won't take comments about the weather, not on game night.

'Now look here,' said No-Conscience Nan, screwing up a paper boat she'd been idly making out of an abandoned bible page, and in doing so damning a thousand sailors. 'You whipsnap,' she said, 'I'd break you in half across my knees if you even think it and –'

'Confound you for a fool,' said Salt-Beef Peg, 'if you think ye'll be getting anywhere with us walking in here uninvited and –'

'Blast you with a thousand blizzards!' said Buttock-de-Clink Jenny, and with a slam of her hand she trumped enough cards to make the rain fall thrice harder all month over his beloved city.

He took our anger, soaked it up. He bowed again, at me this time.

'My name is William Dampier,' he said. 'May I join your game?'

Looking backwise, at this point we might have made everything different, and all right for us; and the worse for you. But at the time there was something about his nerve that made me want to test it for a turn or two.

'Sit,' I said. 'Join us.' The others looked at me, Nan starting to enjoy it, Peg not sure, Jenny fuming like a soggy bonfire. 'It seems safe enough,' I said, 'to add a player for a single round.' I placed a new counter on the board, near the mark that – how was he to know? – signified the *Roebuck*.

Peg saw. 'That's a naughty tidal wave you're sending on, there!' she said.

'Don't tell him,' I said. Peg shook her lovely locks; she wouldn't. Nan's eyes glinted.

'Tell me what?' he said.

'Tell you what,' I said, 'Let's talk stake. I'm telling Salt-Beef strumpet not to tell you I'm betting a wager on your very own *Roebuck*, so help me, but so help you more.' Even Jenny smiled when she saw what I was about.

'Ah,' he said, and I hoped to the great north tradewind that he was beginning to get the weight of what was happening here. Nan whistled in appreciation – and somewhere, off the coast of the Galapagos, a butterfly shuddered at the change in the air and altered its course.

'What do you want to play for?' said Jenny. 'We know who you are. You're an explorer? What's that to us, who've seen the world already? You hothead, layabout sailor, good-for-nothing –'

136

'You needn't bait him any more than we do by our existing here,' I said.

I rolled, I moved the piece. Peg tapped her nails on the board. She had a wooden splinter she was using for her place-marker; it was from the wreck of Sir Clowdisley's *Association*, the naughty girl. That boat was nothing but splinters now. She'd won it off a lucky throw months afore, landed not just that flagship but the *Romney* and the *Eagle* sunk down in the Scillies.

Now, I – what's that, you say? The *Association* sunk in seventeen-oh-seven; and yet Dampier's map came out in sixteen-ninety-nine, and wasn't that when we got our wings clipped, so how could Peg be playing with a piece of driftwood before the ship had even got wrecked? Well, aye. You ask and I'll answer as straight as I can. It's most certainly true that we were put down in our power as the century turned. Dampier did what he done, no doubt of it; but to this day we've still got some strength in us, and some of our bets take a long while to pay off. Old Nan, she was playing with a piece of metal set to go down in northern waters many, many years ahead, in a freezing cold sea and with severe want of lifeboats; she was always a shrewd spreader of bets. I've still a hold of a shapely piece of fibreglass from a vessel that's yet to begin its time on the seabed. Now if you'll let me continue.

'Will you take a turn clockwise or widdershins?' I said. 'I'm to play half-crosswise, old No-Conscience here goes whichever way suits her.' Salt-Beef Peg in the meantime moved a small pawn across a continent of her choice; and rolled a dice to confirm the co-ordinates of her new cyclone.

I do hope you are paying attention to the rules, by the way.

I'll say this for our man William Dampier. We played rings around him, and at our every roll of the dice the currents and the tides and the winds played havoc with themselves over the open ocean, swooping around an erratic course like a child's spinning-top. But through it all he did seem to be trying his best. And also he kept on talking, the rat. Twas all small-talk – none smaller – until just before the seventh round.

'Tis a risky game for a man who travels the ocean,' he said, 'to seek new lands, and chart them. But a greater danger, as I see it, is to seek to know the course of the winds.' His eyes twinkled at mine and I leaned forward to look into them more close-like. It was curious, what I saw.

Now I don't know where the man William Dampier got his information. Don't think us omniscient. We aren't. How he knew what we were, and, further to that, how he knew what our game was truly about, is a mystery to me.

My corset was heaving against the edge of the playing board – I'd pushed it there as a test – but Dampier's eyes didn't flicker there once; in point of fact, Dampier was smiling but not really at my body, nor even at my face. He was looking at the ravaging storms and the swirling currents that swelled beneath the façade of a wench, which I went by in those days. Somehow he knew me for the winds.

It made me daring. 'If only a man had arrows,' I said, 'to shew him a course along those general and coasting winds, for they're pernicious things indeed, or so I hear.' *I'll punish you for knowing*, I thought; *and you can watch*. I dealt him a card and the final round was begun.

Dampier lost. When she tired of following his personal travels, Buttock-de-Clink Jenny took a wider approach and sunk a naval brigade in a vicious typhoon that wasn't to strike for a century. No-Conscience Nan asserted it so Dampier's *Roebuck* wouldn't sink – she was too fond of his lovely dark hair for that, I could see her thinking it – but she did snarl his journeys enough that it would be a decade before he returned home. Salt-Beef Peg whipped up some currents that would get him court-marshalled for cruelty. Twas he and I who were really at chess. I chased his play a whole three times around the world.

Seek to know the course of the winds, indeed. Nobody had known the course of us yet. So I shook his hand at the end of it all, and I told him thus; 'the winds might not be forever at your back, sir, as the old blessing goes – but you've earned yourself a curious stare or two.' And then we four departed about our usual fair and foul business across Port Royal. Ah, what more to tell?

It was sixteen-ninety-nine when the *Discourse* was published, to great acclaim, of course, you'll know this; and a jack sailing into Port Royal brought the newly published map into our company. Nan stole it from him during a tryst, brought it screaming to the rest of us.

A diary of journeys and travels, descriptions of fauna and beasts – not news to us, nothing of interest. No, 'twas one of the charts made us tremble:

A Discourse of Trade-Winds, Breezes, Storms, Tides and Currents. A map much like our playing board without the grid and the counters, without the cards and cribbage sticks, without the dice. But – oh, what it did have, demarcated forever in pen and ink and etching.

William Dampier, I thought.

'He's mapped us,' said Jenny, in a tone that meant murdered us. It wasn't necessary to say so; we all knew. In truth we'd sensed it a long time afore Dampier's damned publication. Somehow, after the game he'd played with us, the game I now consider our last, our dice hadn't rolled the higher numbers, our cards were dealt into bad hands, and our darts had missed their marks.

'Look there,' said Jenny, pointing to the southern edge. In an illuminated strip writ to look like a scroll, Dampier's own spidery writing suggested that navigators 'Note, that the *Arrows* among the *Lines* shew *Course* of those *General & Coasting* winds.' I went to the board, none of my sisters stopped me, and I smashed the counters to pieces. Even as I did so, I knew I hadn't powers to sink. Not now.

Stupid myself, I thought. Fool – the real game had been lost as soon as I'd put the dice into his hands.

For a brief while we continued to meet, playing for matchsticks. But it wasn't the same now our power was pretence. Our monthly games fizzled out like damp dynamite to nothing.

Like Dampier intended when he mapped us. We left Port Royal, one by one, not long after.

A Discourse, published sixteen-ninety-nine. To this day it makes my very breath itch. I'll give you a discourse, my darlings.

I am brought to my main purpose. I say it here. This is my reason for telling you, for finally getting it down into words. I have told this story in order to announce that I, I, yes I indeed, I myself, the very I – I say that I challenge you – yes you, my dear of dears – I challenge you to a rematch.

I will play with any he, she or they who wishes to take me up on the game. There ought to be enough information in these preceding words for you to divine the rules; and this time, of course, the mere sight of play won't be enough. You will be required to win. Now, do not consider me unfair. In the case of your victory I promise you more knowledge, for there is much more you can know and there is much that can yet be altered. In return, we will play for double the stakes – I'll take it all away, I say, and everything will change.

But if you do nothing, I might mess things about in any case. It's in your interest, then, yes? Wait until the moon is full, and find me.

The Chandelier Bid

From the private papers of Irene Adler. Undated; from its tone, possibly intended for posthumous publication. It is in that hope, in any case, that we reproduce it here.

The first time I dramatically left London I had sworn, quite fervently, that I would never return. But such resolutions, broken once, are easily again; especially when one works in the arts. The Imperial Opera of Warsaw was once more touring to London and I found myself drawn by the promise of hearing applause in a familiar language. I was in my dressing room gossiping with a countertenor when a knock came upon the door. It was a smart knock, a series of clean raps with a cane; the knocker was either very confident or had steeled himself to be.

A man in a bowler hat and respectable grey suit, and an even more respectable moustache, stuck his head into the room.

'Pardon the intrusion,' he blustered, as the countertenor stood and hastily bid me good-bye. 'I've a message from an old friend and not much time.'

He quickly looked into the corridor as if to check he hadn't been followed, then closed the door carefully. I wondered at his high level of caution. He removed his hat and bowed, holding the brim tightly in one hand, and coughed politely as if not sure how to begin. I gestured towards the chair the countertenor had so recently vacated.

'I shan't keep you long,' he said. He walked to the chair, with a slight limp steadied by his cane. 'Congratulations on a triumphant performance, by the way! Marvellous.'

I nodded to receive the compliment, maintaining what I felt was a suitably dignified silence. He sat down heavily in the chair.

'You may not remember me, of course,' he said. 'I don't believe we really spoke...'

I smiled. 'Dr John Watson,' I said. 'I suppose we've never had the pleasure of a conventional acquaintance but rest assured I know you.'

Watson breathed out heavily and rubbed his hands together as if to warm them. I always kept it warm enough in my dressing room, believe me; quick changes or no. I therefore determined that he was unsure whether to be relieved or concerned by the news that I, most certainly, did recall him. And I will confess, this is not the best of me, but I let him sit in that uncertainty for a few moments more.

'Well then, Dr Watson. What brings you to the theatre this afternoon? As much as I'm pleased to see you're well, I'm unsure why you've chosen to renew, or even begin, an acquaintance between us now. And I'll confess I didn't take you for a matinee-goer.'

'Then I'll come straight out with it, Miss Adler. My primary reason for visiting was not to watch your performance; although I would wish it known that it was a very pleasant way to spend the time, and I wish my purpose could have been solely one of cultured leisure. You're aware of course of my ongoing collaboration with Sherlock Holmes, and while you'd surely admit to his detective brilliance, I'm aware there may linger a certain quality of... bad blood, between the two of you. He isn't here with me now, by the way, do rest assured about that: and I think he would be adamant against my seeking you out. Hence my concern on entering just now, for I have been trying to get away to see you in secret. I think I just about managed it. I told him I was headed to the market for tripe and onions. Researching a folk remedy for treating the gout,' he added.

'Watson,' I said, 'I thought you were going to come straight out with it.'

'Of course, my goodness; apologies. Miss Adler, I've come to ask you to pay a visit to Holmes and myself at Baker Street this very evening.'

'I understand your desire to widen his social circle, but why?'

'He's in need of your eye. We're working on a case at present that's proving fiendishly tricksy to him. Earlier today I caught Holmes loudly declaring his wish for – specifically, a woman fluent in matters of artistry, if you'll pardon me – with whom to discuss an issue. By chance I had seen your name on the playbills and knew you were only briefly scheduled to be in town, so I thought I might seize the chance. If you do honour myself and Holmes with your presence, he'll be able to fill you in on the nature of the mystery.'

I looked up at the chandelier above my dressing room mirror and spent a moment watching the playful movement of dust around it. It could be amusing, I thought, to illuminate an issue that was confusing Sherlock Holmes, of all people. And where else but here and now would such an opportunity arise?

I took Watson off the hook upon which he was dangling and told him I would call directly after the evening's performance. Or not quite directly; I said I would be late, as I was obliged to mingle backstage with some influential patrons before leaving the theatre. Which wasn't true, but created an appropriate sense of my being in demand.

The lamps cast steady glows across the rain-glinted cobblestones as I left the hansom cab at Baker Street. To my surprise Watson himself answered my knock at 221b, and breathlessly beckoned me inside.

'Do come up,' he said, as I dropped my umbrella into the stand beside the door.

We ascended the stairs, the strains of a violin growing louder as we approached. I confess a certain trepidation. I had been to the front door, of course, but only briefly; and I had never gone inside.

Watson ushered me into the drawing room, where a familiar back stood by the window, one arm moving to draw a lump of rosin across his violin bow. He spoke without turning around.

'Ah, Irene Adler. How very good of you to come.' He replaced the rosin and began fiddling with the strings, re-tuning the violin with small plucking noises. 'I'm delighted you're joining us after your performance –' (*pluck*) '– I'm sure the opera tour is proving is a triumph –' (*pluck*) '– although I hope you didn't have a difficult journey in the cab –' (*pluck*) '– given the traffic difficulties at present north of –' (a high *pluck!*) '– Goodge Street.'

Watson gave a cough of surprise and alarm and muttered something like 'well *really* now Holmes,' too quietly to necessitate a reply.

I took it in my stride, and did not take a seat I had not been offered. 'We took a detour,' I said, 'but I'm glad to have arrived. For my part I'm grateful you've received me; especially given that your housekeeper is away taking the Derbyshire water cure.'

He spun around to face me and for a moment my gaze was locked into his.

He did not look much different from the last time. That same studious air, the utmost confidence in his shoulders. But in that moment his eyes had the coldness of ice.

Watson coughed again, with a spluttering laugh. 'Well I must say,' he said, 'if you're *both* going to be doing this, I'll find myself completely lost at sea. Two of you at it…!'

Holmes' expression relaxed into what I took to be an attempt at hospitality.

'Quite right, Watson,' he said, still looking at me. 'Let us all sit down and set about the mission for which we are gathered.'

He gestured for me to take one of the chairs beside the fire, which I did. Holmes and Watson settled down too, although not before Watson had placed several thick slabs of fruitcake onto the table.

'I hope you're enjoying your return to London, by the way,' said Watson.

'Oh, very much,' I said. 'Less eventful, so much more enjoyable, than the last time: I'm afraid I ended up participating in a botched diamond theft at a high society ball.'

A look of surprise flashed over Holmes. 'So that was you! I recall reading about the caper in the papers. I thought at the time it had something of your nature about it.'

(*I hadn't been acting alone then, of course. Professor Moriarty and I had led each other a very merry dance, and in more ways than one. But of this adventure I have already written.*) I picked up a piece of fruitcake before Watson ate it all.

'Let's hear your reasoning, at least,' he said to Holmes, through a mouthful of cake. 'How did you guess about Miss Adler's journey going via Goodge Street?'

Holmes shrugged. 'An arrival at this late hour must mean joining us after the performance, and there's only one theatre grand enough for the Imperial Opera. It was little work to calculate the most likely route between there and here.'

Watson turned to me. 'And how the devil did you know about Mrs Hudson?'

Holmes flung one leg over the other and tapped his long fingers impatiently upon the side of his chair. 'It is very simple,' he said. 'Miss Adler saw the coffee stains on my right jacket-sleeve, forming the distinctive splash-pattern of a sudden burst of boiling liquid, and correctly surmised that I have been lately forced to tackle that awful stove-top pot on my own. Hideous temperamental thing,' he added.

Watson turned, again, to me. 'Is that so?'

'In fact, it was that postcard pinned to the wall,' I said. '*Greetings from the Wholesome waters of Matlock Bath.* And it was you who let me in, Watson – although that could have been to keep my arrival secret, I suppose.'

'Speaking of attempted secrecy,' Watson gaped again at Holmes. 'How did you know I was bringing Miss Adler here in the first place?'

'Simplicity itself!' cried Holmes. 'First I read that the Imperial Opera of Warsaw is scheduled to perform several dates in London. I adore classical music, a fact of which you're well aware, Watson, since I rhapsodise about it frequently and you kindly indulge me… but suddenly, it is as if the topic is banned by the Lord Chamberlain himself. The Opera is never on your lips, in fact you go out of your way to change the subject when I bring it around. I conclude there must be a reason this particular repertoire makes you nervous around me. A theory forms. I complain loudly during breakfast about the lack of a suitably artistic female accomplice for my present conundrum, and that very afternoon you slink off to the theatrical quarter muttering about onions. It seemed not only natural, but inevitable, that I should find myself sitting face-to-face with Irene Adler before the day was out. And here we are.'

He turned to me. 'Does that sound about right, Miss Adler?'

'Perhaps,' I said. 'By the way, now that you've mentioned it, I should point out there is coffee staining on your lapel as well as your cuffs.'

Watson dropped some cake crumbs onto his plate.

'That damned pot! I ought to throw it out. Let's dispense with these pleasantries,' said Holmes. His face settled into an expression of keen concentration and he laced his fingers together. 'Miss Adler, you might help me to unravel a mystery of peculiar nature. It's a matter of taste; I seek to take advantage of your artistic eye. Do you know W. Bart?'

'Not personally, though I know his paintings sell very well at auction.'

'We were recently visited,' said Holmes, 'by his former art tutor.'

'Oh?' This already sounded like a suitable intrigue for me.

Holmes never touched his cake nor even his tea as he spoke of the visit.

'She had decided that she simply must come and see me. She has picked up many students, as you would imagine, in the wake of Bart's success.

"'I know that I should be proud," she said. "My former pupil's paintings so highly sought. But I spend entire days wondering, frankly, what his collectors see in him – and I cannot for the life of me puzzle it out!"

'I asked her to clarify the nature of her confusion.

"'His paintings, Mr Holmes... they leave me completely perplexed. I am confounded they can be sold at all."

"'I suppose some do like his work, even if you personally can't see its value," I had said. At this point, Miss Adler, the whole thing seemed little more than professional jealousy and certainly not any problem of mine, and Watson put in a reminder that aesthetic preference can be a thoroughly subjective business.

'The art tutor sighed and said: "Normally I would agree with you, of course; I realise this situation is out of the ordinary, Mr Holmes! I suffer such guilt for taking on students in the wake of Bart's success when I cannot understand how it is possible. Others agree with me about his work: my friends; fellow artists."'

At this point I intervened in Holmes' telling. 'If Bart's work is the fashion,' I pointed out, 'that could be enough to make someone desire to buy one. Especially if the purchase looks to increase in value.'

'True,' said Holmes, 'but that only defers the question, it does not answer it. Something has to have made his paintings the fashion in the first place.'

And he continued the story.

"'I was taking a student today," the art tutor told me, "and she spoke of Bart's new painting and had I seen it? When I said I hadn't, she showed me its image clipped from the paper. Mr Holmes, this brought my anxiety to a head. Either through my years of study and expertise I had learned absolutely nothing, or this was a particularly unremarkable painting. I simply had to come here. I have brought a few images of his work, so you can agree for yourself."

'Watson and I duly poured over the images and presently, Watson said that we should agree to take on the case. So, there you have it. This could be a unique mystery with all manner of foul play to uncover, or it could be the mad ravings of an art tutor.'

I replaced my piece of cake on the plate and looked for a moment at the firelight glinting off the currants. 'I still don't see why you need my assistance,' I said.

'I need another opinion,' said Holmes. 'Watson said, on looking at Bart's paintings, that the tutor is quite right about the artist's work. But in truth my difficulty begins where everyone else's seems to end. I cannot go on Watson's word alone. I need someone who has impeccable taste when it comes to the arts, and a good eye, someone with refinement –'

I noticed Watson's shoulders were slumping a little as he stood and went to the bureau.

'– to confirm this beyond question of doubt, in order to properly begin on this case. To be perfectly honest Miss Adler, I do not understand much of contemporary art, and when I saw the images I could make neither head nor tail of them. My question to you therefore is: *are these paintings bad?*'

Watson presented an array of documents, a collection of facsimiles of Bart's oeuvre, torn from newspapers and auction catalogues. I looked over them quickly, then took a few moments to make sure I was certain about what was being asked of me. I looked up again at Sherlock Holmes.

'I can't tell.'

He shook his head.

'Not from these alone,' I said, calling on all my airs of professionalism. 'Works of art need to be seen as they are intended. It simply isn't helpful to draw conclusions from newspaper facsimiles. One must be in the presence of Art to have any real sense of it.'

Holmes leapt up and stood beside my armchair, craning his neck to look again at the pictures. 'You're sure?'

'To really know would take seeing them in person, therefore I cannot yet agree with the tutor.'

Holmes nodded, accepting my judgement, but at the same time he frowned a little, as if he still couldn't quite understand it.

Watson came to the rescue, saying brightly, 'We do have a chance to see one in person. Tomorrow Langford's is having a large auction of contemporary works, the centrepiece of which will be Bart's *The Scene*.'

Holmes stabbed a finger onto the pile of facsimiles. 'That is *that* one,' he said, squinting at it.

The following day had suddenly become much more eventful and so I rose to leave, promising that I would see them promptly at the auction to confirm my judgement of the painting. I looked forward to attending in any case. It's quite enjoyable to watch things grow steadily more expensive.

The auction house stood imposingly on the Strand and a high wind whipped the canvas banner that hung across the large entrance doors, grandly advertising the day's business. I chose to take its wind-bashed rippling as fortuitous, since it put me in mind of a curtain rising. Along the road horses stamped their feet in readiness to get going, as the cabs dispatched their passengers into the blustery street.

I arrived with plenty of time before the day's proceedings, as had most visitors, for it was an additional pleasure to wander through the exhibition hall, where the items were on final display. W. Bart's *The Scene* had pride of place at the head of the gallery and a crowd was already bunched in front of its imposing frame, looking at it in careful silence.

As I contemplated the painting a gallery official sidled up to me in a smart overcoat with brass buttons, peering awkwardly through thick-lensed pince-nez. For a moment I really thought I was going to be informed that the gallery was closing, or that I was about to be accused of trying to steal one of the sculptures.

'Well; what do you think of it?' said Holmes; for of course it was he.

I wanted to laugh at the familiar voice coming from such an unrecognisable visage. Really, it was a dreadful shame the two of us had never appeared on the stage.

'The art tutor is absolutely correct,' I said. I looked solemnly at Holmes. 'It is not a good painting. I had considered that something may have been revealed in the presence of the object itself, telling us some profound truth that the clippings could not. But this has not happened at all.'

Holmes nodded curtly, listening.

'I have acquaintances across the spectrum, Mr Holmes. Life-long experts, practised virtuosos, keen new-money hobbyists, dedicated amateurs; critics at both the professional and dinner-party conversation level; artists and patrons of art; I even know a few who are utterly disinterested in anything to do with it. I am in no doubt that not one of them would pay anything for this.'

Holmes looked again at the painting, craning through his pince-nez over the shoulders of its current audience.

'It's bad,' he whispered, speaking mostly to himself.

'Unquestionably,' I responded, firmly. I wanted no ambiguity on this point.

Holmes turned to me with the air of one making a final decision. 'Now we have confirmed beyond doubt that the painting is bad, let us stay to watch the auction. We will learn much about these perplexing sales if we witness one.'

As if in response, a great gong now shimmered out across the building. Excited conversation broke out between people as they headed towards the auction room.

'I am putting a lot of trust in you, Miss Adler,' said Holmes as we walked along. 'If that painting turns out to be good after all I will not be best pleased.'

We went in separately: I arrived at the auction through the main entrance, and Holmes took the staff doorway at the back, and dropped off the uniform as he went.

I took a seat near the back and waited for the sale to begin. Soon Holmes joined me; no longer in disguise, he stood out instead in the dignified dark suit of his own unmistakable self. I began to hear whisperings at the sight of us together; I heard my name. It seemed the auction was already, to some, slightly scandalous.

The auctioneer sauntered into the hall when the tension of waiting had reached its highest point, a piece of timing I admired. The clerk sat efficiently behind his desk and a row of handlers in white gloves were clustered together. Lining the wall were writers from the newspapers with their notebooks, and photographers with large wooden cameras on tripods, ready to capture the event.

Holmes cast a careful eye over people taking their seats. A respectable gathering, the attendees were easily as interesting as the paintings they were seeking to buy.

Holmes spoke quietly to me.

'Once the sale begins,' he said, 'keep an eye on the crowd, see how they take it. We must try to deduce the *nature* of people's desire for the painting. If what you've told me is true and this painting is as bad as you say it is, we could be looking at multiple crimes, of a very shocking nature, going back many years.'

'I understand,' I said.

He looked at me, surprise flashing over his features. 'My apologies,' he said, recovering. 'Usually I'm speaking with Watson and that's not the response one generally receives.'

The auctioneer announced the first piece (a portrait of some Lord-or-other's niece), the bids duly arrived and we were away. Holmes and I did not speak throughout all this. He was looking about at anyone and everyone, and I settled into my seat. The reader will understand that I am not generally one to dabble in the art market myself. Huge paintings become difficult when one is on tour.

The auctioneer announced he would now take bids for W. Bart's new work, *The Scene*. Whispers broke out in the audience as the handlers brought the painting out. It looked particularly incongruous in the auction room, this space dedicated to informed value judgement in gilt edging and dark wood.

The starting price for *The Scene* was higher than for any of the other paintings, but nevertheless opening bids came quickly from the crowd.

I cast my gaze around the hall as bidding settled into a steady rhythm. The price was rising smoothly as bids passed at a clip.

Sherlock Holmes held up a long finger.

'New bid from the gentleman at the back there: £——!' said the auctioneer. People craned to look.

Holmes was quickly outbid by someone near the front. He waited a second, giving the impression of deep thought. Then he bid again, and once more was countered.

There were more whispers of my name around our seats as people recognised me from the theatre. I wondered whether I had the chance to become a maker of taste – even with a painting as nondescript as this one. A fun diversion, I thought, having never to my knowledge set a fine art trend, and I raised my arm into the air.

'New bid: lady in the opera-gloves,' proclaimed the auctioneer. '£——!'

Holmes glared at me.

Another bid came from a woman in the top balcony.

Holmes raised his finger once more, then I bid again. I was glad of my choice to wear opera gloves; an affectation, perhaps, during the day, but they made my bids strikingly visible and dramatic. Holmes grunted, and bid again himself.

My actions had worked; my name was whispered with a new urgency. A line of women in silk dresses and smart hats, who had not yet bid on anything, joined in now, bids passing across them in a long line. After that, more came from the balcony. Then I bid again. Then Holmes.

His face was etched with annoyance. 'Miss Adler, would you please desist bidding!' he hissed. 'You are throwing my experiment off.'

'I'm conducting one of my own,' I said. 'I never knew I had such influence.'

We had reached a new band of bidding increments: the price was going up by much larger amounts each time, now. The auctioneer was practically leaning over the lectern to search out new bids from the floor.

Holmes bid again. Then I did.

Heads turned to look at us; feathers in hats bobbed. I have already said that I believe my own celebrity inspired some to commence bidding; but to this day I like to think it was the sight of the two of us together – Holmes' apparent wish for *The Scene* as well as mine – that inspired the real excitement. For suddenly it was as if someone had pulled the stopper from a bottle and released a wave of enthusiasm over the room. Hands shot into the air, one after another. The clerk scrambled to note the numbers of all these potential buyers.

I bid again, and made a quick mental calculation. If I bought the painting now I would certainly have to change my hotel; give up the top-floor en suite and take cheap digs in Soho until the tour moved on to Prague.

Another bid came assuredly from the balcony.

I bid again, £———. I would have to secure several more patrons to keep up expenses.

'Will you stop this, Miss Adler!' hissed Holmes, raising his finger once more.

I shot him a sweet smile as I bid again, and there was another flurry of bids around the room. I would have to give up the charitable salon performances that I so loved. And no more lobster dinners between now, I thought, and Christmas. Quite possibly next Christmas.

The auctioneer held his small wooden gavel high in the air.

'Surely there are no more bids!' he cried.

But he was wrong, for Holmes made one and then plenty more burst from the audience in its wake. The doors burst open and more journalists entered the room, summoned by their colleagues. The audience cheered, glad to be witness to this piece of art history.

I heard Holmes say quietly: *Enough.*

He raised his finger again, and in a clear, steady voice declared a price.

There were gasps, and everyone in the building turned as one to stare in our direction. The auctioneer was shocked into stillness, his small hammer paused at head-height. Holmes had put in a bid that soared beyond the highest number we had reached; in truth he had uttered a greater amount of money than I thought possible. The power of it coursed through me as if I were finally accepting a bouquet after a dozen encores.

£————————. The bid was as grand and unreachable as a chandelier glinting at the very top of the tallest ceiling.

The silence was broken by a soft puffing sound and a bright flash, as a photograph was being taken of Holmes as he performed this triumphant final bid.

Then the auctioneer brought the gavel down onto the wood with dazed finality, and the auction house descended into uproar.

Holmes rubbed his forehead with his hand.

'The good news,' he said, his eyes closed, 'is we can say the mystery presented to us by the art tutor is solved. The more… inconvenient news is I appear to be saddled with a painting for my troubles, and a bad one at that, and with no thanks to you, Miss Adler, for driving up the price. Watson?'

The good doctor had appeared beside us, still looking quite agape at this recent turn of events. 'How can I help?' he managed, shouting over the chaos.

'Run outside and summon the first policeman you see,' said Holmes. 'We have the necessary information to make an arrest. And while you're out – I fear, Watson, you ought to do this first – go to the telegraph office and send a message to my brother.' He sighed, then spoke with a voice of flat resignation. 'I'll need to request some funds.'

The auction-room was much emptier now. Chairs were askew and the floor was scattered with torn-out pages from the catalogue. Before us the painting leaned heavily against the lectern. It was now officially the most expensive piece of art Langford's had ever sold. Watson was examining it with his hands on his hips.

'Can't think where we'll put it,' he said. 'So, setting aside what you've spent today Holmes, what's the answer to the mystery? What will we tell the art tutor?'

Before Holmes could explain we were joined by the auctioneer, his hair still plastered to his forehead with the sweat of all the excitement. Standing beside him, looking like the cat who had obtained access to an entire dairy, was a confident-looking young man in elaborately patterned trousers.

'I had to tell him the news personally, and he wants to meet you,' said the auctioneer. 'May I present W. Bart. This is Sherlock Holmes, he's the new owner of your painting.'

'Mr Holmes, I cannot thank you enough,' said the artist, bouncing along on a tide of happiness and unaware of the graveness of Holmes' countenance. 'This is the utter high-point of my entire life's work, and it's all down to you.' He held out his hand, but Holmes did not shake it.

'I'm glad you're here, given what I am about to say,' said Holmes. He waited a moment to ensure he had our attention. Then he declared: 'That you are less the artist and more the criminal!'

The auctioneer looked embarrassed at this turn of events. 'Yet another surprise from you, Mr Holmes,' he said. 'What on earth is your basis for such an accusation?'

Holmes ignored him and spoke directly to Bart.

'I have been... made aware,' said Holmes, 'that no one of taste, not even those with questionable preferences, ought really to show interest in your art.'

The painter stared at Holmes. The shine in his eyes at the recent sale softened at this judgement on his work. The auctioneer did not leap in to defend it, but stared blankly at his own shoes, willing a professionally awkward moment to swiftly pass.

'I'm sure a life devoted to art is difficult. But, nonetheless, let me tell you, sir, you have acted very wrongly by pursuing the hideous practice of blackmail!'

Although I was prepared for what Holmes was going to say I still felt a prickle at the mention of blackmail. It is a crime for which I have particular revulsion.

The painter looked somehow smaller, and less stable, as if half the air had been let out of him. 'Art is my very being,' he said. 'And patronage is an acknowledgment of that. Years of tireless dedication and the Academy continues to refuse me. How else could I secure an endorsement in my position?'

'Of course!' cried Watson. 'The painter who forces his patron's hand! The art world is made up of high society clientele, plenty of incriminating information swilling about. So the blackmail itself was secondary to an elaborate ruse to sell your canvases.'

'If my theory was correct,' continued Holmes, 'I knew that somebody would want the painting more than anyone else. But only when the auction began did the scale of the crime become clear. One victim is bad enough. But, a double blackmail –! And there you sow the seeds for a thrilling auction. The Viscount of Marle (near the front, on the left) and Lady Déricourt (up in one of the top balcony boxes) treated the auction with great importance, and bid with assurance. Marle revealed a tendency to fiddle with his cravat-pin, which he did with ever-increasing fervour; from changes in her stance I saw that Déricourt needed to win the auction. Once I'd identified the victims I decided to bid myself, to see how far they would go, confirming my hypothesis and timing my bids to gauge their reactions.'

The auctioneer was looking at Bart with a face of utmost betrayal.

'What I was *not* expecting,' admitted Holmes, 'was that everyone else would start bidding also.' He avoided my gaze. 'It complicated things considerably.'

'But think what I found out,' I said. 'It seems many would look to us, Holmes, for the question of how to decorate their drawing rooms. I certainly didn't intend to knock your concentration,' I added, and Watson caught my eye and winked.

We both knew that if Holmes wanted to focus, even the auction house catching on fire would not have stopped him.

'I never sought money for its own sake, you must understand,' said Bart. 'And if the Academy had given me a chance I could have developed myself through more noble means.'

'To make a piece of art itself both ransom note and hostage,' muttered Watson. 'Incredible.'

'We have summoned the police,' said Holmes. 'They have been waiting for you.'

Watson signalled off into the shadows, and a pair of constables joined our group. They stood either side of Bart, who didn't pay them much mind. Presumably he was thinking about how art history would surely remember him, one way or another, after this unique incident: if the crime itself was simply a means to an end, no doubt so was being caught.

He turned to me. 'Might I sketch you someday, for inclusion in a future work?'

I made do with arching an eyebrow at him.

'Not to worry.'

The constables clapped their heavy hands onto his shoulders and we watched as he was dragged from the hall. The auctioneer made some small excuse and also left us.

Holmes broke the silence. 'I shall write to Marle and Lady Déricourt directly,' he said, 'and assure them the bribe has been voided and their secrets are safe.'

Then he sighed. 'For now however, Watson, let us summon a cab. I suppose we must get this thing home.'

I had expected to see no more of Holmes after that day, and proceeded to continue my performances with the Imperial Opera of Warsaw. For a week or so the headlines shouted about the hullabaloo of the auction, and the jailing of the disgraced painter;

but soon that news, as all news, was replaced by something else, and in time given my own occupations I thought only rarely of the adventure. On my final day in London however, I received an urgent summons.

COME AT ONCE, the telegram read. *BREAKTHROUGH.*

Naturally my interest was caught, and I put my plans for various romantic au revoirs aside and visited Baker Street en route to the station, leaving my trunks in the hansom.

When I arrived into the drawing room I was surprised to see that W. Bart's *The Scene* had in fact been hung. It covered almost all of one wall, dominating the view as soon as one entered. Holmes was pacing to and fro in front of it. Watson was sitting in his armchair, trying to concentrate on the paper; well-worn marks in the carpet revealed that the chair had been recently rotated to an angle that faced further away from the painting.

Holmes spun around to face me.

'I have been staring at this painting since I bought it,' he said. 'I can tell you the company that manufactured the pigment, and the country where it was mined; I know the artist is left-handed, suffers a minor tremor when deprived of sleep, and used to own a piebald dachshund. I can identify the colourman who supplied the paint to the factory and I know he lives near Green Park in spite of his hayfever. This painting was finished on a Wednesday and stored in an attic that contained a stack of leather-bound bibles damp with mildew, a woollen blanket in rare Highland tartan, and with a hole in the south-facing roof. Miss Adler, using my powers of deductive reasoning I have learned everything about this painting that I can. But I cannot, after all this time, tell you why, as you say, as the tutor said, as even Watson here declares, the painting is bad. I am baffled, Miss Adler. I have spent an unthinkable amount of my brother's money on this. And I haven't the faintest clue why this painting is worse than the next. Perhaps it is because of... this bit? No, never mind!'

I approached Holmes and the painting. 'Developing a tasteful eye,' I said, 'is the work of a lifetime.'

'Forget it, Miss Adler! I sent that telegram to declare to you that as of today I am utterly defeated. Never mind refilling Watson's teacup now, Mrs Hudson!' For the housekeeper had just come in and was waving cheerily to me with one hand, holding a teapot in the other. Holmes motioned for her to put the teapot down.

'Mrs Hudson, please have this painting removed and stored in one of the darkest and remotest cupboards of the house. I cannot bear to look at it a moment longer.'

'Three cheers for that!' she said. 'I must confess I've never liked it.'

Holmes covered his face with his hands.

He was still ranting about *The Scene* as I bid goodbye to Mrs Hudson and Watson, who were both grinning widely as they waved me off at the door. As the hansom juddered me across the cobbles to the station I could still hear his cries of frustration, and I knew the housekeeper and the doctor would already be halfway up a stepladder, relieving the picture-rail of its cumbersome occupant.

Golden Girl

It's dazzling down here.

She's standing on orange sand beneath a bright, molten sky the colour of honey. It's a world that stretches long and far, a rich and infinite shining desert, and it dazzles, and in every direction horizon to horizon the same glowing palette and no shadow, no cloud. Certainly no sunglasses.

(Whatever *they* are.)

Occasionally she sees another, although 'sees' isn't quite the right word. She senses them by the lack of shadow, the brightness moving like flaring heat that creates a flicker of presence. The air wobbles and that, she knows, is a someone, even if it's never for long.

She doesn't know how many of them there are. Certainly enough to fill this place many times over, but never enough to challenge its wide open emptiness and all this shine. If someone, say, ruled over this place, looked down upon it, they might have a sense of its totals, its edges, even (whisper it) its limits. But to her, to all of them, there's nothing but waiting for nothing, and watching for nothing, and wandering in the brightness, with thoughts only of immense stillness and all this luminous orange-yellow.

She knows *shades* is the proper word for what they are, for what she is. She also knows this is something of an ironic name, but she can't get to why.

It goes without saying (as it must, down here), that she doesn't know where she is. Or that she's ever been anywhere else, or, of course, that all this gold is silence. She may have once encountered a fragment of a saying to that effect or some such

161

but she's forgotten it, along with everything else, and anyway, it made no difference to the experience when she got here.

She stands on the glinting sand.

Some time must pass, although there's no sense of measuring that sort of thing, but something happens and that could only be time's doing, surely, she thinks, frowning and blinking a little at the sight of a new figure walking across the sand. First a dark speck in the distance, then they're life-size. And that's definitely something that wasn't so before but now it is. Wait, *life* size?

It can't be a shade, he's too solid. And he's overdressed for the environment. All that heavy cloth on his skin, it's too much, she finds it tricky to look at. Then there's the idea of skin itself, suffocating stuff, and the heavy muscular pressure underneath, with bones stuck solid all the way through. She wonders how she could ever have borne it.

His steps make dark footprints in the golden sand, and even though the grains quickly cover them over again, this is unusual, and she notices that she is noticing it happening.

He's getting closer. He pushes some dark curls of hair from his face and wipes his forehead with the back of his hand. Always his expression is peering into the endless glow of this luminous desert, looking first this way, then that way. This puzzles her; what's he searching for? This place is filled to the brim with emptiness, there's nothing down here except dazzle and gold.

He stares in her direction.

Perhaps, she gave herself away – a brief shudder of bewilderment, or perhaps her confusion registered as a whisper on the wind, or a shape in the gloom, or even (she can't be sure he doesn't see things as she does) as a sparkle in the gold. Or perhaps it was simply luck, on his part, to look in the right place.

After a moment, his face opens.

He runs towards her. His footprints shine before the sand covers them over again, and small specks fly from him, shards so thin they quickly vanish but for a second gleam brilliantly like cold light on water.

He stands before her, looking at her intently, and his mouth moves. More bursts of silver flit into her vision for a moment, then go out.

His face is going through a range of contortions and it is some time before she realises he is trying to speak to her. So *that's* what all this is, this strange movement and the dark shine spiralling out from him. Yes, those must be words he's making, these things that come from his mouth like bubbles of steel. He's trying to talk to her.

His name must begin with an O, because a dark hole opens up in the world and hangs in the air between them, like he's spoken a silver plate.

(Whatever one of *those* is.)

His attempts get more frantic and soon he's jumping up and down and pointing to himself, then to her, back to him again. More metallic words glint in the air and she nods, wanting to both encourage their connection and also stop it here, because it's exhausting even to watch, it's all far too much energy. But she can tell this is important to him. She doesn't know him, and she's sorry to upset him.

She shakes her head.

He shakes *his*, but more quickly, and he takes a few steps backwards on the sand.

He bends his head back and his speech is urgent, sparking fountains of silver, as if he were tossing into the air handful after handful of nails and pins and rings and fragments of mirror and coins.

(Whatever any of *those* are...)

Hang on.

The sky is changing.

The air has intensified, if it's possible. She looks up.

Filling everything above them is a ball of pure fire and its radiance is extraordinary, taking up the entire view, and furthermore it seems to be watching what's going on here with idle interest. This colossal fireball is focusing its blazing attention on the figure in the dark cloak who stands there tiny on the sand, throwing up useless silver spangles. This is *him*, no doubt about it.

And the stranger is staring up into his scorching light, pointing, sometimes waving towards her again, gesturing wildly with his hands.

She drifts closer; many more shades do the same, and before long they've formed a wide circle around the stranger, making the horizon shudder.

The stranger reveals something from within his cloak and holds it up with both hands, as if presenting it for inspection. Light glints off the oval frame and its many taut strings.

The giant sun moves a little, as if nodding towards it.

The stranger lowers the lyre into place before him, and at that moment he must begin to play on it because quicksilver pours out into the rest of the world.

A span of silver blades flickers from the strings and cuts the goldness into pieces, soaring through it, the cleanest cuts imaginable.

Soon silver is everywhere. A jagged crack of the stuff breaks away from the rest, stretching into ribbons that twist and wind around themselves, then untangle again, leaving trails that sparkle as they go. More cracks spread in every direction until they have the landscape in a stranglehold. The goldness shakes, once, indignant at this challenge. Then shatters.

The sky dims darker, the sand an infinite grey. A few tiny pieces of the old world float in the air like so many dust motes.

The stranger stops, and looks around expectantly.

(She wonders what he's waiting for, and wonders why she should wonder.)

The gold returns slowly, a gradual flow of lava seeping into the horizon. But the memory of silver lingers.

She calls out: projects her nothing of a voice as best she can, remembers how he'd gestured towards her and tries to do the same, feeling the air adjust itself around her absence.

A tarnished silver mirror lands heavily into the sand at her feet. The stranger turns around.

She knows him.

The Tartest of Flavours

This is the story of the appalling things Jack Heart did with his tray of desserts.

Yes, Jack Heart! The former petty thief (now renounced) who successfully relaunched himself into society, and with no apparent effort charms his way into every supper and ball – Jack Heart himself, the very same! I would imagine you haven't been to one of the same parties as Jack Heart before now.

Queenie Redford's summer garden party was an anticipated event at the height of the season, hosted each year by the lady herself in celebration of her birthday. This year marked an auspicious milestone, an age she permitted nobody to know, and close attention had been paid to every particular.

'She has surpassed herself this time,' said a young art student in a striking suit, delighted to be a party guest. 'The roses are as bright as if they were freshly painted.'

The gardens had been carefully tended, and the croquet lawn was a neat square of softest green. The air was sweet with the scent of freshly pressed lemonade and music lilted along from the string quartet in the wrought-iron bandstand.

Many were already playing croquet, pulling up trouser-legs and revealing brightly coloured argyle socks. Friends, neighbours and dear acquaintances stood about in good-natured groups, watching those brave souls wielding the mallets; while others sat relaxing beneath the willow trees, spectators to the wider sport of society itself. Lady Red (as she was fondly known by all) fluttered between her guests, making tactful introductions and asking all the right questions, and looking striking in a gown of rich crimson.

Anyone who was anyone was at Lady Red's summer garden party. There were also several people who weren't anyone at all, to add a sense of potential.

Finally, a card in the shape of a heart was brought in to announce that Jack had arrived.

It was a moment of considerable excitement. The news rippled across the manor-house lawns. Guests whispered, 'Here he is!' and some of them added '...at last!' as if to say it had been worth their coming after all. Women who privately longed to lose a necklace to him craned around to get a better look, or else minutely adjusted their croquet stance.

Jack Heart, his beard carefully pointed in the latest style, had just taken a glass of champagne, his golden cufflinks shining in the sun.

'I had half a mind you wouldn't come at all!' cried Lady Red, embracing him with a clack of jet beads. 'I suppose you've been off having all manner of adventures.'

'Have I ever let you down?' he said, smiling. 'In truth, I might be a little late but with good reason. I have a great surprise planned for later, you see, and needed to finish my preparations.'

'Well that does sound promising,' said Lady Red. 'But you were still late, which I may find difficult to forgive. Society simply becomes more interesting when you join it.' Her face took on a mischievous countenance, and Jack shared her joyful look.

Lady Red had been instrumental in helping Jack Heart re-enter society: where she led many would follow and, by now, most people had entirely put behind them his past existence as an absolute scoundrel. Only a small number still needed convincing. He had previously spent vast amounts of energy on petty theft, mostly of precious jewellery and deeds to estate; crimes he pulled off by promising marriage to various persons. But now he stood reformed, with only honest intentions, presenting Lady Red with his most gracious smile.

'It's all very well you grinning at me like that,' she said. 'Some of my guests still disapprove of you, you know.'

He brushed a lock of hair from his face in a dashingly coy manner. 'I hope I'll be able to prove them wrong – or right,' he said. 'Whichever they'll enjoy the most.'

Lady Red's laugh echoed through the gardens, and heads turned as guests tried to watch them without being seen.

The more disapproving members of society gathered together beside the weeping willow tree and whispered to each other.

'I don't know how she puts up with him,' said a young man, a student of law with neatly pomaded hair, who always scowled at moral laxity. 'Once a scoundrel, always a scoundrel. Lady Red will awake one day, he'll have taken this house out from under her!'

'She puts up with him because like attracts like,' said a wise old matron, who had seen a few things. 'She'd be just as much a schemer as Jack – more so, perhaps, Lord help us – if she hadn't been born to be Lady Redford with all the attendant responsibilities. I think she finds it thrilling to have him around. He won't steal anything from her without her express permission.'

'I don't call it *responsible*, to fawn on him like that. Nevermind *thrilling!*' The young man pulled a face as if the word *thrilling* itself had a nasty taste. 'The man's a self-confessed thief, for goodness' sake.'

'A self-confessed *reformed* thief,' added an eccentric milliner who had overheard their conversation. She joined them by the willow tree, adjusting her hat, which was grandly decorated with fruit and an entire bird. 'It makes all the difference,' she said, 'that he's so public about renouncing his former ways. What I want to know is: what has he reformed into?'

'He's never said,' said the matron. 'It does make one wonder what he plans to do next.'

'I'm sure Lady Red will love it, whatever it is,' muttered the law student. 'There are rumours she had her will changed to leave him everything.'

'So that's what he plans to do next,' said the matron. 'Wait.'

But their dour looks went unseen by the party at large. Suddenly there was a great cheer from the direction of the croquet lawn, where Mrs Clubbe had narrowly pulled off a thrilling three-mallet bowl with a risky underhand strike.

Jack Heart cast an eye over the party, which was bubbling as fine champagne with chattering talk; an atmosphere rich with excitement and heady as truffles. The sun shone on salmon-pink gowns, bonnets with flowers in the band, white suits and straw boaters. Lady Red had left him a moment to speak with her elderly aunt, who was up visiting from Cheshire. She was a friendly soul, who wore thick knitted shawls whatever the weather and never stopped smiling.

'I do love it when she comes to stay,' said Lady Red, waving her off. Then she turned back to Jack and her expression faltered. 'You seem preoccupied. What's the matter?'

His manner was exceedingly casual. 'Is Mr Marsh-Hare here?'

'Certainly,' said Lady Red. 'You were insistent that I invite him, after all.'

His voice grew a little quieter. 'In that case I'm indebted to you. Delighted,' he added, although his countenance did not brighten.

Lady Red's brow lowered as she attempted to read him. 'I did not know the two of you were acquainted. Do you have business with him in particular? Now's a good time to kindle a friendship – he's been a beam of brightest sunlight since he and my dear Alison became engaged.'

A wince flashed over his features, as if he had eaten an overcooked goose egg.

'Are you perhaps *not* friendly with Mr Marsh-Hare? Do reassure me that he isn't one of these people from your past you sometimes talk about, whom you technically owe a duel to the death to. I could not abide one of those breaking out here, so close to my croquet lawn.'

Jack Heart made a minute adjustment to his shirt-cuff, then cast another glance over the party. 'I don't mind telling you this, because we are such dear friends, and I owe you so very much. I can promise you...' He tossed his head and said charitably: 'Today I intend to bring any bad grace between myself and Mr Marsh-Hare to an abrupt and permanent end.'

Lady Red's face relaxed with relief, and she took his arm. 'Wonderful news. I am pleased to hear it. Good!'

And she led him off into the party, the two of them chatting away over all the important gossip. They made their way through the crowd, threading through the people and passing the heaving buffet table.

The buffet had not yet been declared open, and many exciting glances were being cast in its direction; so much so that the buffet itself had grown conscious of its importance to the event.

'This is quite the most magnificent party,' said the chocolate cake. 'What a dignified assemblage of the great and the grand!'

'Indeed – we are *almost* impressed with the guest list,' said the cucumber sandwiches. 'Nearly everyone here has a high enough pedigree to associate with us, and we call that a pleasing result.' The cucumber sandwiches were outrageous snobs.

'I can't wait for people to come a little closer,' said the whole trout served with green beans and flaked almonds. 'So that I might better join in with the conversation.'

'You should be more like us,' chirped the vol-au-vents from their high position on the tiered stand. 'We already know most of the gossip. Such an advantage comes from being highly sociable, as we are. We regularly go around the whole party, stopping off to spend time with each and every guest: so of course we hear the latest news. It's your own fault for just sitting there.'

The trout with flaked almonds looked sad at this. 'I would like to be more sociable,' he said. 'But I often find I simply do not have the energy.'

'Because you just lie about,' said the vol-au-vents. 'No wonder you are so tired.'

The conversation was greatly amusing a trio of stately jellies in the shape of castles, who stood at the back of the buffet table in silver dishes. 'Oh hoho, very funny,' they said, and they wobbled about with laughter. 'Amusing indeed. Haha! Haha!'

'We will surely all perk up once the singing begins,' said the kindly chocolate cake, who was a generous soul and wanted everyone to feel included.

'That's true,' said the trout. 'I am looking forward to the singing.'

'It is gauche to sing in public,' said the cucumber sandwiches, decisively. 'Unless one has the proper training.'

The trout looked hurt. 'On every other day, perhaps – but not on a birthday...!'

'I for one cannot wait for the singing,' said the chocolate cake with happiness. 'For then I will blaze with candles, I will learn the Lady Red's secret wish, and then I will be blown out and shared between everyone!'

'Yes, how jolly! How jolly it will be!' said the jellies, laughing away. 'Haha! Haha!'

A purple macaroon piped up from her gilt-edged box. 'I fear this party will be the same as all the others,' she said. 'Jolly enough, but offering little by way of incident, intrigue or lasting interest.' The other macaroons, who were a range of bright colours and just as cosmopolitan as she, sighed in agreement and ennui.

'Well for our part,' said the cucumber sandwiches, 'we *certainly* hope this party will be like all the others! We do not approve of new-fangled ideas or novelties. Progress has given *us* to the world, what is the point of going any further now that we have been invented? Any experiments from now on will always lead to folly.'

'Haha!' laughed the jellies. 'Folly, how funny. Haha! Ha!'

'*Will you shut up!*' came a shrill chorus of voices from the centre of the table. 'Stop laughing! This is a serious matter!'

For at the centre of the table, attracting even more attention than the chocolate cake, was a silver tray of the Lady's famous homemade tarts. The lemon curd tarts were as bright as the sun; the lime tarts glowed like the finest arsenic wallpaper; and glistening orange were the quince tarts.

The lemon tarts spoke up first. 'Your laugh cuts right through us, do stop!'

'There is nothing funny about disliking progress,' added a quince tart. 'You oughtn't to laugh.'

'You should be stately, like the castles you resemble,' said a lime tart. 'But you treat everything as if it were a joke. You are a disappointment to your architecture.'

'And as for *you*,' said a quince tart to the vol-au-vents, 'I wish you wouldn't show off about how much of the party you've seen already. *Some* of us are waiting for our moment. Mind you,' it added, 'when that happens, we will be the star of the show.'

Nobody liked the tarts. Their manner of expression was too blunt; their sense of cruelty was too sharp. This sort of behaviour had gone on for so long the rest of the buffet had little good will left for them.

'There's no need to be so arrogant, we all know how popular you are,' said the plate of cold cheeses and meats – and the olives, who always backed them up, huffed in agreement.

'You'll be sorry when they spit your stones out,' said a quince tart, spitefully.

'This is all so uncouth,' muttered the cucumber sandwiches. 'We were brought up to have a delicate sensibility and would never speak to anyone this way. You severely lack refinement.'

'You look down on us because you don't have any crusts, while we do,' said the tarts. 'Perhaps we lack your "standards", but you made them up, so who is to say?'

'Please!' said the small pork pies. 'Stop fighting!'

At this point, Jack Heart walked straight up to the table, picked up the whole tray of tarts and went away with them.

'I have to say I'm quite glad to see the back of the tarts,' said the salmon rolls. The vol-au-vents piped up in agreement and even the chocolate cake felt things would now be a little calmer; for some time the buffet returned to a state of contented satisfaction in the middle of the party.

But when Jack returned to the table, bearing the tray of tarts, something was very different.

'Egads!' cried the olives, who were easily alarmed. 'What's happened to you?'

For the tarts were now a deep, juicy red, all of them as red as blood. Their redness shocked even the cherries on top of the buns, who knew a little something about the possibilities of fruitstuffs. They sat there on their tray in happy silence for a moment.

'Is everything all right?' ventured the chocolate cake.

The tarts yawned and said: 'Whatever do you mean?' – and their voices were softer, much calmer than they had been before. They sounded blissfully content, as if they were on the verge of falling asleep. 'Isn't this the most gorgeous party in the history of parties,' said the tarts. 'We adore it, not to mention being in your delightful company. How lucky we are to know you all.'

'Ohh, no no no,' said the jellies at the back, and they shook violently from side to side. 'We don't like this at all; very worrying. No, no, no.'

'Something's happened,' said the trout with almonds.

'Frankly, we preferred them before,' said the cucumber sandwiches. 'At least we knew where we stood. This has thrown us rather off.' As has been established, the cucumber sandwiches did not like the idea of change. On this occasion, however, they spoke for the table.

'Shh!' The plate of cold meats had spotted something. 'Look! Jack is coming back – and he's speaking with the doctor! We might be able to learn some answers!'

And the whole buffet listened eagerly.

Jack Heart and the doctor were discussing the major scientific theories of the day. The doctor was a great friend of Lady Red and had been her main supplier of opiates for many years. As they reached the buffet table Jack addressed him eagerly, bringing his voice down to a conspiratorial level.

'Are you familiar with the idea of sympathetic medicine?' he asked. 'Do you use it, I mean, in your practice?'

The doctor adjusted his pince-nez. 'Why, not at all,' he said. 'I thought we were discussing matters of science; *that* is a topic of pure history. Isn't it centuries old?'

'There's nothing wrong with being centuries old,' said Jack, a little defensively. 'I'm sure your thrice-great grandfather is centuries old and remains a respected gentleman of the parish – at least, as far as I am aware.'

'I never said there was anything wrong with age *per se*,' said the doctor, a slight tremble to his voice as if he trod upon dangerous ground. 'But the principles of sympathetic medicine are not applied these days. They are not applied at all. I mean to say,' he spluttered a laugh, 'it's hardly a technique that *works*.'

Jack's smile grew enigmatic. 'I have exciting news, Doctor.'

'You're going to tell me it works after all? You're wasting your time. It has never proved scientifically sound, not once.'

'That's beside the point – by which I mean, it is very *close* to the point, close enough to be very *near* to the point, to *be* as it were on the *side* of the point: but nonetheless, it is not *quite* the point that I mean or wish to make to you.'

The doctor was blinking a little at that, so Jack Heart continued on.

'My theory is this: sympathetic medicine is founded on the principle that there are invisible connections between things that share a key affinity. The idea that *like affects like* has resulted in all manner of foolishness – tending the weapon to heal the wound, that sort of thing!'

Jack Heart laughed at the folly he had just conjured. Then his face became serious again. 'But one never hears of sympathetic principles being applied *adversely*, does one?'

'Adversely?'

'Indeed, doctor. For example: who has heard of a ne'er-do-well utilising the formula?'

The doctor swallowed, a little nervously. 'How do you mean? I must say I absolutely do not –'

'I mean setting out quite explicitly to do harm, using sympathetic resonance. As like does not always cure like, it stands to reason that affinity might, in fact, be working against its subjects.'

Jack Heart picked up one of the jam tarts. 'I made these especially,' he said.

Here the doctor perked up. 'No you didn't. Those are Lady Red's famous birthday tarts. Everybody knows it. I'm happy to listen to your new-old-fangled theories Jack, but you can't go about taking credit for somebody else's tarts.'

'They *were* my Lady's tarts,' said Jack, 'is what I mean to say. But I have injected them with a substance of my own mixing: an ancient formula distilled from red vitriol and two cups of redcurrants. To begin the process of sympathetic poisoning I must add something more. In here –'

And he opened the stone of a ring he wore on his finger, and proffered it towards the good doctor, who lent forwards and peered at it.

The ring's central gem, as it turned out, was hollow. What appeared to be a great diamond was in fact a container of burnished metal filled with fine white crystals.

'This ring,' said Jack Heart, 'contains powder of sympathy. And because I wish to achieve drastic results, Doctor, I am using strong poison indeed. Combined with the concoction in the tarts, the result will be this: mark it, doctor: *I* take this poison, and the *victim* dies.'

The doctor stood back from the ring as if it were about to leap up and bite him. Jack Heart clipped it closed with satisfaction, and placed the offending hand in the pocket of his waistcoat.

'There's no need to be so alarmed,' said Jack Heart. 'I'm only going to administer it to precisely chosen victims. I'm not being cavalier about any of this.'

The doctor looked desperately around the party, but his gaze came back to Jack's mad glittering eyes, which were intensely locked upon him.

The doctor burst into a gale of laughter.

'Oh, this is very funny – marvellous indeed!' he said. 'You had me worried for a moment there, Jack. This is another of your superb stories. I'm glad you retired stealing pearls away from heiresses to become this entertaining!'

Jack stared at him coldly. 'I do not jest in the slightest,' he said.

The doctor chuckled again. 'If you say so. Though I am duty bound to tell you that if you *are* being serious you are quite, quite fried in the head.' He looked about the party. 'I'll take my leave now, if you don't mind. If you're hoaxing me sir you've been very amusing. And if that *is* strychnine you've got there, or any other devilish crystal you're intending to eat, you'll quickly find the only person to suffer is yourself. It really ought to be sugar because those tarts are usually far too astringent for my liking anyway, truth be told. Good-day to you!'

And off he ran to the farthest end of the party, where Lady Red was currently taking aim on the croquet lawn with her personal pink mallet.

Jack Heart stood silently for a moment, then he tucked one hand into a fist, and hit his other hand with it.

'Undermined and doubted; I'm an amusement to them,' he muttered. Then his voice grew even lower, and he whispered: 'The perfect alibi.'

He looked down at the tarts. 'I have confidence on my side,' he said. 'And my own ingenuity to guide me.'

He spent a moment watching the doctor at the croquet game. Lady Red was standing aside for a few hoops to speak with him, but from their arm gestures they seemed to be engaged in discussing hoop and ball strategy and nothing further. They didn't seem to be discussing the doctor's recent conversation, or its abrupt end. Clearly he wished to put it behind him.

Jack looked down nonchalantly at the tart in his hand, then neatly opened the diamond on his silver ring and tipped a small amount of the white powder over the tart.

'My much beloved patron; Lady Redford herself,' he said, and he ate the tart slowly, with great concentration. The tart had been a quince tart, and the delicate flavour mingled with Jack Heart's thoughts of his host. Of all his victims, this made him the most regretful; but, as well as the undoubted financial benefit, somebody as high-profile as she would guarantee attention. He intended to get away with the crime, but the mystery should reach the society pages as well as scientific journals.

'It saddens me to bid her goodbye,' he said to himself, through a mouthful of tart; 'but I daresay she would be thrilled by the audacity of my scheme.'

He put the rest of the tart into his mouth and chewed away.

He immediately picked up another. 'Mr Marsh-Hare,' he said, and his face took on a stony countenance. He poisoned the tart and ate it in a few quick bites. This tart had once been made of lime, and its bitterness inflamed his envy. 'He has slighted me by proposing to the lovely Alison, when I myself had once thought about doing so; I find that to be an insult I cannot forgive.'

Finally he picked up a tart that had once been lemon curd; he sprinkled it with the poison and ate it whole, and the sourness of the taste reminded him of the doctor's scepticism. He thought hard about it, aiming the tart's poison in the doctor's direction.

'If you had believed me I might have shown mercy and done it quickly, to lose the only witness. Instead I will chew on this slowly, so your death is the most lingering and hurtful,' he said, scattering crumbs everywhere. He screwed up his face in frustration, and cast his attentions towards the laughing party about the croquet hoops.

Once Jack Heart had eaten all three tarts, he brushed himself down, and looked about at the party with satisfaction.

'Nobody shall know!' he said. And he rejoined the festivities while he waited for his victims to succumb.

With a few gestures of his hand he communicated with the musicians to play an energetic polka.

He began the dancing by holding out his arm gallantly to Lady Red and there were cries of delight; everyone wanted to dance, and how wonderful that this had begun! They were quickly surrounded with well-wishers and celebrants.

Jack Heart and Lady Red waltzed together for a few steps until, just before they turned a corner by the bandstand, he felt a gloved hand tapping on his shoulder.

'There you are, Jack!' the eccentric milliner held out her arms to him. As if grateful for the distraction, Lady Red let go and spun away, complaining lightly of a headache.

Jack watched her go, with a smile spreading over his face.

'It is beginning!' he said.

'What?' said the milliner, as she began dancing with him. Then she leaned in towards him and said accusingly: 'I invited you to my tea party but you never came!'

'That is because I never celebrate on my birthday,' he said. 'There was no offence intended to you, none at all. I hope you understand.'

'I did not know it was your birthday!'

'As I am orphaned, I do not know when my birthday is. But on that day I did not want to celebrate; so it could well have been.'

'I see,' said the milliner, and her oversized hat slipped further sideways on her head as they danced. 'Well that seems fair enough to me, I suppose.'

Mr Marsh-Hare and the lovely Alison danced past them. Alison looked as charming as ever in her sky-blue dress; but Mr Marsh-Hare looked sweaty and troubled.

'Are you quite all right?' he heard Alison ask him.

'Funny you ask, for I'm feeling quite curious,' said Mr Marsh-Hare. 'Perhaps I am simply overheating.'

Lady Red spun back into Jack Heart's arms. 'I say, I was just speaking with the doctor – he tells me you frightened the life out of him!'

'I do not wish to *frighten* the life out of anyone.'

'He said you're off your head. Can you believe that? *Off your head!* You'll be pleased to know I defended you. I said: you're simply a card, that is all!'

Jack Heart laughed, and with a bow he released Lady Red so she could dance with someone else. 'But how is your headache?' he asked, as she began to twirl away.

'Oh, much better, thank you,' she called. 'I did feel strange, I will admit… but I've taken one of the doctor's delightful draughts of something-or-other, and the pain has gone right away!'

The dancing was speeding up, and Jack was surrounded by swirling fabrics and the sound of merry laughter. He looked about until he found the doctor, who was the picture of health beside the buffet table, laughing with a lemonade. Beside him, Mr Marsh-Hare and the lovely Alison were an image of happiness also.

'Perhaps it was a hint of what's to happen,' said Jack to himself. 'Symptoms that come and go, that sort of thing. Yes, that must be it! Lull them into a false sense of security before their sudden tragic end. I'm about to see the last of them; in fact, it is happening right now; I feel dizzy myself with what must be my oncoming victory. Yes, yes; I can feel the moment approaching – I am losing track of where is down and where is up – my goodness, it is powerful stuff – it is as if I am sinking into an endless rabbit-hole!'

Jack Heart ran into the centre of the party, laughed aloud in triumph and then fell flatly to the ground, perfectly dead.

He opened one eye.

Mr Marsh-Hare was standing over him. 'What are you doing down there old boy? You don't look at all well.'

The doctor pushed his way to the front of the crowd that had quickly gathered. 'This buffoon's just taken a vial of his own poison,' he said, to gasps of horror. 'He's probably trying to kill us all! Albeit going about it in the most backwards fashion you'd ever believe,' he added in a mutter. He began pushing up his sleeves.

'There is no need for concern!' cried a new voice. The milliner joined the doctor at Jack Heart's side.

'Don't get too worried,' she said. 'He's going to be just fine. It was I who sold him his powder. In my trade I know a thing or two about toxicants and I wasn't about to sell anything too strong to this fellow, given the crap he was spouting about inverse revenge.'

'Well well,' said the doctor. 'This is all for the better. Get up, man! You're making the lawn a mess.'

'Oh no,' said Jack Heart, disappointed. The frustrated doctor started gently kicking him in the ribs, while the other guests looked on.

'Oh dear,' said the trout with almonds.

'When it comes to new ideas, experiment at your own peril,' said the cucumber sandwiches.

The Diamond Twenty Thousand Times Bigger Than the Ritz

Some advice I've never heeded: whatever you do, *whatever you do*, avoid your mysterious neighbour and his glamorous parties. Here's a better suggestion: he's had all the advantages you didn't, so go for it. See how the other 0.000078% of the other half live.

I knew I couldn't be the only one who hadn't been invited and my good friend Pearl insisted I join her; she said she knew him personally. She'd popped in for a drink and a snoop, mentioned the bash; *I'd* mentioned that I knew nothing about it.

'You *must* come,' she said, gesturing wildly about, making the ice clink in the tumbler and drops of blue liquor spill over my table, where it fizzed audibly and burnt through the varnish. 'You *must* come and you can join my contingent. You're living on the same planet now, after all, it's only right you're seen at one of his dos. It's the *danse élémentaire* – easily the best night of the calendar.'

And so on. She kept up her pretence of jolly peer-pressure but I was already set on attending, so I let her convince me. I hadn't been long in the area; I wanted to see what was what. Nothing wrong with that. Everyone looks out for illuminous nights.

So we all clambered into Pearl's open-top motor, which was powder-blue and had great oversized headlamps on the orbiter, the chrome bits polished until they shone. The breeze whipped past us as she rocketed wildly through the night, her hands in gloves of pale leather, erratic on the wheel, turning around to continue the pleasant chatter with those in the back and not looking at all where she was going while the night sky, in all its starstruck majesty, spread out before us above the dash.

She'd sat me next to her and we found time to reminisce about days gone by, when she was no one and I was even more anonymous, those fustering studying years of molecular-chem post-post-postdocs (she'd sailed; I'd waded) and nights at the Crystalline with its softly glowing cocktails. Now look at her, and I was still anonymous. Too late I realised my shoes were half a size too tight, but it was good to see her again. We'd always had a bond. We'd had – dare I say it – chemistry.

A wrought-iron gate swung open and we were speeding along a path edged with neatly clipped box hedges. It was a great sweeping curving path, the sort of path that promises you're absolutely arriving somewhere. Pebbles of moonstone and jet made popping noises and the anti-gravity flared out quartz-coloured steam.

'We're nearly there!' cried Pearl.

And then: 'There it is – did you ever see the like!'

We all craned our necks to see it first. Suddenly, it rose as we dipped over a hill.

I was first struck not by the mansion's height, although there can be no question that it towered imposingly, but by the sheer number of its windows: so many windows, neatly aligned from wall to wall, bottom to top. Things were already in full swing. I could hear music, distorted but audible and full of brass, and, with the exception of the tower on the right which was in darkness, all those windows were lit with the brightness of a party begun, their shadows dynamic with dancing shapes.

Rising towers on either side framing the great blockiness of the architecture...

I heard Pearl laughing as I gasped with recognition. That neat grid of numbers and letters, the Table I'd been familiar with all my life, was suddenly rising up before me – transformed into the front plan of a building.

'How often does he host the Elemental Ball?' I asked, finding my voice again.

'Oh, you know, now and then,' she said. 'Periodically.'

I found out later that the mansion had, in fact, one hundred and *twenty* rooms, for at the back was a small entrance-hall, adjoined to a tiny waiting room for deliveries. But they were sparsely decorated, and scarcely talked about. The real interest and point of the mansion was the other one hundred and eighteen, of course.

An entrance on the ground floor took us into Copernicium (it made sense, Pearl said, to go in via a transition metal), where we found ourselves surrounded by whirling dancers in beaded dresses, and cocktail waitresses in black tailcoats and high heels, pouring drinks from silver shakers.

'Come on, let's go up,' she said, raising her voice over the noise. 'There's so much to see between here and the Alkali tower.'

We went straight up, into Mercury, where the lighting was darker and there was headiness to the scent, as people danced through a haze of perfume.

Don't mistake me. I'm saying *rooms* but each was considerable in size, big enough for a whole party in itself – every room was a ballroom, as if the mansion were made up solely of great huge dance halls it took minutes at a time to cross, especially factoring in the need to battle the crowds; for each elemental chamber was filled with party-goers, beckoning each other to come dancing or waving bottles of fizz, and mirrorballs glinted off jewel-encrusted dresses, beaded headbands and the spangled decorations that hung about.

Pearl and I stood there in Mercury. Our other companions melted away, towards a door that had *Au* printed upon it in peeling gilt. Rich light gave them all dramatic silhouette for a moment as they opened the door, and I was tempted to follow – but Pearl beckoned me to her instead, and we kept going up.

'You're lucky; I'm taking you straight to the top,' she said as we went, the light catching the threads of silver in her silk scarf. 'We're going through the transition metals – we can stop at Iron briefly if you wish, take in the view, it's got a lovely balcony – but my goal for us is the highest of Alkali.'

'What an extraordinary place,' I said, watching a contortionist hang from the chandelier by one foot.

'What you can't see from the outside,' said Pearl, with all the happy arrogance of one who knows such things, 'are the two more floors dug down into the cellars. That's where the more experimental and, shall we say, *unstable* partying occurs.'

I took a drink from a fellow passing by with a tray. The liquid was full of bubble and spark, and made me feel immediately more equipped to look upon the tumultuous richness of my surroundings.

Pearl laughed at the sight of me. 'You seem so well-behaved and bashful now,' she said. 'Before too long you'll think nothing of getting tied up and blindfolded down in Plutonium. But we're going *up*, first-off, because I want to introduce you to our host. I wish to show off my social cachet, quite frankly, and as an added bonus it'll prove you're not arriving uninvited.'

'Rot that,' I said, the bubbles in my drink lifting my confidence. 'I'm an honest person. I'll tell him I wasn't invited!'

The revelry around us grew quieter, and I could tell drinks were being gripped a little tighter; there was a strange sudden sense of everyone waiting for something.

Pearl leaned into me and spoke in an urgent whisper.

'*I shall not be doing that because our host does not tolerate gatecrashing,*' she said. 'On pain of… well, I don't know what on pain of but he doesn't want it, that's for sure. Stick an olive in me and down me like a dry martini if I'm mistaken.'

I smiled briefly at the mental image, but was intrigued more by the inference. It didn't seem quite real. 'Does he really hate unexpected guests as much as that?'

I looked around the party; it seemed as if everyone in the whole universe had made their way here tonight, and all the time more were pulling up in their motorcars and long-haul rockets. They were zooming in over the interplanetary expressway. He couldn't possibly have invited them all individually. *Some* of that had to be down to word of mouth, no?

Pearl sensed my confusion, and her face softened. 'It's one gate-crasher in particular he's worried about. Only did it once, as far as I know, but it mightily spooked him. Claimed to be dressed as the God Particle and got him into a fine old flap. He's been looking out for their return with half an eye ever since. So anyone who *has* shown up on the jolly must absolutely not mention it. Nobody really knows why but when he throws such a bash as this, who's to argue the toss?' We had made some headway by now, going along the rooftop path across the middle of the mansion. Pearl pointed up to the tower that rose up before us. Fireworks were sparkling all around it.

'Hydrogen penthouse,' she said. 'Tallest spot in the place where he can look down over the rest of us. He'll be in his element up there.'

Predictably, it was a high point of my evening. Hydrogen offered a view of the house and grounds stretching out all the way to the horizon, where the next mansion along glinted like a faint star – the vista before us, all of it, belonged to our host, and the endless parade of his guests' glittering vehicles streamed down the curving roads towards us. It was as if Pearl and I had stepped into a great inverted glass bowl.

Before us a lone figure stood facing the window. Even with his back to me I felt underdressed; his was a suit you could cut yourself on.

He turned around on hearing our footsteps and greeted us both like old friends, while the night sky exploded with shiny fireworks all around him. He shook my hand warmly enough as Pearl introduced us ('You can tally this one up with my other plus-ones, which I suppose makes him a plus-four? Anyway, he's with me and fully vetted,') and then, quite quickly, my sense of his conviviality somehow faded. I detected a slight heaviness in his voice, and there was a frown somewhere about his eyes that gave his countenance a certain sense of being pinched from the inside.

'It's a pleasure to see you,' he said, and I suppose he was officially addressing me, but even as he spoke he was once more looking out at the view.

Falling back on niceties, I said: 'Marvellous place you have here.'

'I built it up myself,' he said. 'A lot of experimentation and a great deal of patience. Don't think it's always been like this. My several-dozen-greats grandfather lived in a two-up-two-down; earth air fire etc. But one has to begin somewhere, and look at where we find ourselves today...' He spoke the words as if he were following a script while late for a train; a more preoccupied man I had rarely seen.

He wandered back to stand before the glass. I followed and stood beside him, while Pearl kept the tone light; spinning tales about the friends they both knew, opining on what the people we'd passed in Alkaline Earth were calling high fashion at the moment, weighing up what the rising price of rocket fuel was doing to industry these days.

He seemed a little calmer when he was able to stare out of the window. Although we could see so much from up here, the movement and gaiety of the party felt more distant, somehow dampened down.

There was a blot in the starry sky.

'What is that?' I said.

For a moment he looked surprised at my interruption, then his face softened into something more amenable.

'You, my friend, are the first to notice! That is the show-stopping climax of tonight's soiree.'

Pearl twisted her fingers through her necklace. 'That's the size of a small planet, my love. What sort of climax are you planning?'

'A large one, naturally.'

Pearl had made her trillions in the terraforming business; I wasn't surprised to see a flash of interest blaze over her features. 'How did you get a sign-off for a modification to that level? You'll *have* to give me the name of your supplier.'

Our host grabbed me by the shoulders. 'What exactly do you see, out there?'

I'm an honest person; I tried to answer honestly. 'I see a sort of big, heavy nothing,' I said.

'Exactly. That moon wasn't going anywhere of note, was it? Certainly wasn't doing anything interesting. I found it on an idle orbit out in the sticks and had it towed over. What is a moon, anyway? We can improve on such things.'

'I can't make out a moon at all. That looks like a moonless sky to my eyes.'

'You don't see it *now* because it is clamped all about with interstellar equipment, hyper-industrial grade. Imagine a nutcracker machine, with a vice that can hold whole equators.'

'Oh my,' I said, and Pearl's smile showed teeth.

Our host grew more animated as he spoke. 'There's a moon out there, all right. At least for the moment. That device mimics the effect of many millions of years of heat and pressure in only a few short fractions of the time. My guests have no idea they're about to witness the ultimate finale to a fireworks display: when I shall unveil, right before them, the greatest diamond in the galaxy! Perhaps of all time. *Tonight* – all that remains is to remove the supporting frame and do you know, I'm fired up, let's do it right now.

'And *then* we'll see who's a spectacle of themselves,' he said, not really very much under his breath at all.

He recovered himself and smiled. 'I'm not only thinking short-term, of course. Just imagine how desirable property is about to become on the planet with a huge great diamond for a moon.'

He went out onto the balcony. The grounds shimmered as the crowd of party guests looked up at him from the lawns, raising their cocktail glasses. He raised a glass back in a sort of salute, and then turned his attention to a panel beside him I hadn't noticed before; all sleek chrome and glowing buttons. He pressed one.

A trio of huge great lamps came on in the grounds, sending beams of white across the dark sky until they hit the metallic shape that hovered above us. Illuminated, it really did look like he'd trapped something infinitely vast, right above our heads. The sky was filled with it.

He pressed a few buttons more, and there was an almighty crumbling crash, like a thunderstorm taking over the whole weather-system with the whole weather-system with enveloping the world at the top of its agenda. The crusher opened a crack and a gleam became visible, and then, with a series of pneumatic hisses and metal-clanking judders, the machinery lowered itself down and opened itself out. It parted like a clamshell until what hung in the sky was neither moon nor machine but clearly and unambiguously diamond, a great dazzling smooth rainbow-white diamond of impossible proportions, glowing softly over us, hovering like a geometric bright miracle, the whole mansion lit up with the gleam of it. Our host covered his eyes to take in the sound of growing, and soon absolutely roaring, applause.

'It's a wonder,' said Pearl. Quietly to me, she added: 'Do you know what my first thought was? Add a gold band to that.'

Our host removed his hands from his eyes to stretch his arms out and bask in the adoration, and at the very moment his hands were fully stretched his face became a rictus of fear, and he raced to the balcony and leaned over it at such a sharp angle I felt he might topple over. I followed his gaze. A long white starcruiser limousine was zooming steadily through the grounds of the mansion.

'It's *her!*' he said, his voice a ghastly whisper. 'Stop – *must* stop her coming in.' He took several woozy steps backwards until he leaned against the thick glass wall of the penthouse. He sank to the floor, muttering. 'She mustn't come in.'

Pearl knelt beside him and began loosening his tie. She looked up at me. 'Go and stop her, will you? Nobody knows who you are and nobody else has the faintest what's going on yet. You'll slip through the crowds easily.'

I remembered again that my shoes were too tight, but I followed her words immediately. I raced down the steps, to the top of the Alkaline Earth tower, ignoring the pinch in my toes all the way down the steep stairs that took me back to the transition metals. I went through the rooms, which were still full of party and revelry, looking out of every window I passed, the view newly brightened with the glow of the great diamond, watching the crowds swirl around the approaching limousine. Through the window in Cobalt I saw a door opening near the back of the long white vehicle. A woman in a shining evening dress got out and walked smoothly towards the mansion, the crowds parting to let her through – or perhaps recoiling backwards; it was tricky to tell.

I raced down and down again, almost tripping several times in my haste, trying to ignore my shoes pressing into my heels.

Before I reached the ground floor I started turning corners, going up and down and tracing out a path – it was the thought of a moment to know exactly where I needed to go. I could detect the sound of gleeful uproar curdling, joyful music turning into discord, glasses being smashed for the wrong reasons.

I entered a room where a group of partygoers stood facing a woman in a shining dress. She had her back to me. I planned to creep up and surprise her, but somehow I lost my footing in those damn shoes and bumped into a pyramid of champagne glasses; it made an audible chorus of chimes. She turned her head slightly to follow the noise, and must have seen enough to realise my presence and know my purpose. Off she ran, straight through the line of revellers and further into the party.

I was right behind her. Her dress was low in the back and made of silk that could have been woven entirely of chrome thread, such was the way it caught the light. She wore her platinum hair loose and long, and it trailed out behind her as she ran.

She tore through the party, and I followed.

Twice, three times I reached out to grasp her shoulder, but always she slipped from me. In the Zirconium hall, she stopped beside the martini-fountain, turned and looked directly behind her. It brought me up short: I stopped too. For a few seconds we stared at each other. It seemed she was smiling at me, mockingly so, but in truth I couldn't make anything out through her intricate silver mask. And all the rooms had their great windows, of course, through which the impossible diamond waited: the brightest moon, adding drama to our shadows.

I followed her up to Titanium, then through Scandium and Calcium, and then up through the rooms of the Alkali Tower – and only then did I realise she wouldn't let me reach her before she got to our host.

By the time she disappeared up into the Hydrogen penthouse my breath was coming heavily and my feet were screaming a protest of their own. I ascended once more into the great skydome, but too late.

Our host was at the furthest end, practically pressing himself into the wall to get away, and Pearl stood beside him. Between us all was the gate-crasher. Pearl glared across at me with the disappointment we reserve only for our closest friends.

'And what of it?' our host was shouting, as the new arrival took another step towards him. I was feeling very familiar with the back of her dress by now, especially as I still hadn't seen her face.

He had the frightened energy of a fellow cornered. 'How could you try to take this moment from me? I won't let you – you can't!'

The gate-crasher reached up and took off her mask.

I have thought about the following moment many times since and have come to believe the phenomenon I will describe to you had something to do with angles. What *seemed* to happen was our host was suddenly blasted with a new and terrible brightness, a much more intense dazzle than when he unveiled the diamond. The new surge of light came either from the diamond itself or perhaps some scattered beams reflected from a multitude of other sources I had not noticed, my attention focussed upon the cumulative effect. He reached up to cover his eyes.

For a moment the two of them were pinned to the spot. Then our host staggered backwards.

'Damn you!' He squinted into the brightness. 'You did warn me – didn't you? – that you'd show up and ruin it all!' He began to laugh. 'You know I almost dared you here, practically summoned you, doing this. Perhaps that's exactly what I did!'

And, while the gate-crasher waited unmoving, the whole place swimming with light, he went out to the balcony.

With a shaking hand he pulled a lever on the control panel and the pneumatic machinery whipped into action, coming back up to cover the diamond. It gripped the jewel on either side and the sudden darkening made new shapes swim across my vision.

Our host kept his hand on the handle until everything started to shake, and a few sparks zipped from beneath his fingers. Eventually it became possible to hear a groaning sound coming from the sky and through the thick glass walls.

'What's he doing?' I said, not quite knowing who I was talking to: everything was becoming so extreme and I had to say *something*, I suppose, to prove to myself I was still there. 'Can he reverse the procedure?'

Shadows moved as Pearl shook her head. 'He knows he can't. That's not it.'

The diamond exploded. It filled the sky, and suddenly we were all of us plunged into a world of dappled, shimmering crystals of light. I found myself waving my hands in front of my face, as if the room itself had been filled with sharp splinters of the stuff that I might usher away. This carried on for an amount of time impossible to count, until I noticed the gate-crasher had vanished.

Our host ran out of the room.

For a moment it was only Pearl and me, looking at each other across the illusion of infinite pieces of shattered diamond.

She came to me, through the light, and put her hand on my shoulder. 'Thank you for your efforts,' she said. 'Frankly I doubt she could have been stopped by anyone. Besides, what kind of party would it be without a few surprises?'

'But he destroyed it.'

'Of course he did! Didn't you see how she looked at him?'

I stared outside, lost for speech, at the fragments that filled the sky, jostling for attention with the stars, like a scattered, shattered galaxy.

I consider myself a rational person. 'This is all too much for me,' I said. 'I'm going to reach her this time. I want answers. I think I can do it. '

'My dear, everyone thinks so. And answers to *what*?'

But I was already running. Pearl shouted something at me as I left the glassy penthouse, but I didn't hear what it was.

Once again it seemed as if I were intuiting exactly where to go; but when I think of it now, she must have been waiting for me at the foot of the stairs. I saw a flash of her luminous gown and we were off again, chasing through the metals across the mansion and into the metalloids, and when we reached Arsenic I knew I wasn't alone in the chase, that this time the word had got out about who had spoiled the party and I was heading a crowd and everyone reached out to her as she ran, but each grasp just missed her, she bolted clean through the attempted blockades, the force of momentum pushing through linked arms, upending the tables, spilling the fizz; nobody could catch her.

She tore through Phosphorus with dancers falling to the floor to get out of her way, then Sulphur, scattering the coals that thickened the smoke, and then Chlorine (upending the tables and spilling salt everywhere), until she came to the door that led through into Argon and I thought: *aha, you're trapped now*, for the door into Argon was locked. Pearl had explained it to me: all the rooms in this wing were kept in stillness and darkness, with sheets over the furniture, for this part of the mansion stood for the noble gases; and so it remained fastened, and it was forbidden to enter the Helium penthouse at the top. My feet panged again in my shoes but I laughed because I knew I could catch her now.

Then, instead of trying to enter the locked room, she went down.

I'd got her, surely. She was still running, ultimately, towards locked doors, she couldn't smoothly go through into Oganesson on the ground floor, so we'd got her, and naturally as she and I descended through the metals everyone got more reactive, and a group burst out in an ambush, throwing paper streamers and firecrackers up into the air, catching her in the middle –

But she quickly slipped by and turned, running towards the door to outside and I followed, gaining on her all the time –

The fresh air hit me, and it was brighter here, the light moving I chased her across the gravel –

Her dress was mere inches in front of me –

A mob of revellers burst upon her, and she was surrounded –

My fingers *just* touched the glittering fabric at the back of her dress –

And the silk was fluttering down in front of me, empty.

I blinked in the light of all the drifting shards of diamond. A piece caught my vision, appearing to move at ease through the sky but in truth racing at colossal speed: it had all the facets of a grand hotel but must have been heaven knows how many times the size. As if I were hovering along with it, I felt myself looking down from above at the partygoers as we stood around the empty dress that lay there on the grass, the silver shoes lying sideways and no sign of their owner, only empty champagne bottles and confetti stars scattered as far as you could see. Uncertainty had torn through the neatly patterned rooms, and here all of us gathered, in the effort to get to the single soul trying to play God.

Mrs Pepper's Ghost

Of all the ghosts appearing that season in theatres across the creaky town of Trippingly-on-the-Tongue, most agreed the spirit hovering about the wings of the Repertory was fast becoming the biggest nuisance.

It began by appearing on the stage very briefly, and always just before the interval. The more pragmatic theatre-goers took it as a cue to rise from their seats and get in early for ice-creams.

The proprietor of the Trippingly Rep did not mind the ghost at first, as she was convinced these momentary flickers brought character to the place. But quickly it became a problem.

'Did you see it?' she would hear punters ask each other as they left the theatre. 'High point of the show, I'd say!'

Its appearances became sporadic, unpredictable, flashing across the stage *exactly* as the detective named the murderer: 'Now I've missed who did it!'

Soon it was on stage for whole scenes at a time: 'My aunt thought it was part of the plot!'

And as the snow fell over panto season, cries of *it's behind you* were far too frequent.

This wouldn't do. Mrs Pepper had successfully navigated the Trippingly Rep through many a disastrous season: box-office flops, last-minute replacements, emergency closures; there had been the year of the actors' strike, when she had played many of the parts herself; there had been the summer of the heatwave, when nobody wanted to sit in hot darkness and watch a play (discounted ice-lollies had come to the rescue there); and there had been fraught rivalries with other theatres, which was something Mrs Pepper felt particularly proud of seeing off. The Trippingly Rep, thanks to her vivid and varied programme of entertainment, had overtaken the town's more prestigious Trippingly Grand in popularity. All its gilt-and-velvet splendour proved no match! She was certainly not about to lose her Rep to so insubstantial a problem as a *ghost*.

There was no denying that audiences seemed more interested in the ghost than the plays themselves. To counter this, Mrs Pepper decided to put on a very famous play, a classic they would definitely want to pay attention to, and chose the great tragedy *Tarquin of Rome*. She spent a lengthy teatime convincing a local legendary actor to leave retirement and play the title role. Rehearsals went well, with the rest of the company honoured to play alongside such a celebrity and spurred on to do their best. Expectations were high – until opening night, when the ghost appeared during Act One Scene One, in the guise of the legendary actor himself, but a younger version – from when he had first played the role, many years ago.

The actor tried to ignore it, but his distraction was clear. In Act Two Scene Four the ghost appeared as the most famous actor to *ever* play Tarquin, hovering sinisterly as the actor struggled through the lines, sometimes even speaking over him. The rhapsody of the ghost's delivery, evoking a performance from nearly a century ago, made the poor fellow on the stage nearly inaudible. For the rest of the play the ghost continued to reappear as various other Tarquins, and Mrs Pepper's actor spent the whole night navigating through them.

'We'll go the other way,' said Mrs Pepper, who was not to be deterred. 'If the ghost is bothering my canonical drama, let's try a crowd-pleaser. It might be a cultural snob.' And so posters went up announcing the Rep would that night play one of the most popular pieces in its programme, the outrageous farce *The Kicked*

Bouquet, set in a florists struggling to provide for multiple weddings on the same day as a funeral (for a man who was faking his death).

But that did not work either. The play moved through its series of misunderstandings, plot steadily gaining absurdity and speed – and in the second half the ghost appeared in a vicar's collar, which was coming loose, as it ran from door to door and back again, ghostly trousers around its ankles, confusing the audience as to what belonged to *this* farce and what was the play. The curtain call was a mixture of applause and confused muttering, and the actors went home glum.

Drastic measures were now called for. The following day, alone in the theatre (more or less), Mrs Pepper unlocked her desk and opened the secret compartment, from with she withdrew a faded letter from the previous proprietor of the Rep, recommending a course of action for exactly this emergency. Then she went down to the darkened props store, following the letter's directions until she found a corner that had not been touched for many years, and rummaged around until finding the object she was looking for. She held it out before her and examined it.

'How curious,' she said. Then she frowned. 'And oddly familiar.'

Finally, she dispatched missives to the stage crew to meet in the theatre that afternoon.

'I have an answer to our current problem,' she announced, standing centre stage. She held up a diagram drawn on the back of an old playbill. 'Can you make me something like this?'

The crew stood in a semicircle around Mrs Pepper. Beside her was a sheet covering a bulky shape: the object she had found hidden in the props store.

'Shouldn't be too difficult,' said the head carpenter, peering at the diagram. 'What's that, a mirror?'

'Better than that and even simpler,' said Mrs Pepper. 'It is a pane of glass. We shall place it beneath the stage, angled to reflect the action above. Strength of the limelight will ensure it *acts* as a mirror, and then it shall merely be a matter of keeping watch.'

She looked around the company as the same doom-laden thought settled upon all of them. There was a long pause, and an anxious shuffling of feet.

'This is to do with getting rid of the – *presence*, miss?' asked one of the more superstitious stagehands, knotting her fingers together over her pinafore.

'You have it exactly,' said Mrs Pepper, smiling. 'And we can ensure our efforts will be successful. By using this.' She pulled the cloth away, and the assembled stagehands gasped at the sight of the contraption.

It was made from brass and resembled a blunderbuss, with a greater number of pipes than might be expected on a blunderbuss and with the addition of several valve-like buttons similar to those on a trumpet. The end of the barrel widened out like a gramophone, or a metallic flower seeking the sun.

'I'll be depending on you all to hold your nerve,' said Mrs Pepper. 'This will be a true test of our powers of stagecraft.'

'Sounds like forbidden stagecraft to me,' and, 'Dangerous business, that.' Mutters of this kind rippled across the company, but Mrs Pepper overrode their reluctance with the promise of a ghost-free existence.

'Besides,' she added. 'I shall be the one operating the device. The rest of you have nothing to fear. Just help me set it up.'

That evening, during the performance of *Tarquin of Rome*, Mrs Pepper stood beneath the stage, balancing the ungainly gun on her hip. Before her, leaning against the far wall of what would have been the orchestra pit, was a pane of glass. One of the carpenters had detached it earlier from a window he hadn't been using. The theatre itself was a full house, and Mrs Pepper could feel the warmth and energy of hundreds of restless spectators. Her chest butterflied with anticipation.

Up there on the boards, the legendary actor crept along holding a lantern out before him, exploring a spooky ruined fortress. This was a famous scene: Tarquin's big monologue.

The theatre ghost appeared, this time looking exactly like the legendary actor when he played this scene a few nights ago. The audience murmured with recognition. The ghost copied how the actor had moved about the stage, going left when the actor, tonight, went right, and making similar gestures but slightly out of time. Suddenly the ghost strode forward with determination, which the actor was too alarmed to do, and so the ghost passed right through him. From the balcony came a few cries of alarm at the sight.

'All right, that's quite enough of that,' said Mrs Pepper, and she turned the contraption on.

For several moments nothing visibly happened, but the brass grew warm beneath her hands. The actor continued to totter through the lines up on the stage, followed closely by the pale image of how he had done it previously. Sharp blue electric light emanated from the contraption's widened end, getting steadily brighter until it shone fully on the pane of glass and made it glow. Mrs Pepper watched the glass carefully until the image of the ghost was there, perfectly reflected from the stage.

The actor said a particularly famous line, and the ghost raised its arm triumphantly. Mrs Pepper flicked the switch.

The entire theatre was bathed in blue light.

Crackles and sparks shot from the blunderbuss, bounced off the glass and made straight for the ghost, who seemed to explode in a shower of shimmers. The light was blinding; everyone in the theatre covered their eyes.

When Mrs Pepper opened hers, the light in the theatre had returned to normal. And the ghost was there before her, trapped within the pane of glass.

'Hard to imagine it going much better!' cried the legendary actor, raising his drink to everyone. 'Thank goodness we got through the rest of the play without any drama.'

Mrs Pepper nodded her agreement, but couldn't stop herself frowning a little. She had noticed just how politely the audience had applauded after the play, how quietly they had filed out of the theatre. She put it down to their being overwhelmed by the spectacle of it all, but couldn't deny that she'd hoped for a standing ovation.

'What did you do with the beasty?' asked one of the younger actors, who had decided to keep wearing his cricket whites from the matinee.

The famous actor raised his eyebrows, still in his laurel wreath from *Tarquin*. 'Good point. Where did it go?'

'Never you mind,' said Mrs Pepper. 'Somewhere it will never bother any of us again.' And the whole company cheered.

That evening, when the actors had gone home and the final stagehand had locked the doors for the night and departed, Mrs Pepper lit a candle in her otherwise darkened office and approached the curtain that newly hung upon the wall. She tugged on the rope and drew the curtain. There hung the pane of glass, with the ghost still trapped inside it.

'Thought you'd outsmarted me, didn't you?' Mrs Pepper wagged a finger at it. 'Thought you could interfere with my plays and face no consequence? Well, let's see how you like it. You're going to hang there on my wall and see how my theatre flourishes without your meddling.'

The ghost only looked at her through a wavering eye. It did not look squashed exactly, but might prefer freedom regardless.

Feeling triumphant, Mrs Pepper closed the curtain over it and went home for supper.

The Trippingly Rep continued its ghost-free season, putting on a great range of plays, none of which were interrupted or suffered any spoiled effects. The theatre continued to play to full houses and receive positive notices in the *Trippingly Post*. But it was becoming clear that something, somehow, was ever so slightly wrong, that a night of entertainment at the Rep was losing its lustre. Responses were more muted, laughter was polite, applause hesitant. Mrs Pepper could overhear confusion as audiences left the theatre, asking each other what had happened or what a particular moment had signified, or even admitting they'd nodded off.

After *The Tragedy of Lancelot and Gwenivere* (of all things) had, like everything else, played to indifference, Mrs Pepper stormed into her office, pulled the rope that opened the curtain and angrily faced the ghost.

'You've been doing something to my theatre,' she said. 'I don't know what, but things are altered. Worse.'

'How can I do anything from in here?' said the ghost. It held its palms up innocently. Disgusted, Mrs Pepper drew the curtains back over the glass and stalked down to see the actors. They were in costume already for *Length by Width by Death*, a murder mystery set in a quantity surveyors.

'All right,' she said, as she faced the cast in the dressing room. 'Tonight I want you to give it all you've got. Make the Trip Rep proud.' But something in the tone of her words sounded hollow and she felt it miss the mark, while the actors stood there wanly, stripped of all energy. Their performance that night was dire – resembling a tired group of exhausted people, going through the motions of something dull, having long forgotten their reason for doing it. The meagre applause hadn't even died away when Mrs Pepper drew the curtain and spoke to the ghost again.

'What are you playing at?' she snarled, as the ghost looked back at her with blurry, wobbling eyes. 'Why doesn't anyone seem to know or care what they're doing any more?'

'It's just like I said. What can I do for you while I'm in here? It's no surprise to me your audiences are all lost. Without me, there's nothing to remind them of what they're watching or why. So they forget; and the actors, too.'

'Forget *what*? What do they need to be reminded of?'

'Why, anything and everything that has gone before, on your stage or any other.'

'What do you mean?'

'Theatre,' said the ghost, in a voice full of pomposity, 'is a cultural technology of ritual and repetition above all else. When you watch a play, you don't just watch: you *remember*. Now you've done this to me, how does anyone have the foggiest idea what they're looking at? No wonder something feels off. You've stripped your stage of time, and everyone can feel it.'

Mrs Pepper put her hands on her hips. 'You're the ghost of history-plays in history now, are you? The spirit of pantomimes yet to come? Don't give me any of that. You're nothing but a menace, and now you seem to have placed us all under some sort of curse. Well, turn it off. My theatre doesn't need you and my audiences certainly don't.'

'If you say so,' said the ghost. 'But might I suggest you'd've been better off thinking of me as an opportunity?'

'You're just trying to trick me into letting you out,' said Mrs Pepper, closing the curtain. 'I'll take you off the wall and throw you into the Tongue before I do that.'

The ghost continued to speak from behind the curtain. 'I can't get out,' it said, its voice muffled by the material. 'There's no reversing your little procedure. Now we both have to watch the theatre fail. For shame!'

That idea sat heavily with Mrs Pepper, a gnawing feeling that grew ever more dreadful. Performances were increasingly grim. The actors mumbled their words before half-empty stalls. They forgot their lines, and the prompt forgot to prompt, leading to even more emptiness. The stagehands got the set-changes wrong and nobody noticed, the furniture or backcloth clashing with scenes that were hardly happening anyway. Stragglers dotted about the near-empty theatre, whistling to themselves distractedly, and they left without applauding, sometimes long before the end. The final straw came when the posters announcing the plays for the following week, which Mrs Pepper had been very firm about and had told the printers the details of repeatedly, were pasted up completely blank.

Mrs Pepper stormed up the stairs into her office and once again faced the ghost.

'All right,' she said, her voice weary with defeat. 'You win. What do you want me to do?'

'There's nothing you can do,' said the ghost, its tone mournful. 'If I may be melodramatic for a moment, it's too late.'

'So you say?' Mrs Pepper looked around desperately.

In the corner of the office stood a bucket, which held an ancient set of carpenter's tools. She picked up the hammer, swinging it slightly to enjoy the weight at the end of her arm. Her eyes were wide. 'You'll do no more mischief from in there. I'll see to that.'

'I wouldn't if I were you.' The ghost's eyes on her were mocking, and it made some rude gestures along the flat plane of its thin existence. 'You won't fix anything that way.'

'That's what you think,' said Mrs Pepper, reaching back with her arm to get a full, good, clear swing. 'Watch this – and see what we remember!' And she smashed the hammer into the pane of glass.

A giant sound echoed through the theatre like sudden thunder.

In the dressing rooms, all the mirrors shattered. The lamps along the walls burst with a flare, the smoked glass cracking as it dropped to the floor. In the carpeted foyer all the windows smashed themselves to bits, and in the auditorium the great chandelier splintered into a thousand crystal droplets that showered onto the seats and lodged forever between the stage boards. Onstage, all the pasteboard windows over the scenery flats were wrenched in half, tearing like the flimsiest paper until the pieces floated down gently to the ground, and the wine and whisky glasses on the props drinks trolley popped and exploded, and the entire stage floor was suddenly veined with cracks. The company looked at each other for an alarmed moment – then as one they all raced off the stage, through the theatre, up the stairs, and along the corridor, until finally they arrived breathlessly into Mrs Pepper's office to find her there, standing among a thousand smithereens of glass, still holding the hammer, and laughing.

Helen/Hermione

Hot country, high summer: the sun's glare over an expanse of white sand, and the horizon shimmering. Thin silver line of the sea. Certainly, a sense of great distance.

A high outcrop looking over the rocks to the coast, and two figures. The wind pulls gently at robes of purple and yellow. Jewellery flashes in the sun.

Mother and daughter. It's long after the war.

'Do you know, after everything, what people ask me about the most?'

'Not your love life?'

Helen laughs, and leans out to peer further down the rocks. Hermione, as an act of support, tries to laugh too.

'They ask *you* that, perhaps. But that's the one thing people will contort themselves *not* to ask me about. They're almost afraid, I think. No, it's something much more prosaic. Silly really.'

Even at this distance, the sound of the sea.

Helen of Sparta became Helen of Troy, and a war followed. The most beautiful woman in the world; so the poets say, anyway. She has a daughter. Imagine that, Helen with a daughter. For that matter imagine having Helen of Troy for your mother.

'Say it then. We both know what it's going to be.'

'Ha! They *always* ask me about the ships!' Hermione laughs with genuine delight; Helen claps her hands.

'Such fascination with the size of the fleet.'

'How would I even *know*?'

If they were to meet like this, high on a cliff, long after the war. Helen, and her daughter Hermione. What would they say?

'It was never anywhere near a thousand, I know that much. Although it sounds impressive. It should be obvious, including to someone who wasn't there. Or at least you'd think so.'

'I always knew instinctively it wasn't a thousand. Impossible.'

They walk a little further, passing large rocks, some bearing script – the names of those who've been this way before.

'When they ask, how do you answer?'

'I say it's rounded up. It was eight hundred and four. They assume I have authority on the matter or realise I have no idea. Either way, they stop asking.'

Dust rises in the wake of their footsteps. 'And don't necessarily trust the answer.'

'It can be like that.'

What would they say, this woman and her daughter? And would we even tell who was speaking?

They come to a stop, looking out to the thin ribbon of coastline.

'I don't doubt people must want to ask me all kinds of things. The stories I could *surely* shed light on, being who I am... but they ask about that, then run out of conversation.'

'It would be worse for them, I suppose, to hear something that contradicts what they imagine.'

'Mm. Better not risk it then.'

Silence settles over them. Hermione fiddles with a gold bangle.

'After all, would you say this life has been an easy one?'

'Aside from the mess?'

Helen nods, and they both spend a minute looking off towards the sea.

'It is strange. To be so close to the centre of things and yet to feel absent.'

The waves break into sprays of white over the rocks, fizzing then draining away.

'It's been such a long time.'

'We've spent a long time apart by any measure, and no wonder, think how long it all *took*. Ten years before a war even began, all that preparation, it didn't happen instantly – *then* a whole decade of war; and a long journey back, and now finally here…'

White specks of boat sails move across the ocean.

'I was shocked when I first saw you.'

'How so?'

'How much you'd changed.'

The moment hangs.

'*Really?*'

'I know it sounds ridiculous. But I had to hold on to such… *young* memories for a long time. Tender memories. I didn't want to imagine how the years might change you.'

Some shouts come up from below; male voices on the beach.

'I always hoped I might learn from you.'

'Whatever could *I* teach *you?*'

The dry grasses are bending in the wind. More shouts from down below. It resembles battle cries and so there's no avoiding it now.

'So much death.'

'So much glory.'

'The sun glints off bronze, but also bleaches bone. The same people. It's all the same.' A deep sigh that was years in the writing. 'That's how I've come to see it.'

'Time has made you cynical.'

'Think yourself lucky you were never on the battlefield.'

'You think I don't know battlefields? That every step hasn't risked danger?'

A rising urgency in their voices brings a question. 'There's something I want to know that I think only you can answer.'

It's very much as if they make each other nervous.

'Go on.'

Helen takes a breath; Hermione keeps her expression controlled.

'Can you see it? In my face?'

'See what?'

'Can you see the most beautiful woman in the world?'

A moment of mutual examination.

'Is she there?' A touch of desperation.

Helen's face drops into sadness.

'Oh...'

'Sometimes I look in the mirror and... Where *are* those sounds coming from?'

They break off with relief to follow the noise. An echo of metal on metal reaches them from below, great blows carried all the way on the wind. Two soldiers at practice, sparring with one another on the sand. Helen points them out, the gold thread in her sleeves catching the sun. Hermione shades her eyes to get a better look.

'Which of them are you betting for?'

An eyebrow arches. 'Come on now. I know better than to answer a question like that.'

'Ha! Perhaps you *can* teach me something after all.'

'If you haven't learned it by now...'

At this distance, the clang of metal is out of time with the vision of the fight. Blade clashes on shield in painless dumbshow, then the sound of the blow.

The distraction has lifted Helen's mood. Hermione sees it, wonders at the effect.

'Can I ask? Do you feel any blame?'

A stiffness; some defensiveness here, walls raised. 'Should I?'

'Some guilt, perhaps, I would understand.'

'Nothing like that. I wasn't in control of how things turned out. How could I be? I live in the shadows of other people's decisions.'

'Everyone does. Think of it this way: you have been lucky enough to know as much.'

The soldiers give up fighting and stretch out in the sun, weapons down. They're not to blame; it's a time of peace, and the afternoon is chokingly hot.

'What do you long for?'

A wave bursts up over the rocks again.

'Now – or before?'

The sea swells.

'I used to long for it to all be over.'

'And now…?'

The breaking wave folds in on itself, pulling everything down with it.

'Do you feel…?' She bends to the ground, picks up a handful of the dry earth and lets it fall between her fingers. 'That you've been able to have an understanding of your life? – or do you feel it's been overshadowed by the scale of things around you, whether you feel part of them or not?'

Hermione and Helen stare at each other.

'You never answered my question.'

'I'm not sure I can.'

'*Try*, for gods' sake. What do you see when you look at me? Do you see the most beautiful woman? People look at me and I can see it's what they're searching for –'

'Yes, I know.'

'So you claim but you have no idea, *no idea* of the difficulty. They see *me* but they're looking for "Helen". They look through me – clean through me – they look at my features, they look around me, they see everything but who is there in front of them. She's a trap: like a costume. Something you'd choose now and again, certainly, but it doesn't fit you or perhaps it never really did, perhaps it was made for someone else. Certainly someone laid it out for you, and tied you to it before you could have a say. But there's no taking it off. Let's have another look at this possible "Helen". How thorough *is* the resemblance, or lack thereof?'

'I'm so sorry.'

'And I never asked for any of it.'

'Of course not. I know.'

Distant temple bells from the city.

'Sometimes...' She hesitates, unsure if this will be welcome. 'At times the likeness will be unmistakable?'

'Oh, yes. In the right light. If I am so inclined. I can decide to be seen that way. I have more control over that than people might imagine.'

'You can suddenly enter, as it were.'

'Sweep in after keeping them waiting. Or have my back to them, speak with them a while, busy myself pouring wine or gazing out at the world. Then, at the right moment, I can be coy and show my profile – or, depending on my mood, turn and fully look at them. Then I watch their reaction. "Can it be, do we see Helen here...?"'

A flock of birds pass overhead, singing out to each other.

'And then, what happens?'

The shadows of the birds flit across the grasses, quick and dark.

'They never quite see what they may have expected.'

The birdsong flutes through the air, mingling with the sound of crashing waves.

'People will always be searching. It mustn't make you sad. Think of it from their perspective. To feel you have the remotest chance to glimpse the most beautiful woman in the world. Of course they'll wonder if you're close to such a description.'

Scraps of cloud briefly cover the sun.

'That's the impossible thing, nobody is.'

Hermione looks down at her hands. Helen lightly pushes a stone about with her foot.

'The truth is, I've often wondered what my life would be without "Helen of Troy".'

A laugh of pure surprise. 'Ha! If *you* think that just imagine how *I* feel.'

They seem to be finding comfort with this agreement; if everything is not solved, exactly, they can at least clasp hands. Further up the hill, the rocky path takes them away and higher.

'I know the family has had its troubles.'

'Yes, all that.'

'Do you think we can put it behind us?'

The wind picks up, streaking through the heat of the air, lifting it slightly.

'I don't think we're in a world that wants to forget it.'

'Come now. Perhaps people will.'

'Would you really want that?'

'What? I'm not so proud. I'd relish the chance to live without all that –'

'You'd miss the legacy if it wasn't there.' They are making their way further over the rocks. 'To be a part of such a story. Which you *are* and you could never not be, even though you've been somehow hidden in the middle of it, and nobody knows what you really think, even if they try.'

'Are we both part of this?'

'Some people don't know Helen of Troy had a daughter. Never mind what I wanted, how I felt, what I did. It's not about that.'

Looked at, spoken for, spoken about, painted, drawn, carved; the sheer number of odes you wouldn't believe, some about the one body part even, I'll spare you the details; a dream museum, a pawn, a legend, the very idea of this woman inspiring tales in the thousands – now, you'd think the great Helen of Troy could finally tell all, but she's here with her daughter, and either of them could have said any of this, and all I can think about is the three of them, mother and daughter and legend, high up there on the rocks.

'Well, there you are. Right at the centre, and how many will know you? You have anonymity as well as its opposite.'

They climb on, taking a route that might, eventually, lead back to city walls.

The Arousing Adventures of Gelato Parlour

Hooray for Gelato Parlour!

I'm supposed to demonstrate narrator neutrality, I know. But I can't! Hooray for Gelato Parlour, I say.

There he is now, look: climbing up a drainpipe, rescuing a baby pigeon that fell from its nest, and kicking out his candy-striped trouser legs he's off, scampering over the rooftops.

Morning in the city. There's dew on the topiary, and nobody's turned the water features on yet. The sun is shining through the mists onto the awnings of the cafés, the large glass windows of the ballet school. A few jaunty street sweepers are skipping along, whistling. The nobility have only just gone to bed. So has our Gelato. But he's up, now! See – he just leapfrogged a chimney! Oh my!

He's making his way along the roof of the opera house. And there she is, the lady in the white lace nightgown opening her window and leaning out to wave a handkerchief at him as he goes. He blows a kiss before disappearing from her sight, sliding down the bunting from last week's festival with an improvised pulley made from one of his sock suspenders. She sighs and returns to her room, pulls the cover from the bluebird cage, prepares to begin the day. It will be another long one, signing endless political papers, trying to talk some sense into the Chancellor of the Exchequer, beating the Minister for Bricabrac at archery. Again. She takes one last look at the bed; and there –

oh look, oh yes, see what he's left on the pillow there, in elegant pale yellow with a mint leaf on top and a small spoon made of silver: it's a glass of sorbet! She fans herself with relief: he hasn't left a goodbye sundae as is his wont sometimes, or (worse) the banana split when he doesn't stay the whole night. No, this is quite a different message altogether. A sorbet is merely a refresher between courses. He'll be back!

He's reached the ground now and dodges elegantly through alleyways. The newly swept cobbles leave no dust on his shiny shoes. Gelato Parlour jogs along until he finds a gap between a hot chocolate emporium and a boutique offering bespoke ladies' fans (he sees his likeness inked upon several – not a terribly good likeness, it's got the nose all wrong, they really shouldn't have delegated such a responsibility to an apprentice, but never mind, it isn't important); and he stops, leaning against the wall, breathing in a manner just exhausted enough to still be attractive. See him there fixing his moustache with wax, adjusting his pale pink, candy blue and green striped barber jacket. Finally, he checks the silver pocketwatch in his waistcoat, clicks it closed with a satisfied nod, and smooths down his trousers (not that they need it). He's got a pressing engagement to get to now, has our man Gelato Parlour. He has to return a priceless object to a lovesick duchess. Of course he does.

Famous in the city, is Gelato. Infamous among the nobility, who frown upon his ambiguous parentage. Doubly infamous with le Guard, who are ever playing catch-up, scurrying along in his freshly ploughed furrow. This is going to be a particularly risky mission for Gelato. The robbery of the priceless object had not come easy. It happened a few days ago, and was still being spoken about in the lacemakers, at the boules courts, in the queue for the boulangerie, at the aquarium, by the mango stand. Gelato Parlour, everyone said, had only just got away.

(This wasn't true, of course; but in the days following the escapade, as he dined with friends and duelled with acquaintances throughout the "laying low" period, Gelato had hinted at near-disaster in the getaway. Greasing the gossip, he liked to think of it, to make it move faster.)

A rare instance of violence in the city; several members of le Guard had felt faint at the sight of blood on the empty jewellery boxes. Only the sergeant was brave enough to examine it closely, upon which she felt the first glimmerings of a suspicion. She removed a glove and tasted the redness, which was fat, slow moving and sweet.

'This isn't blood; it's strawberry syrup!' she cried. 'This is the work of Gelato Parlour!'

Gasps all round; le Guard hummed with indignation, excitement, and fear. The sergeant was prepared for imminent victory, provided her team acted with competence. 'Hold every exit; perimeter double-check; immediate reports!' she cried.

Her team ran to and fro and hither and thither and came back with conflicting sightings. A pink trouser leg doing a triumphant high-kick as it disappeared around a distant corner into the market square; the click of a pocket-watch behind the gauze curtain flapping in a newly opened window; a faint laugh carried on the breeze from the moustache-wax shop. The sergeant's team tramped back to her, their heads bowed in embarrassment and frustration. 'We tried to catch him, Sarge, but he melted away.'

Damn. He could be anywhere now. And the sergeant knew well that Gelato is a fugitive with many allies in the city; essentially, anyone who isn't le Guard. His clients are often powerful, secure in their wealth and adoration for him; and if they decide Gelato is worth protecting, the sergeant of le Guard can do little about it. Hence, our Gelato's successful career. Sometimes, the sergeant – for she is not stupid – suspects her endless chasing after Gelato is somewhat... decorative. She's been playing the game a long time. The money is good, anyhow.

He's stolen many things, has our Gelato Parlour. He's stolen hundreds and thousands.

Back in the alleyway. Gelato adjusts his pink waistcoat, and wonders who he will visit tonight. Perhaps the lady in the white lace nightgown (so soon? but, then again, why not so soon?), the lady Victoria Sandwich, diplomat. Or perhaps he could pay a visit to Genevieve Raghu, she of the full black curls and the ruffled red dresses, who even now is probably returning from yet another forbidden midnight trip to the tango district. Or perhaps he might visit the handsome Monsieur Jean de Bouillon, leader of the shadowy underground network of rapscallions known as the Croutons, the team of renegades and rogues who bob throughout the city carrying stolen goods and information. A night of dice and strong beer in the underground tunnels followed by a fumble or three in Jean's private tent might be just the ticket after a day at the duke's jardin party, which Gelato fears will be a stifling few hours exchanging pleasantries with the gentry by the arboretum (he'd have more satisfying tête à têtes with a horse chestnut); even if he plays his own private game of smuggling as much *double entendres* as he can muster into the endless conversation, nibbling suggestively at the canapés with the crusts cut off.

Or perhaps he could visit all three! Nights in this city stay young, after all! The world is his coconut-dusted oyster.

Don't think it is an endless party, this life. He has those who set themselves against him, our man Gelato Parlour, the dashing gentleman thief. Being he is not easy. He has a real nemesis, a real threat, a real undoing: and only a lick away. But let us forget that for the moment, we better not dwell, or else Gelato will move on without us. See, even now he has decided on a safe house to get ready for the jardin party and is adjusting his cravat in anticipation.

First, he must collect the priceless object from its hiding place.

After the raid on the pawnbroker's, Gelato – contrary to le Guard's sightings – did not actually go anywhere. Instead, he settled down and watched the whole chaotic episode unfold from behind a box hedge. And so he now returns, sitting for a moment beside a fountain that depicts a troupe of mermaids engaging in a harmless team sport. The fountain has been switched on, the trickle of water joins the birdsong in the air and – if you listen closely – a distant accordion wheezing away from a busker somewhere in a different square. He drinks a double espresso from a small portable cherrywood case containing a copper bean grinder and a silver thermal decanter. Then he washes the cup in the fountain, throws a silver coin into the fountain, reconsiders, throws another, reconsiders, throws a *gold* coin, mutters a wish we are not privileged to overhear, stands, and, with the effortless grace of a fencing master (which, naturally he is) leans across and pulls the priceless object from where it is hidden: a subtle groove in one of the mermaids' intricate stone hairstyles.

It resembles a cigar case and is intended to house chocolate flakes. Naturally it is made of gold.

We shall skip the intimacies of Gelato's readying himself at the safe house. Needless to say he is looked after and his host and hostess find themselves extremely well catered for in return. Gelato has a very brief nap, then changes into a mint-green ensemble with pale brown cravat. He makes sure the priceless object is safely tucked away somewhere about his person and ventures out again into the city. As he nears his destination, he smells freshly cut grass.

See Gelato now, sauntering up to the gates. He is let in with an air of confusion by the servants; they are happy to see him, of course, but are more accustomed to admitting him in secret through one of the back doors. No, today Gelato saunters as a privileged guest, bursting into the jardin, fashionably late, to the delighted applause of all assembled. He is immediately accosted by the Knickerbock sisters, the three daughters of a senior politician and her pastry-chef husband (they are, respectively: also a senior politician; an artist, noted for her particular genius with watercolour nudes; and the manager of a city-wide architectural consultancy, specialising in deep window-ledges, wide crossable roofs, secret passages, and sturdy drainpipes). They are pleased to see him, and he them; they have a lot of catching up to do. It would not hurt to engage in pleasantries with the Knickerbocks before delivering the priceless object to the duchess. After all, she is not even here yet. The jardin party crowd subtly shifts its constellations, refiguring itself around the presence of Gelato. Wait – what was that in the crowd, was it a trouser-leg of dark green tweed? At a *springtime semi-formal?* Surely not! It must have been a trick of the light.

But let us not forget it. Things are not as well for Gelato as they might seem. For the moment his life is easy as a sundae morning, but he will soon discover he has ninety-nine problems. For now, though, he has detached himself from the Knickerbock sisters and, exchanging compliments as he goes, makes his way to the dessert trolley.

Waiting there is a little girl, eight perhaps, or nine. In a pink dress of ruched and tucked satin, frosted with yards of frothing white net and lace and pearls. She's far too young for pearls – and for net and lace, for that matter. It is much as if the dress is wearing her, but she stands within it confidently nonetheless, as if it shields her from the nonsense going on all around. She has blonde hair in ringlets and a pale face in freckles. She's adorable. Gelato suspects her of secretly pulling the wings off dragonflies.

But he cannot complain in this instance as she folds her hands below her knees and strains upwards and begs him to tell her all about his adventures, and would he mind awfully passing her a slice of that cake? Pay attention for here we will see Gelato's downfall. She snatches the cake slice from the trolley (somebody has thoughtlessly left it languishing by the meringues) and holds it towards Gelato like a ready sword.

Gelato takes it and turns towards the cake to serve up a slice – servants rush to help, but our Gelato is a man of the people – and slides it onto a plate made of delicate china. He can ask her about her schooling, he thinks; maybe they can laugh together conspiratorially at the pomposity of the place. It would do him good, he thinks, refresh him somewhat, to chat to this youth with the slightly spiteful eyes. But when he turns back, the little girl has gone. He sees her taking a cornet from the other end of the trolley; then she vanishes into the crowd. He waits a moment for her to reappear; but he only sees more fully grown revellers being polite to each other in pantaloons. The little girl seems to have left the party altogether. Ah, the short attention span of the young, reflects Gelato, wondering whether it would be bad form to eat the cake himself. Gelato thinks very fondly of cake; not many people know this, but he was born and raised in the gateaux.

Within moments the pianoforte screeches to a halt and the guests look in silent horror at the presence of the unwashed le Guard standing, oh, so unthinkingly rudely, in the middle of the lawn.

Gelato thinks nothing of the fact that he does not recognise any of them. He does not tend to retain memories of le Guard as individuals.

'Gelato Parlour, you are under arrest on suspicion of stealing a priceless artefact what is formerly property of the Museum Of Confections, what is owned by the Impresario Mister Razberry Rip,' says one of them. 'We 'ave been sent to recover this item and return it to its rightful guv'nor.' A distant alarm bell rings for Gelato; a solitary red flag waves in his mind. The cadence is off. It sounds as if they had to memorise the lines by the syllable.

He knows it will be useless to tell them that Mr Rip pawned the golden flake holder in secret to cover his gambling debts, and that by giving it to the lovesick duchess Pina Pistachio he is performing an act that will cheer her up beyond measure: an objectively good deed. He does not wish to argue at such a civilised jardin party. And so, Gelato lets them take him. He gestures to the stunned and silent party guests that it is all right; he will go along until this nonsense is resolved; and he winks at le Guard as they tie his arms behind his back. 'I tend to prefer strawberry bootlaces for this sort of thing,' he tells them, but they don't get it. He doesn't bother with any further quips as they lead him out of the mansion grounds.

But our man Gelato is surprised to be marched straight past the municipal prison. He was expecting a short stay in the clean marble cells with their ornamental bars, was actually rather looking forward to the spartan prison diet of focaccia bread, sparkling spring water and olives until the morning – by which time the lovely Lady Bree Lemonsponge & her half-sister Poppy Seed, or perhaps the perennially bored Prince Frederick Mountbattenburg, or any of his other great allies, learned of his plight and arrived, tearful but overjoyed to help, trailing a long line of servants carrying the requisite bail gold in hessian bags.

But no, the guards take him through the city (windows are opened, distraught citizens look out, fanning themselves at the sight of Gelato arrested, turning away in distress, assuring le Guard that they will not, cannot hold their man for long) and finally reach a shadowy district where a series of knocks on the back door of a disreputable crêperie reveal a secret entrance in the brick, and a spiral staircase that leads further down than would be strictly necessary if the destination were merely the standard crêperie cellar designed to hold barrels of golden syrup. No, something is off and it isn't the batter. By now Gelato has noticed the misspellings in le Guard's motto embroidered on the uniforms of his captors, and how the uniforms in any case do not properly fit; and he has seen the way they do not quite know how to do the signature march of le Guard, an engaging albeit unnecessarily complex jaunt in 3/4 time. But it is too late. They throw him into a cell down there and leave. Bowing his head in frustration and anger, Gelato hears their laughter, followed by their plans for the next job down at the docks. (They're going to ambush a trawler, by the sounds, a scallywag cove who's been smuggling diamond necklaces in the calamari. Gelato would like to meet them.)

And so, Gelato languishing in a cell beneath the city, in dark, cavernous quarters; Gelato in the clutches of his nemesis.

Argh! That little girl. He should have known.

He hasn't seen her since she was much younger, cradled in the arms of a long thin man in dark green tweed and brass buttons. But that look in the eyes: unmistakable. That mischievous grin (he is reminded of Genevieve; will they ever tango again?) and the way she snatched the cake slice away – just a little too impatient – he'd taken it as a child's love of sugar, but in retrospect it was clearly the giveaway of the naive villainess. It was Petit Filou!

And there she is, Petit Filou, still in pink tucked satin but cut and tailored differently; with less froth and decoration, a more practical dress this time, still with bows on but fewer, hair in a swinging ponytail. Petit Filou in her work duds for guard duty. She's ignoring the prisoner, playing a game with a ball on a string attached to something in the shape of an ice-cream cornet. She has a high success rate of getting the ball into the cornet. She wins the game with a neat swing for the fourth time and finally deigns to look at the prisoner.

'You're *so* in trouble,' she says.

~ Intermission ~

How are you getting on? Are you all right?

Maybe take a moment while the lights come up. Have a look around. It's all happening in a bit of a rush, isn't it, the soaring score – and no denying it's effective, plenty dramatic and all that – but the thing's galloping along like a horse. Actually, a friend told you there is a horse at some point. Although that bit hasn't happened yet. Maybe they were joking.

You've got a lot to think about.

It's perfectly understandable if you don't fancy an ice-cream.

Eavesdropping. Naturally. You can't help it, even if you don't mean to.

A couple, perhaps, or at least very old friends; it's certainly a familiar way they have of touching each other on the arms. In front. Oldish, dignified. One's looking through the programme; the other's eating chocolate in loud wrappers.

'I didn't really get the bit with the sock suspenders. And how come everybody just let him get marched away from the jardin party?'

'Mmm.'

'Surely they could have prevented him being arrested in the first place? And why did he get arrested by a fake guard?'

'You're right. What city is it supposed to be, anyway?'

'In the programme it just says neapolitan. But, I don't know.'

'It's melodrama, is it?'

'It has to be.'

There's a pause.

'And what's going on with the golden flake holder? It wouldn't surprise me if we don't hear anything about it again.'

Pause.

'Who wrote the libretto?'

'I'll check. It doesn't say.'

Pause.

'Do you want a chocolate?'

'Are there any strawberry ones left?'

Pause. Some investigation. The box rattles.

'No.'

'I'm fine then.'

'Sorry.'

The voices go down to more of a mutter as they discuss the various performances. People are arriving again. Shouldn't be long now.

Maybe you wonder if there's a grand scene change going on. But it's prose and it's all in the mind. There is and there isn't. Nothing you need take fifteen minutes out for.

'Well, I don't know. There's excitement and whatnot, I'll give it that,' says a plummy voice behind you, velvety, knowledge-y tones. They continue their thesis with quotes and examples. Nobody replies; it isn't clear who they're speaking to, if anyone at all. But it would be too obvious to turn around and look so they'll have to be left to get on with it.

Anyway.

We've all got things to do. Things we're worried about.

~ Act II ~

Gelato kneeling on the floor in the cell, head raised at a proud angle, the prison bars making dramatic shadows that flatter his jawline and lend emphasis to his smouldering stare. There's a single cut on one of his cheekbones. Where did that come from? The distant rumble of the market outside, flashes of laughter as people go about their day up above, enjoying themselves in the crêperie that hides the way to reach him. People will be assuming he is in le Guard's comfortable cells, that he will be free any moment now. The sound of those outside, unaware of our hero's tragically subterranean situation. The sound of Petit Filou playing the cup and cornet game.

Gelato knows Petit Filou is his way out of here. But he wavers. How to turn a child against their own parental figure? He's done it before, of course – it rarely takes more than a packet of sweets. But Petit Filou has had a formidable upbringing.

'I say –' he begins, but he gets no further. We'll never know what charming strategy he had planned. A long thin laugh emanates from the shadows outside his cell, and a long thin person stalks into the light, to whom Petit Filou bobs a curtsy. Gelato balls his fists for a moment, narrows an eye with an unspoken curse. Damn!

And now we can gaze upon Gelato Parlor's nemesis, a long thin man in dark green tweed and brass buttons. His long thin hands are on his hips. He stands contrapposto, chewing on a runner bean.

'Well thrice, Gelato Parlour. Fooled by a child's trick with a cake slice,' says that devilish cad, the vile and unsavoury man in the tweed, who goes by the name of Mange Tout.

'I'll be out of here before you reach the dessert course, Mange Tout,' says Gelato.

'There will be no such course, Gelato. Not this time. I've had it with your adventures around my city, scampering across my rooftops, your romantic daydreams with every damn citizen – while I work here, below, on underappreciated things. On achievements of infrastructure, on our city's architectural glory!'

'This city's architecture is a Knickerbocker glory.'

'Pah! She merely outsources. She might add a fire escape to a public bath every now and again, or bugger up a tea set by making a crucial bit out of chocolate…'

Gelato, who does own a Knickerbock tea set, is mildly offended, but with admirable restraint he does not let it show.

Mange Tout continues. 'Yes, she may concern herself with trifles. But when there is real work to be done she is desperate to hire one of my many aliases. It is I who am responsible, for example, for the efficiency of the sewage works.'

'I'm sure the people would like to thank you. Why don't you go aboveground?'

'Pah! They don't care about what is good for them! They long only for parties and festivities and… and… and all that nonsense *you* do!'

Petit Filou has picked up a book. And why shouldn't she? The nemeses look set to trade barbs for hours.

'You may call it nonsense, Mange Tout. But of the two of us, it is you who are angry. You should try spelling *stressed* backwards.'

'It's *desserts*,' adds Gelato, helpfully.

'I have no time for your games, Parlour,' says Mange Tout. 'Now I have you frozen to the spot. Ha! What a scoop! It's pav*lova* for you, Gelato!' And he laughs, as if he has been waiting to say these things for a long time.

Our Gelato cannot cope with any more monologuing from Mange Tout. 'A cheap trick, having your brat point me out with the cake slice,' he says. (Petit Filou shrugs uncaringly as she reads.) 'Trust you to hire labour so cheap they can't even be depended on to recognise me. Some scoop *that* is.'

'Ha ha. I come up with so many schemes to capture you, Gelato. In fact, I aim for five a day.'

Petit Filou turns a page.

But wait – what's that? There's a crash that sounds like the secret door to a disreputable crêperie door being broken down, followed by a clatter that sounds like a troupe of vigilantes rattling down a spiral staircase. And you're right!

Mange Tout's underground HQ is overwhelmed with members of the Croutons!

Mange Tout wrestles and curses but they have heard worse, and are able to block and parry his feeble blows with ease (they have practiced these moves in the tunnels, sometimes greased up with caramel and hot fudge sauce for extra difficulty. Mange Tout is no match for them.) They gently push Petit Filou away as she scratches and bites. Monsieur de Bouillon doffs his cap at Gelato as he races by.

And there – over the mess and the chaos – hear the sound of a horse's hooves?

Enter Genevieve Raghu, leading the victory charge!

And she is on a horse. A chestnut stallion, naturally, it is the champion racehorse Meringue M'Lord. He will go down in history for managing the rescue and the spiral staircase (in that order) with little to no complaint. Gelato Parlour holds up his hands in delight.

No sidesaddle for Ms. Raghu (Dr. Raghu by rights, she has a degree in natural philosophy); her red dress billows behind her, her hair braided into a thick plait as protection from the wind as she gallops through the city. A young Crouton in a flat cap unpicks Gelato's cell lock (it's Minnie Stroné with the short ginger hair and the delightful nervous laugh, how joyously he will thank her later) – the cell door swings open and Gelato stands and staggers towards it as another Crouton – a muscular fellow called Broth – reaches towards his boot for the short knife he keeps there. He pulls it out now and cuts through the ropes binding Gelato's arms, just as Genevieve sweeps into the cell and pulls Gelato up to ride behind her. The moment his arms are free they hold Genevieve's waist.

'We'll leave the Croutons to absorb the rest of this mess,' she says. 'Yah!'

The stallion knows to power back into action at that sound and does a big dramatic rearing-up-on-his-hind-legs manoeuvre. The Croutons cheer as Genevieve and Gelato clatter up the spiral staircase again and away. Mange Tout stops fighting for a moment to shake a fist.

The city is drenched in golden sunset light as they return above ground. (Can you believe it has all happened in a single day? Quite the wrap, even for Gelato.) The stallion takes them through the streets. Windows open, citizens look down upon the latest developments. Gelato waves and salutes. Someone has found some confetti, leftover from a festival the week before (or was it a wedding?), and throws it from their balcony. It floats gently over Genevieve and Gelato, covering them like sprinkles.

Genevieve has no wish to hang about in the gutters covered in crepe paper. 'To the tango house?' she says, with a hint of impatience. A daring rescue is not all she wishes to lead on today.

'Without delay,' says Gelato. 'And then to party with the Croutons for an all-night fondue!'

Hooray!

We'll not follow them as they ride off. We can surely agree that privacy has been earned by now.

Alone underground, the defeated Mange Tout washes the cell with a mop and bucket. In completing the rescue mission the Croutons left their vegetables all over the floor. Petit Filou is changing the bedclothes in the cell, after Monsieur Jean de Bouillon slashed them with his sword in a fit of overexcitement. They are both undoubtedly disappointed, but there is, also, lying beneath it all like a fine biscuit base, the undeniable satisfaction of a full day of activity. And Mange Tout has plans to interrupt the escapades at the Grand Racetrack tomorrow, where he believes Gelato intends to deliver a smuggled theatrical manuscript to an earl. Its playwright needs support from the nobility to stage this new piece, for it contains – so the rumour goes – some unspeakably controversial material. Mange Tout thinks he can get the play rewritten to star himself, with speeches inserted that finally reveal the greatness of his contribution to the populace. Petit Filou has some actresses she wishes to meet. It's a plan with something to please everybody.

And then there's the hot air balloon show the week after that…

But, in truth, Mange Tout's ward is less sure. Petit Filou has witnessed many of these failed attempts to discourage Gelato Parlour's adventures across the city. She suspects that without Mange Tout's interventions, Gelato's endeavours wouldn't be half so spectacular. She has observed how le Guard help Gelato's reputation as they attempt to constrain it, by racing to the scenes of his crimes and bungling things up so reliably. And although she loves her legal guardian, she fosters some individualism, and wonders whether he knows that he is only enabling Gelato's achievements of greatness. Perhaps, she thinks, things would be better if the nemesis relationship were over. Perhaps, she hopes, this adventure might even be the last one...?

But Petit, what's that on the windowsill?

Looks like a sorbet to me.

Here we go again!

About the Author

Rose Biggin is a writer and performer based in London. Her previous books are the punk fantasy novel *Wild Time* (Surface Press) and gothic thriller *The Belladonna Invitation* (Ghost Orchid Press). She is author of *Immersive Theatre and Audience Experience* (Palgrave), and is an Associate Lecturer in Creative Writing at Birkbeck.

Acknowledgements

Thank you very much to Ian Whates for inviting me to compile this collection, and to Keir Cooper for working on the final edits with me as each story was revised for the book. Thank you to Jared Shurin for the introduction and all the encouragement over the years; and to the original publishers: Mark Beech, Joy Crelin, Maxim Jakubowski, Andrew Kaye, Rebecca Kilroy, Eileen Lavelle, David Thomas Moore, Bennett North, Aimee Ogden, Bre Stephens, Heather and S.D. Vassallo, Arden Young. And much gratitude to the readers, comrades and friends who have come along the way.

ALSO FROM NEWCON PRESS

ANIMALS – Geoff Ryman
From the multiple award-winning author of *HIM*, *Was* and *The Child Garden* comes a powerful new novel. *ANIMALS* tells the chilling tale of a family caught at the heart of a terrifying and transformative epidemic. Geoff Ryman delivers an astonishing fusion of beautiful writing and pure horror as the world we know falls apart.

The Hamlet – Joanna Corrance
A fabulous tale that dances between horror and science fiction with an added dash of weird. Screens go blank, radios go silent, and a government announcement advises everyone to stay indoors. The residents of a rural Scottish community abandon their picnics and return home. Everyone can sense that something is wrong...

The Other Frankenstein – Melissa F. Olson
Elizabeth Frankenstein and Heck Saville's parallel, intersecting stories encompass murder, intrigue, loss, trauma and ultimately empowerment, in this stunning feminist saga that grasps the classic tale of *Frankenstein* and uses it as a springboard to weave a potent tale of horror, love, and revenge, with Elizabeth, a minor character in Shelley's original novel, given full scope to shine.

The Creator – Aliya Whiteley
When Phillip receives a distraught call from his sister-in-law, Patricia, to say that his brother is dead, he doesn't hesitate in dashing to her side. Little does he imagine the tragedy and horror that awaits, as he uncovers what really happened to Reynold – the genius behind ThinkBulb, the invention that changed the world – and where his latest obsession has led.

Futures to Live By – Ana Sun
Ana Sun spent her childhood in Malaysian Borneo and grew up living on islands. Her stories of the near future reflect this, approaching fiction from a different perspective and telling tales of solar punk and more. They have already brought her award shortlistings and considerable critical acclaim This, her debut collection, is a volume to savour.